"Don't Tell Me You're Working Late?" She Asked.

She arched a disbelieving eyebrow at Casey. "If I recall correctly, you resigned today."

"That doesn't mean I intend to sit on my duff until my last day." Casey smiled as he took in her casual appearance. "You look a lot more like the Drew I remember now. I enjoyed her a great deal. She knew how to live life to the fullest."

Stung, she retorted, *"You* were the one who refused to take a chance in Houston. I could have supported both of us until you found a job."

"I wasn't about to be kept by a woman, Drew," he snarled. "Not even you."

LINDA WISDOM
is a California author who loves movies, books and animals of all kinds. She also has a great sense of humor, which is reflected in her books.

Dear Reader:

Romance readers have been enthusiastic about Silhouette Special Editions for years. And that's not by accident: Special Editions were the first of their kind and continue to feature realistic stories with heightened romantic tension.

The longer stories, sophisticated style, greater sensual detail and variety that made Special Editions popular are the same elements that will make you want to read book after book.

We hope that you enjoy this Special Edition today, and will enjoy many more.

The Editors at Silhouette Books

LINDA WISDOM
Business as Usual

Silhouette Special Edition

Published by Silhouette Books New York

America's Publisher of Contemporary Romance

SILHOUETTE BOOKS, a Division of Simon & Schuster, Inc.
1230 Avenue of the Americas, New York, N.Y. 10020

Copyright © 1984 by Linda Wisdom
Cover artwork copyright © 1984 Robert Maguire

Distributed by Pocket Books

IBSN: 0-671-53690-7

First Silhouette Books printing September, 1984

10 9 8 7 6 5 4 3 2 1

Map by Ray Lundgren

SILHOUETTE, SILHOUETTE SPECIAL EDITION and
colophon are registered trademarks of Simon & Schuster, Inc.

America's Publisher of Contemporary Romance

Printed in the U.S.A.

Books by Linda Wisdom

Silhouette Romance

Dancer in the Shadows #39
Fourteen Karat Beauty #95
Bright Tomorrow #132
Dreams from the Past #166
Snow Queen #241

Silhouette Special Edition

A Man with Doubts #27
Unspoken Past #74
Island Rogue #160
Business As Usual #190

To Penny, for her cheerful boosts when I'm down and her well-aimed kicks when the ego tends to take off a little bit. For just being a friend and being there on the other end of the phone when needed. Thanks, friend.

And for the real life Shadow, who's more than just the crazy cockatiel portrayed in this book.

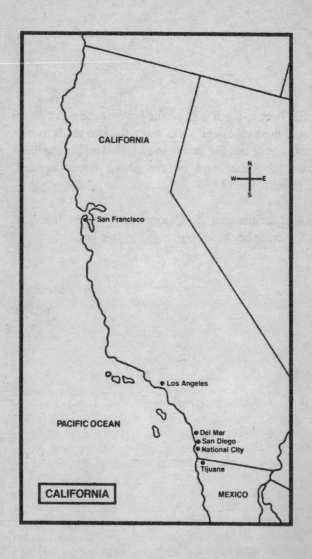

CALIFORNIA

San Francisco

PACIFIC OCEAN

Los Angeles

Del Mar
San Diego
National City

Tijuana

CALIFORNIA

MEXICO

Chapter One

$\mathcal{A}$ muted roar like a tiger's purr followed the sleek black Ferrari as it moved down the tree-lined street and turned onto a boulevard facing a park. The driver's shoulder-length, honey-blond hair danced loosely in the wind, alternately masking and revealing her delicate features. Her amber eyes, shaded by oversize sunglasses, were supposed to be looking straight ahead, even though there was very little traffic on the road at that early hour. However, they kept straying toward the large park, where several joggers could be seen. Her brain wouldn't accept the fact that she might be looking for one particular jogger. Then she saw him.

He was running just ahead of her and to the left; he was tall, with the body of a man used to regular exercise. His tawny-blond hair was plastered to his head, a silent testament to his early morning workout, and drops of sweat clung even to his neatly clipped moustache. A pair of dark green nylon athletic shorts hugged his well-muscled body, and a matching bandanna was tied around his forehead in an attempt to keep the sweat from dropping into his eyes. His bronzed muscular chest gleamed brightly in the early morning sun.

The moment the woman saw the jogger, her body jerked slightly and her foot hit the accelerator harder than she had intended. A squeal and the smell of burning rubber permeated the air as she shot down the road. The jogger paid her no notice.

Twenty minutes later the woman parked the Ferrari in a slot marked D. Sinclair. She flashed a smile of greeting to the guard at the door and walked briskly across the lobby toward a bank of elevators. After getting off at the top floor, which housed the company executives, she made her way down the cream-colored, plushly carpeted hallway to the last set of doors, which were guarded by a large secretarial desk. She walked through the ornately paneled doors and placed her soft leather briefcase on the teak desk, then paused to look out the huge picture window. No one else would be in the building for at least an hour, plenty of time for her to get in some extra reading. There was so much for her to learn! She dropped into the high-backed soft leather chair and opened one of the desk drawers.

When Drew Sinclair had taken the position of temporary executive director of Fantasy Toys two months ago, she hadn't realized the extensive work that would be involved. Hard work had never scared her before, though. She thrived on it the way plants thrive on sunlight. That was how she had become an expert in her field. She was a troubleshooter, working with companies that required a shot in the arm to get them back on the road to excellence.

The pile of folders in the drawer had slowly dwindled as she studied each one carefully to familiarize herself not only with the company, but its employees, as well. Only one folder could safely remain unopened, or could it? If she studied it as carefully as she had the others, she might find out something she hadn't known before.

Drew rummaged through the personnel folders and extracted the one marked Carstairs Langdon McCord. She looked at the name typed neatly on the label and smiled. Poor Casey, saddled with such a ponderous family name. She slowly opened the folder and began reading, although she already knew most of the information.

Thirty-seven, six-feet-one, four years in the Navy before obtaining a B.S. degree in engineering from M.I.T., he had worked as a mechanical engineer until three years ago, when the influx of new engineers combined with fewer available jobs had meant layoffs. Casey had turned out to be one of the victims. More than willing to change fields, he had worked for the Sundance Novelty Company in Boston as part of their sales force, until Fantasy Toys, here in San Diego, recruited him as a regional sales manager. He was presently their director of sales, with a vice-presidency in the offing, judging from his outstanding work record.

Drew knew so much more than the dry information recorded in the files. She knew that his actress mother had traveled to Montana to work in a film years before, met his father, a cattle rancher, married him and never looked back to her glamorous former life. Casey had grown up in cattle country, but had no love for ranching. His love was tinkering with machinery and working with his hands, not with the land. After deciding to learn more about his first love, he had applied to and been accepted at M.I.T. He was ambidextrous, enjoyed classical music and dinners for two, and hated large parties, loud women and rock concerts —although, just once, he had overlooked that dislike. She knew that he preferred to shave with a blade rather than an electric razor, and what he looked like without his clothes. . . . She shook her head quickly to chase away her disturbing thoughts of the man in question while she closed the folder firmly.

"Don't you ever sleep?"

Drew looked up at the sound of her secretary's exasperated question. The woman standing before her placed a coffee cup, with the proper amount of cream added, in front of her.

"I'll try to do some sleeping next year." Drew smiled as she picked up the welcome cup and took a sip. "Um, I needed that." Still holding her cup between her palms, she leaned back in her chair. "What's on the agenda for today, Viv?"

"You're meeting with the department heads at nine-thirty, which will probably take all morning; you have a luncheon meeting with Mr. Wilson from Legal; and Mrs. Thornton would like to talk to you sometime this afternoon if you're free. I penciled her in at three. You also wanted to see the Christmas ad layouts if they were ready. They'll be delivered sometime after lunch. Not to mention that this is also the evening for your exercise class, if you're so inclined, and if you have the energy left to walk out of here." The gray-haired woman looked at Drew over the top of her glasses. "If you don't feel that's enough to occupy your day, I can fit in a few more people."

Drew wrinkled her nose. "What do you say we run away to Tahiti, find ourselves a couple of good-looking beach bums and build ourselves a grass shack?" she asked flippantly.

"When Robert Redford asks me, I'll go. Until then you'll just have to make do with the handsome men around here," the secretary returned pertly. "And speaking of handsome men, Casey McCord would like to see you this morning before the meeting."

Don't let the memories intrude, her brain warned her. She shook her head. "No can do," she said firmly.

"If he needs to see me, tell him I'm free sometime tomorrow morning. Or am I?" She raised a questioning eyebrow at the woman who ran her office so competently.

Viv laughed. "For him, I'll make room." She gestured toward the stack of envelopes on Drew's desk. "I've already made notations on the ones that need your immediate attention."

"Oh, Viv, what would I do without you?" Drew breathed a sigh of relief. Though she had only been at Fantasy Toys a short time, already she didn't know what she would do without the efficient woman. From the beginning the clear-thinking secretary had been her savior in times of crises. And the crises just never seemed to stop as each day passed and Drew became more involved in her work.

"Commit hara-kiri?" Viv smiled. "Any dictation this morning?"

Drew looked shocked. "And when would I have time for that, pray tell?" she demanded, mischief in her heavily lashed amber eyes. "Personally, I think that's why you keep me on such a heavy schedule. You figure if I'm busy with all these meetings, I won't have any free time to put you to work."

"You got it," Viv agreed cheerfully as she walked out of the office.

Drew finished her coffee, wincing as the hot liquid burned its way down to her stomach. "All I'd need right now is an ulcer to go along with everything else," she muttered, putting the coffee aside so she could concentrate on the mail.

When Marty Watson had called her into his office ten weeks earlier and told her that she was finally going to get her chance to prove her worth on a large-scale project, she hadn't realized what would be entailed. CHEM Corp., a conglomerate, had purchased Fantasy Toys when its owner had died and the heirs had decided they could do without the burden of running the company. That it was in financial trouble had been obvious, that it needed a firm hand, equally so. Drew was to step in as executive director for Fantasy Toys, study every piece of paperwork she could discover, and deliver her findings to the board before the end of the year. At that time a new executive director would be appointed, probably one of the vice-presidents within the company, and Drew would be sent to a new assignment. That gave her a little less than ten months. In the eight weeks she had been there, very little of the information she had seen on paper was encouraging. The sales figures might continue to rise, but even they couldn't compensate for the rapidly rising costs of labor and materials, or rising salaries. All these factors combined could very easily run a company into the ground. Preventing that was Drew's job.

It hadn't helped to find that the department heads didn't appreciate a woman coming in to tell them how to run their company. Drew wasn't one to remain low-key for very long, and she had immediately taken steps to let them know that. Like it or not, she was there to get their company back into shape. In a job like that, feelings were taken into consideration, but the company came ahead of anyone's damaged ego. They were determined to make her odd woman out, and she was equally determined to do the job she had been sent there to do.

"Ready to face the lions in their den?" Viv's voice intruded on her thoughts.

Drew smiled briefly. "Not really, but I guess now's as good a time as any. They'll do their best to smile paternally, pat me on the head and talk in that obscure masculine language that we women aren't supposed to understand. Where did Colin Wakefield dig up all these old chauvinists, anyway?"

"I think they all belonged to the same Edsel club."

silver hair cut in short curls and her angular features, she presented the paradoxical picture of youth after sixty. "The least I can do is pamper you this evening and bring your dinner in here."

Drew grimaced as her sore muscles protested the slightest movement. "I hope it's something light. I had a fairly heavy lunch today."

The older woman's eyes narrowed. "It's all this pressure you've been under these past few weeks," she announced. "If you keep up the way you've been going, you'll get an ulcer, if you don't already have one."

"The food was too spicy, that's all," Drew protested.

Kate's motherly lecture on stress and the effect it had on a person's health was interrupted by a high-pitched sound from a corner of the room.

"Hello, Drew; hello, Drew."

She smiled and pushed herself to her feet, then walked over to the large square cage where a gray cockatiel hopped excitedly along its perch.

"Hello, Shadow," Drew greeted the bird as she opened the door and watched the cockatiel climb out onto her arm, his yellow crest standing high in the air.

"Hello, Shadow," he piped back. "Hi." Then he began a series of high-pitched whistles, slightly off-key.

Drew smilingly shook her head. "What's this supposed to be?" She turned to Kate, who had just reentered the room carrying a tray of food.

The older woman cocked her head to one side in concentration. "Hard to tell. I think it's the theme from one of my movies. I don't think he can tell any of them apart."

Drew rolled her eyes upward. Kate's avid interest in her videotape library was well known, including her penchant for watching certain films over and over again. It was difficult for anyone to imagine that the serene-faced grandmotherly woman standing before her preferred science fiction and horror thrillers to the more sedate films of the 1940s. "You'd think after hearing the music so often he'd at least get the tune right."

Kate shook her head in disagreement as she set the tray on a nearby table. "Why should he? A tone-deaf bird is more of a conversation piece."

"Kiss Casey!" the bird squeaked. "Kiss Casey!"

Drew divided her accusing glare between Shadow and Kate. "Have you been prompting him again?" she demanded of the older woman. She sat down to sample a bowl of hearty clam chowder, then had an oven-warmed crusty sourdough roll topped with butter. "I was hoping that time would let him forget that phrase."

"He stopped by a while ago with a letter from Sara." Sara was Casey's mother, and Kate's sister. "Naturally Shadow greeted him."

The cockatiel hopped up and down on her shoulder. "Hello, Drew," he chirped happily. "Sexy Shadow." He leaned over to tug on her gold earring with his beak.

"How was your day?" Kate spoke up.

Drew sipped her hot coffee cautiously. "Busy, much too busy." She shot Kate a sideways glance. "Did Casey tell you about our conference?"

"Only that one of your most important accounts reduced their order. He also mentioned that he had the problem well in hand."

"Glad to see his confidence level hasn't wavered," she muttered, leaning back in her chair. "I really should get out those files I brought home and look them over." She was hoping that if she spoke the words out loud she would somehow find the energy to live up to them.

"You're working much too hard," Kate scolded maternally. "You're going to have to slow down before you become ill."

Drew shook her head emphatically. "Too much to

do," she argued mildly. "Don't worry, I know my limits." She broke off a tiny piece of her roll and offered it to Shadow, who happily nibbled on his prize.

"You should be married and worrying about what school to send your children to."

Drew sighed inwardly at this familiar tactic. Kate was one of her favorite people, but this was getting to be too much. Drew hadn't been in town more than a week before Kate showed up on her doorstep, breezed into her rented house and calmly informed the younger woman that she was moving in to take care of her. By that evening Kate was installed in the guest room and taking charge of the housekeeping duties.

"Tell me something, Aunt Kate." Drew posed a question which had been plaguing her from the beginning. "If Casey is your favorite nephew, why aren't you keeping house for *him*? After all, domestic chores were never his forte."

"Oh, my dear, no." Kate picked up her crocheting and continued her work on an afghan. "I'd only cramp his style." She smiled blandly.

"Of course, I should have realized," Drew replied dryly, returning to her meal.

If Monday had been bad, Tuesday wasn't promising to be much better.

Drew received a telephone call from Marty Watson first thing in the morning demanding to know the status of Fantasy Toys. After a lengthy and thoroughly irritating conversation with her boss, she swallowed two antacid tablets, calmly informed him that an updated report would be on his desk the following Monday morning, and hung up. She cursed softly when the intercom buzzer sounded.

"Casey McCord is here to see you," Viv announced.

"Would you please inform Mr. McCord that I moved

to Siberia and did not leave a forwarding address?" Drew sighed, staring at the never-ending pile of file folders on her desk.

Before she clicked off she could hear Viv saying, "You can go right in. She's expecting you."

The door opened, and Casey walked in with his usual indolent grace. His tawny good looks were accented by a chocolate-brown three piece suit and cream-colored shirt.

"What ill tidings are you bringing me today?" she asked caustically, damping down her leaping senses at the thoroughly sexy picture the man presented. "Don't tell me. Toy Faire canceled the rest of their order, right?"

"You're making me sound like some prophet of doom," he returned lightly, dropping down into a chair opposite her desk.

"Then tell me one piece of good news," she ordered sardonically.

"You've got the sexiest pair of legs I've ever seen on a woman." Casey's husky voice carried easily to her ears. In her agitation Drew crossed and recrossed the appendages he had mentioned. "Not to mention a body that belongs in a bedroom where only your lover can see it, totally unclothed and flushed from lovemaking."

"And you have the mentality of an oversexed adolescent," she replied pleasantly, wishing his words wouldn't send volcanic shock waves up and down her spine. "Now, I only have five minutes. What problem do you have today?"

Casey's features hardened at her crisp tone. "Back to business, eh, boss?"

Drew's eyes gleamed with anger. "That's not funny, Casey."

"I didn't mean for it to be." He withdrew a folded sheet of paper from his inside jacket pocket and tossed it onto her desk.

She stared at it with a sense of foreboding. "What is this?" She glanced up with a suspicious frown.

"Some reading material for you, when you have the time." He looked totally at ease and much too relaxed for her peace of mind.

She picked up the paper, unfolded it slowly and scanned the contents. Her face drained of all color as she read the typewritten words.

"It's my letter of resignation," Casey explained patiently when Drew looked up.

"I can see that," Drew replied through clenched teeth. She took a deep breath to steady her quivering nerves. "Whatever you've been offered elsewhere, we'll match it. We'll even go higher, if that's what you want. I'm sure we can come to an amiable agreement," she stated crisply.

Casey's lips twisted in a wry smile. "You're enjoying the feeling of power, aren't you? That's what it comes down to, doesn't it? Offer the poor sucker more money and he'll stay. It doesn't work with me, though. Don't worry, Drew; I'm giving you a month to replace me. You shouldn't have too much of a problem finding someone by then."

Drew was no fool when it came to recognizing the importance of certain of her executives, and as far as she and CHEM Corp. were concerned, Casey headed the list. In a split second her feminine instincts took over. She forced her lips into a dazzling smile, then stood up and walked slowly around to the front of the desk. She perched herself on the edge, knowing the front slit in her cinnamon linen skirt would afford him a good view of the nylon clad legs he had professed to admire.

"Now, Casey," she purred, "surely we can talk things over before you come to any definite decision. After all, it isn't as if we're only business associates here. You and I go back a long way." She slowly lowered her lashes, then glanced up in a thoroughly provocative manner guaranteed to raise a man's blood pressure. Unless the man knew her too well and realized what she was up to.

"Cut the maudlin pose, Drew," he rapped, instantly seeing through her seductive act. "We only lived together, we weren't married."

"We lived together for five years!" Her voice rose right along with her temper. "That's longer than a good many marriages last nowadays! Even that would have lasted longer if you hadn't revealed such a stubborn streak!"

"Speaking of the number five"—Casey interrupted Drew's tirade as he glanced down at his watch—"I see that my five minutes are up." He stood and walked over to the door. Just before he opened it to walk out, he turned back to her, flashing a panther's grin. "Have a nice day, Ms. Sinclair."

Chapter Two

$\mathscr{D}$rew returned to her chair before her wobbly legs gave out. Her mind was still spinning from Casey's announcement. She wasn't sure if she was more stunned by his letter of resignation or his casual dismissal of their five years together. Of course, she should talk. When it came right down to it, *she* was the one who had walked out of their relationship.

"Damn him for this," she whispered brokenly, losing the cool composure she had been showing to the world for the past five years. She had done so well at pushing the memories of their time together to the back of her mind that days would go by before something would jog her memory. That was until she came to Fantasy Toys and met their director of sales, a meeting that brought her past flashing back at her with a vengeance.

She had been a junior at Harvard, majoring in business administration, when they first met. As part of her part-time job for a singing telegram company, she had been sent to a local manufacturing firm to deliver a birthday greeting, which read in part *To Casey with love from Gloria*. What she had found was a tall, good-looking, blond man in his late twenties. Casey had stared transfixed as Drew had gone into her birthday song set to the tune of a Broadway standard. Her brief congratulatory kiss had lasted longer than usual, thanks to Casey. After Drew had finished her routine Casey had followed her out to the parking lot, asking for her telephone number as she walked the short distance to her car. For the first time in her singing career Drew had given a man her number. She had even hoped he would call. Casey had wasted no time. She had heard from him the very next day, and in less than a month they had become inseparable, with Drew moving into Casey's apartment soon after. They had lived together for five years before it all fell apart. Drew groaned, willing herself not to give in to the painful memories. At the same time, how could any woman forget her first lover? Casey had been that and more; he had been her closest friend and confidante. He had known secrets that she hadn't dared to reveal to anyone, but Casey had been different. He was Casey, pure and simple, and she had loved him.

"Drew?" Her secretary's questioning voice brought her back to the present with an abrupt bump. She looked up to see Viv's face etched with concern. "Are you all right?"

Drawing upon the reserves of strength that had kept her going for the past five years, Drew managed a bright smile. "Fine."

Viv didn't appear to be convinced. "I buzzed you several times, but you didn't answer, so I thought I better check on you," she said, explaining the reason for her intrusion. "Mrs. Perkins from Accounting is here."

Drew sighed wearily. It looked as if it was going to be a long morning. She glanced down at the slim gold watch on her wrist. Casey had given it to her for her birthday their first year together. As it kept perfect time, she had seen no reason to replace it. "All right. Oh, do me a favor. When Mrs. Perkins leaves, would you please get Mr. Watson on the phone? Also, please cancel any appointments I have for this afternoon. I won't be coming back after lunch. There's some personal business I need to take care of. I'll be coming in this evening, so if anything comes up, just leave a note on my desk."

Viv smiled. "Meaning I won't be able to get hold of you if the place decides to fall down around our ears. There are going to be some people who won't appreciate hearing that you're unavailable."

"Too bad," Drew replied ruthlessly. "Could we have some coffee in here please?"

Viv nodded as she went out the door and gestured to the woman seated in the small waiting area. Drew pulled her professional mask back in place and was able to greet the assistant accounting manager with her usual charm.

An hour later Drew talked to her boss on the phone. Since CHEM Corp.'s corporate offices were in Houston, she usually got in touch with Marty Watson once a week to recap her progress in revamping the administrative offices. She knew he was going to wonder at a second conversation in one day, and he wasn't going to appreciate the news she had for him.

"Drew!" The gruff-spoken man greeted her effusively, as if their earlier argument had never happened. "How's it going out there? I have a lot of trust in you, darlin'. Now, what can I do for you?"

Drew grimaced at Marty's hearty greeting. She knew it was only part of a carefully planned facade. Beneath the teddy bear exterior lay a heart of pure stone, buttressed with profit and loss statements, with the emphasis always on profit.

"Everything is going along fine, Marty." She mimicked his exuberance sarcastically. "I thought I'd let you know that Casey McCord tendered his resignation today. I'll be looking for a replacement, so if you have anyone in mind for the position, I'd certainly give them first consideration."

There was a cold silence on the other end. "What company snapped him up?" Marty demanded, reverting back to the cold-hearted businessman she knew so well.

"He didn't say," she admitted, then winced at the sound of the explicit curses coming across the line. "Marty, it won't do any good to threaten the whole world," she told him mildly, all the while torn up inside at the idea of Casey leaving. And not because of their business relationship, either.

"Don't accept it," he ordered. "Tear his resignation up and offer him anything, but don't let that man go anywhere else."

Drew was surprised by the vehemence in Marty's voice. Usually when employees threatened to leave, and if Marty thought they were only holding him up for more money, he said, "Fine, go for it. More power to you," and didn't give them another thought. This wasn't going to be his way with Casey. Why?

"I already offered him more money, and he said that that had nothing to do with his reasons for leaving," she told him quietly. "He's giving us a month to find someone else. Marty, this man is extremely stubborn. If he doesn't want to stay here, there's nothing we can do to persuade him otherwise, believe me." She felt a wrench of sadness at her own statement. Could she be conceited enough to think that he was leaving because of her?

"He's a man, damn it!" he roared over the phone, almost blasting her eardrum out of existence. "Use some of that sex appeal you have! No man in his right mind could resist you if you put all your weapons to work. I've seen enough men panting around you when you were working here to know that you've got what it takes. If there's one man this corporation needs on its side, it's Casey McCord. If he's going to get ahead, I want to make sure he's on our side. Now, I suggest you start practicing some feminine wiles on him and persuade him to stay. Do whatever you have to," he commanded.

"What you're asking me to do is prostitute myself. That's not part of my job description, Marty," she reminded him in an icy voice. "It's also not part of me, period. I won't go to bed with a man just to keep him on the payroll. If that's what you want, you better call in someone more suited to that type of work." She wasn't going to tell him that she had tried just that and it hadn't worked.

Marty snorted with disbelief. "Isn't Fantasy Toys' annual sales conference coming up soon?" he asked so suddenly that he almost threw her off balance.

"In a few weeks." What was he getting at? she wondered silently.

"You are attending, aren't you?" he suggested smoothly.

She immediately understood his meaning. "I'll see what I can do," she murmured.

"You better," Marty said darkly. "I sent you out there, sweetheart, because you told me you could do the job. If you blow this, be prepared to spend the next ten years in our Alaska office. Without central heating!"

"You're so good to me, Marty," Drew said sweetly before hanging up. She looked down at the phone and stuck her tongue out. It might have been a childish gesture, but, oddly, it made her feel better.

After a quick lunch at a nearby fast-food restaurant

Drew decided to head for home and just relax. She didn't really have any personal business to take care of; she just needed some time alone to figure out how to deal with Casey.

"What are you doing here at this hour?" Kate greeted her with open surprise.

"I live here," Drew reminded her dryly.

"But it's only two o'clock." The older woman regarded her with suspicion. "Did something go wrong at work?"

"Not exactly." She shrugged as she pulled off her suit jacket and walked into her bedroom. A few minutes later she came out wearing well-worn jeans and a loose-fitting T-shirt, her hair pulled back into a casual ponytail. At that moment she looked a far cry from the modern businesswoman she presented to the world.

"What happened?" Kate persisted, shutting off the vacuum cleaner and setting it aside.

"Your dear darling nephew handed in his resignation," Drew stated bluntly, walking into the kitchen and heading for the refrigerator. "Do we have any soda?" she inquired, hunting through the contents.

"In front of you," Kate pointed out. "What do you mean, Casey quit?"

"I mean he handed me his letter of resignation effective a month from today." She withdrew a can and popped it open, then poured the contents into an ice-filled glass.

"And because of that you're home early?"

Drew shook her head. "I'm going back tonight, when it's a lot quieter. Right now everyone sees me as CHEM Corp.'s hatchet person, and they're coming to me saying how indispensable they are. Now I know why Casey's been so quiet on that subject. I thought I'd come home, take a quick swim and recharge my batteries before finishing up my report for Marty

Watson, who, by the way, is livid that Casey has the audacity to leave. He seems to think that Casey would be a valuable addition to CHEM Corp.'s corporate family. It seems that I'm to persuade dear Mr. McCord to stay with us at any cost."

"*Any* cost?" Kate's eyes twinkled merrily. "Hm, that should prove interesting!"

Drew took a healthy swallow of her soda and turned around to lean against the kitchen counter. "Kate, did it ever bother you when Casey and I lived together?" she asked quietly. "After all, it wasn't exactly something that was done in your day. What I mean is, were you ever angry that we dared to do such a thing as 'live in sin'?" She smiled wryly at her choice of words.

Kate smiled, understanding Drew better than the young woman understood herself. She poured herself a glass of ice tea and added lime juice to it, then walked over to the kitchen table next to a window which overlooked a small patio. She gestured toward the opposite seat before sitting down herself.

"My dear, I loved you as one of my own from the first moment I laid eyes on you," she said honestly. "I loved you for putting a sparkle in Casey's eyes and for giving him a purpose. When he came back from Vietnam he was withdrawn and quiet, not at all the smiling, happy young man I had known from a baby. I knew things hadn't been easy for him over there, but we hadn't wanted to pry and ask him to talk about his experiences. He spent time with his parents after they moved to Oregon, but he knew the time would come when he would have to get on with his life. His first step to his new life was his acceptance at M.I.T. He worked hard in school and didn't seem to care that he had very little free time. Oh, I'm not saying that he was some kind of a monk, because I doubt he's that kind of man. He certainly had his share of girlfriends, but none of them stayed around too long. And he never asked any of them to live with him as he did you," the older woman added gently.

Drew set her glass down and leaned forward, resting her elbows on the table, her hands clasped in front of her. "He was my first lover," she admitted quietly. She still felt a sense of pride in having pleased a very special man. "I'm not ashamed to admit it, because he always made me feel as if I were someone very precious to him. To be honest, the feeling was mutual."

"You shouldn't be ashamed," Kate told her. "There were many times when my Hank and I were tempted to anticipate our vows." Her face lit up with love and joy as she remembered her husband.

Drew nodded. For the first time the memories didn't hurt, perhaps because they were being shared by someone who could understand what they meant to her, maybe even more than she could herself. She had met Casey at the age of twenty, and not long after her twenty-fifth birthday they had parted. She hadn't expected ever to see him again, and had worked long, body wracking hours in order to keep her memories at bay. It had been all for nothing.

"Did Casey ever tell you his feelings when he learned I would be coming here to take over Fantasy Toys temporarily?" she asked soberly, adding wryly, "He was the one to tell you I was in town, wasn't he?"

Kate nodded. "He called me one evening and said that you had been appointed to be CHEM Corp.'s representative, but my coming here to take care of you was entirely my own idea," she informed Drew in her brusque voice. "Heavens, girl, I remember how you worked so hard at school, not to mention at that part-time job that Casey continually nagged you to quit. I was never so glad as when you left that telegram place."

"After I had delivered that anniversary telegram to you, you mean." Drew chuckled, remembering the older woman's look of shock when Drew had shown up in a brief costume at the surprise anniversary party Casey had given for his aunt and uncle. It was a party they all remembered, since Hank Wilton had had a stroke a month later and never recovered.

Drew sighed wearily. "My boss is having kittens because Casey is resigning. He's demanded that I do everything in my power to keep him at Fantasy." She decided that reminiscing hadn't been such a good idea after all.

Kate laughed at that. "Anything within reason, or has he suggested you play the slinky siren?" she asked slyly.

"Marty would say anything, although I was never one for low-cut silk gowns and black stockings," Drew said dryly, finishing the last of her cold drink.

Kate leaned forward, all signs of teasing gone from her face and voice. "Do you still love Casey, child?"

"Does love enter into it, Aunt Kate?" she evaded quietly, refusing to look up for fear Kate would see the truth in her eyes. Love did enter into it a great deal. Their relationship had been based on a deep, fulfilling love from the beginning, but in the end that love hadn't been strong enough to endure her immaturity and his fragile male ego. "Pardon my bluntness, but we were good together, in all areas. Isn't that all that should matter in the type of relationship we had?" It was hard to remember how many times Casey had told her that he loved her while they made love, all the dinners that had turned cold because Drew and Casey couldn't wait to reaffirm that love by worshiping each other's bodies. It hadn't been just a physical love, either. There had been many times when they stayed up all night sharing a bottle of wine and one glass between them, talking about everything and anything. There was so much more, but it hurt to remember too much about those years.

The older woman patted Drew's hand. "I wonder," she mused, rising from the table. "Enough of this lazing around for me. I thought I'd make a seafood quiche for dinner. Does that sound all right to you?"

Drew nodded, her mind now thousands of miles away. Kate had been a source of strength for her from the beginning. She and Hank had lived in a small town in New Hampshire when Drew had been in school and shared Casey's apartment. Many weekends had been spent at the rambling farmhouse, and not one word of censure had ever been spoken to the young couple. They had been given a loft bedroom with a large double bed and a warm comforter that shrouded them on cold winter nights. How wonderful those nights had been!

She hated to admit that she had subconsciously compared every man she had met since then with Casey, and that every one had always been found lacking. She had even gone so far three years before as to become engaged, in hopes of banishing her sensual memories. After a short time she had realized that she would only be starting out her marriage with a lie, and she had promptly broken it off.

Sighing deeply, she got up from her chair and walked over to the sink to rinse out her glass. This wasn't the time to brood over the past. She had enough in the present to worry about.

That evening, still dressed casually in jeans, Drew returned to her office long after everyone else had gone home. After signing in with the security guard she went directly upstairs.

The first thing she found on her desk was a note from Viv informing her that Marty had called and was taking a late flight out of Houston. He would be in her office first thing in the morning.

"Damn," she said under her breath, crumpling the note and tossing it into the wastebasket.

"Tsk, tsk, ladies shouldn't swear." The mocking male voice came from the open doorway.

Drew's head snapped up. "Don't tell me *you're* working late?" She arched a disbelieving eyebrow at his informal apparel of jeans and a body-molding knit shirt in forest green. "If I recall correctly, you resigned today."

"That doesn't mean I intend to sit on my duff until my last day." Casey entered the office and sauntered over to her desk. A half smile curved his lips as he took in her casual appearance. "You look a hell of a lot more like the Drew I remember," he murmured. "Except your hair was longer then. Down to your waist. It used to hang like a golden curtain."

Drew couldn't keep the betraying flush from her cheeks at his subtle reminder of the way he would bury his hands in her hair while he made love to her. Sometimes he would teasingly refer to her as his sexy Rapunzel.

"She doesn't exist any longer," she whispered tersely. "That Drew grew up a long time ago."

"Turned into a business machine, you mean." His mocking smile appeared briefly again. "What a pity. I enjoyed the other Drew a great deal. She knew how to live life to its fullest. She could make an afternoon in the park a special occasion. There were no airs, no dreams of driving expensive cars, no striving for power. Just a vibrant love of life and the people and the world around her."

Stung by his words, she retorted, "*You* were the one who refused to try your luck in Houston. It wasn't as if we needed to worry about money. I was already doing pretty well. I could have supported the both of us until you found a new job. I told you that then."

"*I* was the one meant to lend financial support," he snarled. "I wasn't about to be kept by a woman, even you."

"Yet it was all right for you to insist that I give up my job while I was in school."

"It was cutting too much into your study time, and your grades were beginning to show it," he reminded her arrogantly. "I made good money, and I was willing to share all I had with you—which was a hell of a lot more than others would have done in our situation."

Tears burned her eyes. "Then why wouldn't you let me do the same for you?" she whispered, tipping her head back to look him square in the eye. "Why couldn't I share what I had?"

A swift yank had Drew out of her chair and into Casey's arms. "Five years ago is past history, Drew," he murmured in that sexy bedroom voice of his. "I used to pray I wouldn't ever see you again, but Fate decided it just wasn't to be. Who am I to argue with that?" he growled, lowering his head just enough so that his tongue could trace the barely parted softness of her lips. "You still taste of peppermint." He teased a corner of her mouth, leaving a moist, heated brand on the ultrasensitive skin.

"It's my—my lip gloss." She stumbled over the words. She had forgotten the warm strength of his arms around her, the silky brush of his moustache against her mouth, the musky, male scent of his skin that no other man could duplicate. "D–don't, Casey," she pleaded.

"There was a time when you enjoyed my kissing you," he breathed over her glistening lips. "We used to do a lot of it, remember? Among other things. It didn't matter where we kissed, just as long as we could hold and touch each other and kiss when the need struck us.

Even that time in the elevator." He chuckled at the memory and received a faint answering smile from Drew.

"And that elderly lady caught us," she murmured, unconsciously sliding her arms around his waist. "I really don't think she wanted to get off at the next floor. She probably thought she should leave us as quickly as possible."

"It was always good between us, Drew," he purred, leaning against the edge of the desk and pulling her between his parted legs until she was cradled against him. "We not only spoke with our bodies, but with our souls. I have an idea that magic is still there."

"We'll never know, will we?" She strained to keep her breathing even. This situation was getting out of hand, and she had no defense against the whispers of desire in her veins. She could feel his lips touching the sensitive spot just behind her ear, his teeth grazing the soft skin. He hadn't forgotten any of the erotic spots on her body.

"Why not?" His voice was deep and sensual with meaning. His lips moved lightly and teasingly against her jaw, creating dangerous sensations in the pit of her stomach. One hand slipped up to caress her breast, unerringly finding the pointed tip begging for his touch. "I think we're already finding out," he murmured roughly, dipping his head to outline the nipple with his tongue through the soft cotton of her shirt, then tugging on it gently with his teeth.

Drew gasped as the heated dampness seared her. Without thinking, she had already let her hands tunnel under Casey's shirt to explore the smoothly muscled skin of his back. She could feel him tense in response.

He lifted his head and captured her mouth with his, flicking his tongue over her lips until they parted in surrender. Soft purring sounds were torn from her throat by the kiss that catapulted her back into the past.

How could she forget the fierce hunger he always displayed for the moist recesses of her mouth, the way his tongue would delve into every dark corner and seek out the flavor that was uniquely hers? Her own tongue participated in the love dance, darting out to tease his, inviting him farther into the shadowy caverns until there would be nothing left but for them to take that one last step. They had never been able to begin this way without tumbling into bed to continue their intimate exploration of each other's bodies.

Casey's hands had found their way under Drew's shirt and even farther under her bra to seek out the thrusting fullness of her breasts. As always, the pearly mounds shaped themselves to his palms, relishing his knowing caress. Drew whimpered and pressed herself even harder against Casey while allowing her own hands the same privilege of roaming over his chest and finding the tiny male nipples that hardened as easily as her own did. She buried her face against the warm skin of his neck as his tongue traced the delicate line of her ear. In answer, she used her own tongue to draw lines along his throat, tasting the salty skin and noting the faint sheen of perspiration with feminine satisfaction. She moved suggestively against his body and felt his answering desire. She wanted him more now than ever. It had been so long since their last loving! It was some time before sanity began to assert itself and she began to realize just where they were.

"Casey, please don't do this," she pleaded breathlessly, trying to pull away from his embrace, but he merely tightened his hold, not wanting to let her go just yet. "The guard . . . he might come by."

"No problem there, love," he chuckled softly. "The door is not only safely closed, but it's locked. Of course, if it bothers you so much, we could always go to my place. It's been a long time since you've been in my bed, sweetheart. I'd like to have you there again."

"For *auld lang syne?*" She smiled bleakly, finally able to free herself from his arms so that she could think clearly again. "No, I don't think so."

Casey pulled back slightly and looked down at her with a strange expression on his face. "You certainly were more than willing enough a few minutes ago," he stated bluntly. "In fact, we probably could have had a high old time on the carpet or on the comfort of your couch if I had pushed a little further."

Drew hated to admit how right Casey was. There had been several moments when all that had mattered was that he assuage the erotic ache in her body, no matter where they were. Luckily, she had come to her senses in time. Now all she wanted was to get as far away from him as she possibly could. The two of them made a dangerous combination, and their passion would be likely to erupt again if she didn't escape.

"Oh, come on, Casey." She injected an airy note in her voice. "Surely you can't expect us to take up where we left off five years ago. Although you have to admit that there is a bit of *déjà vu* to this, because next month you'll be out of work again. Unless, of course, you do have another position to go to." She looked up and flashed him a brittle smile.

All passion was now gone from his face, leaving behind a stony mask. "That's what this was all about, wasn't it?" he asked with a deadly quiet. "You're still wondering where I'm going. Well, I guess you'll just have to wait until next month to find out, won't you?" He turned away and thrust the tails of his shirt back into his jeans. "You were right; that other Drew is gone. Too bad. At least she wasn't just a facsimile of a living and breathing woman. CHEM Corp. did more than just train you to be one of their hatchet men. They turned you into a hollow mockery of a woman, a shell with no life of its own. I wish you luck, lady, because you're going to need it when the time comes for your retirement and all you'll have to show for it is the list of companies you've gone in and revamped. You'll have nothing else. There'll be no man standing in the wings, because no man wants to play second fiddle to a corporation. I only hope your memories and your pension will keep you warm on those cold winter nights." With that he strode over to the door, unlocked it and pulled it open, closing it behind him with unnecessary force.

Drew found her way back to her desk chair. She couldn't shed any tears. She could only feel a chilling numbness from Casey's words.

It was a long time before she could rouse herself enough to leave the building and return home. Luckily Kate was out for the evening and wasn't there to witness Drew's paper-white face and tousled clothing. There would have been no way Drew could have explained her appearance satisfactorily. She crawled into bed, hoping to fall into a deep slumber where even dreams didn't come to haunt her.

Chapter Three

*W*ednesday morning Drew stared at her reflection in the bathroom mirror and winced at what she saw. Her restless night had left its mark with lavender shadows under her eyes and paler than usual features.

"You look terrible," Kate announced when Drew walked into the kitchen for her morning cup of coffee.

"Thank you. My dented ego is now a complete dud," Drew said dryly. She had hoped that extra touches of makeup and the coral silk dress would give her some color, but they obviously weren't going to be enough.

"Sit down and eat your breakfast," Kate ordered kindly. "You'll feel better."

"I hate breakfast." Drew voiced her usual argument, yet knew deep down that it wouldn't get her anywhere. She had long since learned where Casey got his stubborn streak. Kate was the original immovable rock. "I would be ecstatic if they would abolish breakfast and we could start with lunch every day."

"Why? You rarely eat lunch unless it happens to be

for business reasons." Kate set a plate containing a poached egg on toast and several slices of bacon in front of Drew. "I don't know how you coped with Casey, since his favorite meal is breakfast."

"If he wanted breakfast, he cooked it himself." She grimaced, but proceeded to eat every bite under Kate's watchful eye. She tipped her head to one side and looked across the table at the older woman. "Why are you bringing up your traitorous nephew's name? He's putting me in a spot, and he knows it. My boss flew in from Houston last night, and I just know that today is going to be horrendous. Deep down, Marty has a sadistic streak, and he enjoys watching his staff suffer. I think he'd be in seventh heaven if he could get me to cry."

"Then you'd better eat every bit of your breakfast," Kate advised. "You're going to need all the strength you can get."

"Strength." Drew gave a hollow laugh. "I'm going to need a miracle."

Forty-five minutes later, when Drew parked her car at Fantasy Toys, she instinctively knew that Marty was already there. It was as if she could sense a big cat nearby, and she was its quarry. Squaring her shoulders, she slid out of the Ferrari and walked into the building.

One look at the faces of the people she passed as she walked down the hall to her office told her that they hadn't found out that the so-called head honcho, meaning Marty, was there. It was just as well, because she'd have even more problems with the department heads if they thought that she couldn't sneeze without the boss coming out to take over.

"I suppose Genghis Khan has taken over my office already," she murmured to Viv, stopping at her secretary's desk.

Viv nodded. "Syd at the gate told me that he's been here for almost an hour."

"I'm not surprised. He's hoping to catch me off guard." Drew smiled pleasantly. "Take a word of advice from an old veteran. His bark is definitely *not* worse than his bite. At least a rattlesnake gives you some warning before he strikes. The only reason Marty warned me ahead of time was because he was hoping I'd have a sleepless night." Which she had, but it hadn't been on his account.

"I told him you had an emergency dental appointment yesterday," Viv confided.

"Thanks." Drew winked. "Do me a favor and get us a pot of coffee. A spoonful of hemlock in one of the cups would be greatly appreciated."

She walked toward her office door, took a deep breath and opened it. As expected, Marty was seated at her desk, going through a pile of folders.

"It's about time you got here," he growled, not bothering to glance up from his reading. "Doesn't anyone start work at a decent hour around here?"

Drew walked over to Marty and picked up his arm to look at his watch. "You forgot to change to Pacific time," she pointed out dryly, setting her briefcase on the only clear corner of her desk. "I certainly hope that you'll clean up this mess before you leave." From the very beginning she had learned that he didn't appreciate people who fawned all over him. Meet the man head on and you were in his good graces; back down and you'd find yourself in one of CHEM Corp.'s out-of-the-way offices with little chance of seeing civilization again. Drew had always privately thought of Marty as a bulldog who held on to his victim and refused to let go.

"Why bother when I won't be here long enough to worry about the time change?" His voice even resembled a bulldog's growl. Marty was short and stocky, and was never without a cigar in his mouth. His graying dark brown hair always looked as if he never combed it properly, and invariably a lock dropped over his fore-head.

"Would you like a tour of the facilities?" she asked, walking around the desk to the other chair. She knew very well that Marty wasn't about to give up his chair even if it was hers. "You *do* want to see the rest of the building, don't you, Marty?" she pressed, seating her-self.

"I've already seen it. Don't ask for my impressions just yet." He looked up from under a pair of bushy eyebrows. "Your secretary said you lost a filling and had to go to the dentist. Don't the dentists around here have evening hours?"

"If I decided to take my sick days and vacation time all at once, you wouldn't see me for months," Drew said lightly. "Just be glad I only took a few hours."

"I want to meet with McCord," Marty announced, but she wasn't surprised to hear it.

"When?"

He cast her an exasperated look, as if he thought her mind was failing. "Ten minutes ago would have been perfect," he rapped out, taking his cigar out of his mouth and waving it in the air. "Get him on the phone and arrange a meeting for lunch."

Drew clenched her teeth, wishing just once she could cuttingly inform him that she wasn't a secretary—as if it would make any difference. She leaned forward and buzzed Viv on the intercom.

"Viv, would you please get Casey McCord on the phone for me? And if he isn't in his office, have him paged."

"Sure thing."

Marty held a folder in his hands and perused the contents. "How did a run-down company like this get hold of someone as on the ball as he is?" he mused. "McCord is a genius in sales. He's ten steps ahead of the world when it comes to figuring out what the public will buy. We can't afford to lose him, Drew. Hell, even if we dump the company later on, we can always find something for him somewhere else." He laughed. "I'd put him on my staff, but if I wasn't careful he'd probably take me over on his way up the ladder. This guy's got what it takes, and I want him with us until long past retirement age. According to his personnel record, sales isn't even his field. How did he fall into this?"

"He was a victim of being the last one hired, as they say," Drew explained, knowing that her boss knew all of this already. He was just testing her. "The job market was flooded with too many engineers. Luckily he was willing to switch fields, and he found a sales position with Sundance." She knew she had to tread carefully so that Marty wouldn't realize just how knowledgeable she was about Casey's past career.

The intercom buzzed, and Viv's announcement that she had Casey on line four interrupted their conversation. At Marty's nod Drew picked up the phone.

"Good morning," she said a shade too brightly.

"Hm, I was afraid you might not be talking to me today." Casey's husky murmur was a little too suggestive for eight a.m. "What can I do for you?" He chuckled softly. "Or would you like some suggestions?"

"I thought we could meet for lunch." Drew felt a light tap on her arm and looked up to see Marty point to himself and shake his head. It was obvious that he didn't want Casey to know he was going to be present.

"Sounds fine to me," he agreed readily. "How about I come by your office around twelve-thirty?"

"All right." She hesitated, wishing she could tell him the real reason behind her lunch invitation. She had a strong idea that he wouldn't appreciate her deception.

"Drew," Casey said, sensing that she was preparing to hang up, "I'm glad you called."

"Yes, so am I," she murmured, hastily cutting off the connection. She replaced the receiver and looked at Marty. "He'll be here at twelve-thirty."

"Fine." He smiled broadly. "Don't worry, kid; I'll handle all this. You just sit back and listen to the expert. You're going to learn a lot from my little talk with McCord."

"Why are you here and why are you doing this?" she demanded bluntly. "You promised me that this project would be all mine. You're already going back on your word, Marty. All along you tell me how much you trust me, that this is my baby. Yet at the first obstacle you're here." She unconsciously stuck her chin out stubbornly.

The expression on Marty's face was not pleasant. "This *is* your project, Drew," he replied seriously. "At the same time, there could be trouble if McCord leaves. You've read all the reports. The people here look up to him. He's a natural leader, and I intend to make sure he stays with us. You're still pretty new to the bargaining table, so I'm going to try to find out what he wants so he'll tear up his resignation. Don't worry, you're going to be present at this lunch, and I want you to listen very carefully to what I say. Call this a hell of a good learning experience for you, because the next time something like this happens I'll let you work it out on your own. And if you fail, you'll fall on your sweet tush all by yourself. Understand?"

With a mutinous gleam in her eye, Drew nodded reluctantly. She understood only too well.

"Now, why don't you have your secretary get us some coffee and you can bring me up to date on what's going on." His former good mood was returning.

The morning passed quickly for Drew. Much too fast for her peace of mind, in fact. She had a pretty good idea that Casey wasn't going to appreciate having Marty present at this luncheon, especially when he thought that she had invited him to a lunch for two. She had realized that Casey thought she was trying to renew their relationship. The husky suggestiveness in his voice when he had spoken to her had been proof of that.

When Viv announced Casey's presence, Drew asked to have him wait while she hurriedly put on a new coat of lipstick and an extra touch of blusher. Marty watched her with open amusement.

"Not one word," she warned darkly. "Or so help me I'll let everyone in Houston know about that secretary who waylaid you in your office late one night about a year ago."

"Blackmailer." He groaned in memory of the shapely young woman who had thought that seducing her boss would gain her an instant promotion. She hadn't realized that he was very happily married, and her efforts had been all in vain. Her dismissal had come the next day. Marty's marriage was something Drew always wondered about. How a sweet, gentle person like Julia Watson could put up with a gruff, overbearing man like Marty was beyond her comprehension, yet their long-standing marriage was proof that opposites did attract.

When Casey entered the office a few minutes later he halted immediately, sensing that something was wrong. He might not have met Marty before, but he knew the kind of man he was facing. In addition, Drew's shame-faced expression easily gave her away.

"McCord, I'm Marty Watson." The older man stood and offered his hand. "Since I was in the area I thought I'd come by to see my star organizer. I also wanted to meet you while I was here. I've been receiving glowing reports on your work." He smiled expansively.

"Oh?" Casey gave Drew a cool smile. It hadn't taken him long to see that the lunch invitation hadn't been her idea. "I'm sure Ms. Sinclair has been much too generous."

Drew could already see that it wasn't going to be a

good lunch. She knew what Casey could be like when he wanted to act difficult, and she had an idea that this was to be one of those times.

Still talking a mile a minute, Marty steered Drew and Casey outside to his rental car. Drew hid her smile at the large Mercedes parked haphazardly in a marked slot.

"I'm surprised CHEM Corp. doesn't get upset over your car rental bills, Marty," she teased him lightly, waiting as he unlocked the passenger door.

"I wouldn't ride in your hot rod even if there were enough room for three. I almost got whiplash from your crazy driving the last time," he grumbled as he gestured for the two of them to get in the front seat. "Go ahead, there's more than enough room."

Drew didn't like the idea of sharing such close quarters with Casey, and even protested mildly that she would sit in the back to give the men more room up front, but Marty quickly overrode her suggestion.

"He drives like a maniac," she muttered under her breath to Casey while Marty walked around to the driver's side. "As long as you keep your eyes closed you'll be fine."

One thing Drew was grateful for was that Marty didn't smoke his cigars in the car. Before she had left her office she had passed Viv a note to *please* air out the room before they returned!

She sat stiffly in the car, wishing she could shift her position even a little bit, but the burning sensation along her right side where Casey's body pressed warmly against hers warned her against that. There was no point in letting him know that she felt any discomfort, a discomfort due not to the limited space, but to the man seated next to her.

"It was a shame you had to leave the engineering field, Casey. You don't mind if I call you Casey, do you?" Marty went on without bothering to wait for an answer. "Especially with your impressive background. I won't complain, though, because you've been a major asset to CHEM Corp. I'm sure I don't have to tell you that Fantasy Toys wouldn't be where they are right now if it hadn't been for you and your sales force keeping them afloat. Hell, no one else wanted to market that crazy little troll character that came out a year ago, yet you hung in there and actually helped get the contract. A good piece of work. I like a man with foresight about marketing trends."

Drew concentrated on looking at the dashboard. To this day she wondered how Marty had gotten his driver's license, since he ignored stop signs—and even red lights, when he could—not to mention that he disregarded posted speed limits.

"I still took a chance," Casey replied, shifting so that his left arm rested along the back of the seat very close to Drew's shoulder. "The Fuggles"—he pronounced the name with a long *u*—aren't exactly the cutest characters in the world, but they have an appeal to small children, and even some adults."

"Tell me about it." Marty shook his head in amusement. "My grandchildren have every one of those ugly little monsters. And how a movie about underground critters like that could be a hit is a mystery to me."

In no time Marty parked in front of a small Mexican restaurant in Old Towne. Drew shook her head in amusement. It never seemed to fail. Marty could be in a town for only a few hours and still find the best restaurants. San Diego was proving to be no exception.

"Marty, when was the last time you were in San Diego?" she asked.

He shrugged. "During the war. I shipped out from here."

"Did this restaurant exist back in the forties?" she persisted.

"Who knows? I just asked around and a few people recommended this place." He ushered them inside.

Drew winced inwardly at the thought of digesting hot, spicy food. Her stomach had already been protesting against all the coffee she had drunk that morning, and she knew that Mexican food wasn't going to make it any better. Although the men ordered drinks, she asked for iced tea. She wanted to keep a clear head while she watched these two circle each other. Marty was right: It was going to be a learning experience. In more ways than one.

"Drew mentioned that you're thinking of leaving us," Marty said later as they finished their meals, getting right to the heart of the matter.

"Not thinking, definitely leaving," Casey corrected.

"You know, of course, that no matter what anyone else offers you, we can top not only the figures but the perks to go with it." He smiled confidently. "I won't beat around the bush, McCord. You're a good man, one we'd like to keep no matter what the cost, and I don't say that lightly."

"I'm sure you don't." Casey smiled briefly. His eyes were enigmatic when they turned to Drew. This was one time when he wasn't going to allow her to read his thoughts, and she shuddered to think what they might be. One thing she was certain of: He was blaming her for this meeting. "I just feel it's time to move on."

"Because of Drew acting as your superior?" Marty asked, his eyes narrowed in concentration.

"A woman boss doesn't intimidate me," Casey replied evenly.

"Not even when the woman is one you lived with at one time? You two were together for close to five years, if I recall correctly."

Drew's moan was barely audible, but the shock on her face told the whole story. Casey snapped around to face her with accusing eyes.

"I never said a word, Casey," she whispered, shaking her head for emphasis. "I never saw any need to."

Marty smiled wolfishly. He was obviously pleased with the results of his bombshell. "Don't blame her, McCord. She's telling you the truth. She never said anything about the two of you. All I had to do was work a hunch and look over past work histories and previous addresses. At one time you two had the same address in Cambridge, Massachusetts, including the same apartment number. It wasn't too difficult to figure things out from there."

"My reasons for leaving Fantasy Toys have nothing to do with Drew," Casey told him in a stony voice. "I can't imagine what all this fuss is about. I'm resigning in a month; that's all there is to it."

Drew decided to put a word in now while she still had a voice. "Would you consider staying on a few weeks past that?" Seeing his instant negative response, she added hastily, "As you know, the sales conference comes up soon, and I thought a one-to-one meeting with the regional managers would give us an idea of who to promote to your position. You've maintained an excellent sales record with your force, Casey, and it's going to be very difficult to keep that up unless we come up with just the right person to take over. With your input, we just might be able to do that. Personally, I would prefer promoting someone from within the company rather than looking on the outside. That way we would have someone who already knows the ins and outs of Fantasy Toys. If you stayed on a little bit longer, you could help us fill him in completely. Will you at least consider my suggestion?" she asked softly, her eyes echoing her plea. "If it will make you feel better, we'll keep you on in a consulting basis. It's just that the company is going through so much upheaval right now that I don't want to create any more problems than I have to."

Marty sat back and watched his protégé go to work. His plan was working just fine. He had known very well that Casey wouldn't go along with any of his suggestions, but Drew's soft amber eyes were a different story. The fact that they had been more than close friends in the past would help even more.

"Why should I want to help you?" Casey muttered, forgetting about their avid audience of one.

"Because I need you," she replied without hesitation.

They silently studied one another, Casey wishing he could forget how the gold flecks danced in Drew's eyes when she was happy, or how the deep amber of her eyes deepened when she was serious, as she was now. He wondered if the past really could be buried. Drew's work had come between them five years ago, and it was doing the same thing now. The painful part was that Casey would walk away from her and they'd never see each other again unless she was able to do something about it.

"Your little lady here deserves a raise, Watson," Casey said harshly, finally breaking the fragile web surrounding them. "She knows how to use the tools of her trade very well." When he shifted slightly in his chair he made sure that his hand covered her thigh and inched its way upward in an insolent caress.

Drew smothered a start of alarm at his intimate touch, although it wasn't unfamiliar to her. But this time there was no tenderness in his touch, only the knowledge that he felt she was selling herself to keep him at Fantasy Toys for a while longer. She wasn't sure if it was that realization that was beginning to make her sick to her stomach or the spicy meal she had eaten while Marty talked. Either way, she knew she had to get out of there fast.

"Marty, I believe you mentioned an early afternoon

flight back to Houston," she murmured, casually moving her leg away from Casey's touch and feeling sorely tempted to stamp her heel down on the toe of his soft leather loafer.

He glanced down at his watch and nodded. "I've got just enough time to drop the two of you back at the office. I'm proud of what you've accomplished here so far, Drew," he said sincerely. "You've come a long way from that green kid I hired almost six years ago. You're going to go far with us."

She managed a weak smile at his praise. It was praise she had worked hard to hear, but now it didn't seem very important.

The drive back to the offices was quiet except for Marty talking to Casey about CHEM Corp.'s corporate offices, mentioning a hope that Casey would come out there for a look. Marty seemed to think that if Casey could be persuaded to stay a little longer at Fantasy Toys, there was no reason why he couldn't be convinced to stay with the company itself. Yet even the gold carrot of a vice-presidency dangled in front of the younger man brought no response. Marty shrugged inwardly and decided to leave any further corporate romancing to Drew. He hoped that she had picked up some pointers during lunch. She was a comer, and he was determined to see her rise to the top of her field.

Marty dropped them in the company parking lot and drove off with a screech of tires.

"His cars must not last too long," Casey observed cynically.

"Usually a little over a year," Drew said dully.

"Well, I hope you're happy, Ms. Sinclair," he said harshly, turning to walk away. "You did achieve your purpose, didn't you? Am I in store for any more surprises before I leave here?"

"I didn't know Marty was coming until last night,"

she argued. "And I certainly didn't ask him to come. I figured I could handle this problem on my own," she maintained stubbornly.

Casey looked back at her, a smile tugging at the corners of his lips. "That's the first time I've ever been referred to as a problem."

His mood had suddenly lightened, and with it Drew's hopes rose. More and more she had stopped seeing him as an important asset to the company and was seeing him as the man she had lived with and loved for five years.

"It seems that if you're going to persuade me to stay here, you'd better pull out all the stops." His smile was a little too dangerous.

"What do you mean?" She looked genuinely puzzled by, and just a bit wary of, his sudden good nature.

"Simple," he murmured, allowing his eyes to roam over the graceful curves beneath the soft coral dress. "If I'm to stay here, you're going to have to court me."

"Court you?" Now Drew was really confused. She stared at him as if she thought he was truly demented.

"That's right." Casey nodded. "And I mean the full treatment. I want to see and hear all the advantages in staying with Fantasy Toys, and I don't mean that none too subtle offer of a vice-presidency, either. I want to see how far you'll go to keep me here." His soft velvet voice was even more dangerous than his smile.

"You're crazy!" she flared up, uncaring who might hear her. "I should think a substantial raise and promotion would make you more than happy. It's certainly a good indication of how much we want you to stay."

"Not exactly." He shook his head, enjoying her frustration. "I want to know just how badly I'm wanted by *you*." His meaning was all too clear. "Oh, I still intend to look over the regional managers at the sales conference to find my replacement, but just in case I decide to change my mind, I want to know how *you'll* make it worth my while."

"Right now you can consider yourself lucky that I don't give you a well-deserved kick in the shins. Especially after that crass act back at the restaurant. Pawing me as if I were some hooker!" Drew glared at him.

"Aunt Kate wouldn't appreciate you beating up her favorite nephew," he chided. "No matter. It's getting late, and I have a meeting this afternoon. I'll stop by your house tonight and we can go into this further."

"There's nothing to go into," she argued. "This is purely business, and it will be conducted in the office. If you want to stop by to see Aunt Kate, I can't stop you, but that doesn't mean I have to talk to you."

"There are a few personal matters we have to attend to," Casey informed her blithely.

"Such as?" She regarded him suspiciously.

"Since we were living so far apart, I couldn't have visitation rights with Shadow. I think I should have him every other weekend or so now," he said calmly.

Drew definitely knew he had lost all his marbles. "Visitation rights to a bird?" It was becoming an effort to keep her voice down. "You've got to be kidding!"

"He's my bird, too," he responded.

"You gave him to me when I left because you didn't think you'd be able to give him the proper care. He's my bird now!" she protested, unable to comprehend the insane turns this conversation was taking.

"He said my name before he said yours."

"Only because you told him your name more than you told him mine!" Drew took several deep breaths. This conversation was getting ridiculous! "Fine, every other weekend then," she said sharply. "Now, as you said, we both have work to return to." She turned away, intending to get as far away from him as possible.

"I'll be by around seven for dinner," Casey called

after her. "I know Aunt Kate won't mind an extra person."

"No, but *I* will," she muttered to herself, heading for her office and her bottle of antacid tablets. "If work doesn't give me an ulcer, Casey McCord most certainly will. I can't believe this. We lived together, we split up, I got custody of the bird and later his aunt. I just don't think this is the way things are supposed to work out," she moaned.

When Drew entered her office, Viv took one look at her boss's troubled features and decided that lunch must not have gone very well. With the intuition of the well-trained secretary she brought Drew a glass of water and left her alone for a while.

But Drew wasn't about to brood over her misfortune. If Casey wanted to be courted, then that was exactly what he would get. Usually it was done when a company wanted to lure someone away from a rival. Although she didn't have firsthand experience in the art of luring prize employees into the fold, she suspected that with Casey, falling back on her feminine intuition would be more than enough. By the time she was through with Casey McCord, he would be tied hand and foot to Fantasy Toys for the next fifty years!

Chapter Four

*E*ven with all that went on that day, Drew was able to leave her office in time for her evening exercise class.

But the night didn't go well for her, either. The regular instructor was out sick, and the substitute, an athletic woman in her late twenties, kept up a pace that would have killed a racehorse. By the time the session was over Drew's bright turquoise and white striped leotard was dark with sweat, and her ponytail drooped as wearily as her body.

"And to think I pay good money to be tortured this way," she gasped, walking slowly to the locker room. Too tired to change her clothes, she merely pulled on a pair of faded jeans over her damp leotard. In her casual outfit and an old pair of jogging shoes she looked a far cry from one of CHEM Corp.'s up-and-coming executives.

She drove home looking forward to a leisurely hot bath and a relaxing evening doing nothing more strenuous than breathing.

Drew parked in the garage and activated the automatic garage door as she removed her bag from the passenger seat.

"Aunt Kate?" she called out, walking into the kitchen.

The older woman appeared in the doorway. Her agitation communicated itself immediately to Drew.

"Where have you been?" Kate demanded in a whisper.

Drew gave a puzzled smile. "Exercise class. It's Wednesday, remember?" She walked through the kitchen and into the den. "All I want is to get out of these grubby clothes and into a robe." She stopped short at the sight of a visitor seated in an easy chair, with Shadow perched on his shoulder.

"The part about getting out of those clothes sounds fine with me," Casey said affably, greeting her with a wicked smile.

"What are you doing here?" Drew demanded. She had never been more conscious of her bedraggled appearance.

"I told you that I'd be by tonight to discuss taking Shadow this weekend."

"Hello, Shadow," the bird piped up. He inched his way across Casey's shoulder and reached over to draw his beak over Casey's moustache.

"Don't forget that he isn't exactly housebroken," Drew reminded him acid-sweetly.

"I invited Casey to dinner," Kate spoke up brightly, entering the room.

"Wonderful," Drew muttered sardonically. "If you two don't mind, I'll go change my clothes." She headed for the stairs, anger burning in every line of her body.

Drew had never showered and dressed so quickly in her life. Not wanting to take the extra time to blow-dry and style her hair, she pulled it back in another ponytail, then braided it. She donned a peach-colored

V-necked silk tunic and pants, teamed with gold strappy sandals. She might not be happy to see Casey, but she certainly wanted to look her best for any confrontation they might have.

The warm glow in Casey's eyes told her that her efforts hadn't been wasted. She would bet he even knew that she had brushed on an extra coat of mascara.

"My, don't you look nice!" Kate beamed maternally from the kitchen doorway, then turned back to her cooking.

"Need a pick-me-up?" Casey handed Drew a glass.

She didn't even need to taste her drink to know that it was vodka and tonic. Hadn't he forgotten anything about her?

"Kiss Casey! Kiss Casey!" Shadow chirped from Casey's shoulder.

A slow smile illuminated Casey's face. "What an excellent idea," he murmured, moving closer to Drew.

"Aren't you afraid that I might bite?" Drew challenged, her eyes sparkling with amber lights.

"There were times when you did just that," he returned smoothly. "It certainly never bothered me before."

"Aunt Kate!" Drew's alarmed voice rose in a shriek. "Is dinner ready yet?" She swiftly turned away, missing the devilish amusement in Casey's eyes at her discomfort.

"I'm putting the last touches on it now. Come on into the dining room." The muffled reply came from the kitchen.

"Good, I'm starved." Drew's voice was more animated than usual. She took a large gulp of her drink and hurried into the dining room.

Her eyes widened at the attractive floral centerpiece. Kate had even set out the good china!

"If we're having fatted calf for dinner, I'm leaving," she muttered to the older woman.

"Cornish game hens stuffed with wild rice," Kate replied serenely, indicating that Casey should sit at the head of the table.

Drew drained the remainder of her drink, set the glass on the table and took the chair on Casey's right.

"I don't remember you ever downing alcohol as if it were water," he murmured as Kate went into the kitchen for the soup tureen. "Generally you were pretty cautious with your drinking."

"Not when it's an emergency." She presented him with a tight smile. Where was all her composure when she needed it?

"And I'm an emergency?" he guessed.

"More like the beginning of a national disaster."

Casey threw back his head and roared with laughter. "This is what I miss the most, love," he told her in an engaging drawl. "You could make me very angry one minute and have me laughing the next."

"I'm surprised you can remember my idiosyncrasies after five years' worth of women," she retorted tartly. She ignored the flash of bitter jealousy flaring through her body at the thought of the faceless women Casey would have been with over the past five years. She told herself that she shouldn't be jealous. They, as a couple, were a thing of the past, and Casey was very much a man, with a man's physical desires—as she knew only too well. It would be natural for him to find other women to grace his bed.

Drew was glad when Kate returned with a tureen filled with homemade vegetable soup. Now she had something else to concentrate on besides Casey's proximity. His suit had been discarded in favor of a pair of jeans and a white V-necked sweater that highlighted his tan. It didn't help her to see tufts of dark gold hair peeping out of the V-neck, or the narrow gold chain nestled against his throat. Gold chain! She had given him a gold chain their last Christmas together. Could it be the same one?

"It is," Casey murmured, accurately reading her thoughts.

"What?" She looked up.

"I'm still wearing the chain you gave me."

"I don't know what you're talking about," she evaded, damning him for having the ability to read her thoughts even when he couldn't see her face. In fact, they had always been in perfect tune with each other's minds. That was one aspect of their relationship that had made it so special.

Casey smiled before turning to speak to Kate, who had seated herself across from Drew.

Drew found it difficult to concentrate on her food during the meal. Luckily she didn't have to worry about carrying on a conversation. Kate was more than capable of keeping the talk going as she and Casey caught up on family news. Drew knew that Casey took Kate out for dinner at least once a month, and that aunt and nephew had always been close. After dinner Kate suggested having their coffee and brandy in the den. Drew didn't mind that Kate had taken over the hostess duties. Right now, she wasn't feeling very hospitable.

"You did say you wanted to attend the sales conference, am I right?" Casey inquired politely.

"That's what I thought." She was surprised by his question, and even more puzzled by his wide smile. "Is there any reason why I shouldn't?"

"None. I'll have my secretary take care of your air and hotel reservations for you," Casey continued, still grinning.

"What's so funny?" Drew demanded finally.

"Not a thing." His smile was replaced by an expression of sublime innocence which didn't fool her for a second.

"Where is it being held?" she asked curiously. She lifted her coffee cup to her lips. She couldn't recall seeing any information on the conference, although with all the reading material she had been perusing lately, it wouldn't be surprising if it had slipped by her.

"Hawaii."

Drew choked and began coughing. Casey took her cup out of her hand and clapped an unconcerned palm against her back.

"Y–you're going to kill me!" she finally managed to gasp. Her fingers were splayed against her throat in a defensive gesture. Drew sat up straight and took several deep breaths. She took her coffee from Casey and sipped it, wishing it were something a great deal stronger.

"We'll be staying on the island of Kauai." Casey continued unperturbed, naming a hotel that started Drew choking again. "My, you do have a problem there." He winced an innocent concern for her distress. "Your coffee must have gone down the wrong way."

"Something certainly did," she gritted, shakily replacing the cup in its saucer.

"The arrangements were in the planning stages more than six months ago," Casey told her quietly, accurately guessing the cause of her difficulty. "You weren't here then, and I didn't see the need to bother you with them once you arrived."

"There was no reason to consult me. Setting up the annual sales conference is your department, not mine," Drew said stiffly.

"I think I'll wash the dishes," Kate said brightly, jumping to her feet. "You two just sit here and talk." She bustled out of the room that was rapidly becoming a battlefield.

"I didn't realize staying at that particular hotel would upset you so much," Casey said in a calm voice.

"It doesn't," Drew denied, feeling the muscles in her

stomach contract as memories intruded. She and Casey had spent their vacation there one year. Even now, thoughts of those blissful days could warm her body.

"About Shadow . . ."

She looked up, amazed that he could change the subject as easily as he changed his clothes. That was another characteristic she preferred to forget. "You wouldn't mind if I took him this weekend, would you?"

Drew took a deep breath. "Don't you think this sounds just a trifle crazy?" she asked him, matching his matter-of-fact tone. "After all, he *is* only a bird."

Casey got up from his chair and walked over to the cage, where the cockatiel sat on the open door. The bird hopped happily onto the back of Casey's hand and then climbed up to his shoulder.

"I remember that you carried on a good many conversations with this bird," he replied sardonically. "In fact, it was because of your attention that he talks as well as he does."

"Hello, Drew." Shadow then launched into one of his off-key songs.

"Courtesy of Aunt Kate's taste in movies," Drew said dryly. "He's trying to imitate a theme song. Don't ask me which one he's working on now. None of his efforts sound the way they're supposed to."

Casey returned to his chair and sat back, allowing his tawny eyes to roam over Drew's slim figure. They lingered at the point of her neckline, where the shadowy cleft of her breasts was revealed. His memory could easily fill in the curves and hollows that the material covered. How much he would give to reacquaint himself with every inch of that tantalizing skin! If he closed his eyes he could still recall the special scent of her skin and the way she tasted.

For all Drew's outer sophistication, Casey could still catch glimpses of the little girl inside. He remembered the Drew who had been frightened to attend a cocktail

party given by one of his co-workers for fear of saying
or doing the wrong thing and embarrassing him. The
Drew who had been so shy when meeting other people,
but who had always acted the totally sensual woman
when they were alone. There was no doubt that they
had always been perfect together. Drew was right;
there had been women after her. Hell, he had thought
he'd never see her again! But none of them had kept
him interested the way she had. With Drew, he had
never been sure what would happen next, and he had
always enjoyed her spontaneity. They had lost a lot
when they parted five years ago. He only hoped it could
be regained before it was too late.

"What would you say to going out for dinner Friday
night?" he asked softly. "We could talk over old
times."

Drew knew only too well that "old times" would
probably have them end the evening in bed. Even now
her fingers itched to tease the hairs peeping out over
the neckline of his sweater. She wanted to rediscover
the hardened contours of his body. Her nostrils
twitched slightly as they picked up the fresh clean scent
of his skin. Once she had given him a very sensual
backrub, using his after-shave instead of alcohol. What
a night that had been! Her cheeks warmed at the
memory.

"I don't think that would be a good idea, Casey," she
said quietly, raising her eyes to meet his. The mask had
lowered over her face, and he could read nothing of the
thoughts that were tormenting her. "I don't care to give
the company gossips any new material. You and I as a
romantic duo would give them a field day."

Casey's eyes narrowed to tawny slits. "What you
mean is that you don't care for anyone to find out about
our past—" delicate pause— "involvement." The
deadly quiet of his tone was warning enough.

"It's best," Drew clipped defiantly.

"Best? Best for whom? Me?" he condemned, sneering. "I can't see you covering this up for *my* sake. It's all for your own precious reputation, isn't it, Drew?" he rapped out, standing up, the bird, now forgotten, perched on the back of the chair. "I was proud of you, woman! I still am. You've achieved a great deal in a short time. I also know you accomplished it with nothing more than hard work. You're the last woman who would reach her goals by lying on her back."

"Damn right!" she shot back, jumping to her own feet. "I took every stinking job they could find, but I didn't complain once. Instead I worked twelve to sixteen hours a day and finished each of those projects ahead of schedule. Fantasy Toys is my chance to show them that I can handle larger scale jobs. I can't afford to blow this!"

"And the best way to do that is to turn into some asexual being? You can't try to pass us off as a one-night stand!" Casey roared. "Damn it, I took you everywhere with me when we were together. If someone had the nerve to say, Oh, by the way, McCord, don't bring your girlfriend, I didn't go. Not because I was acting like some kind of martyr, but because I always wanted you with me. My friends were your friends. You might not have been my wife, but you were certainly accorded all the privileges of one."

"If the people at Fantasy Toys knew we once had an affair, I'd have to be extra cautious in my dealings with you. Otherwise they'd believe we'd taken up where we had left off," Drew declared stonily.

His features hardened. "I've never thought of what we shared as an affair, Drew." His low voice was encased in steel. "I guess you've changed more in the past five years than I thought you had." He turned away to walk out the room, then spun around again. "Damn your stubborn pride," he growled, reaching out and hauling her into his arms.

Drew had only a brief glimpse of Casey's grim face before he blotted out her world. Considering the cold anger in his manner, his kiss was anything but arctic. The heat of his mouth branded her the same way it had two nights before. The hot thrust of his tongue seared the dark recesses of her mouth to find each sensitive nerve. It taunted her, teased and curled around her own tongue, drawing it back into his mouth. Drew linked her arms around Casey's neck and arched her pliant body against his aroused form. At that moment there was no past, only the present. Their desire for each other instantly rekindled the dormant flames in their bodies. The soft brush of his moustache against her skin, the wholly masculine taste of his mouth, reminded Drew of the heated nights they had once shared.

Casey's hands slipped under the silk of Drew's tunic to roam possessively over her bare back. His fingertips urgently glided around to her midriff and slid up under her soft lacy bra, stopping to cover the pulsating peaks of her breasts.

Drew was equally aggressive in her suggestive movements against Casey's body. She was drugged by the warm, musky scent of his skin, influenced by his caresses, dominated by his masculinity. Soft moans were torn from her throat, only to be swallowed by his own.

It could have been five seconds or five minutes—she had no idea—before he stepped back, though he didn't release her.

"Don't worry, Ms. Sinclair." There was only the barest hint of a ragged edge to his voice to reveal the high state of his arousal. "I won't expect these kinds of tactics when you come to court me."

"Co—court you?" she asked numbly, forced to grip his forearms to keep her balance.

"How quickly we forget," Casey mocked softly. "It's

going to be interesting to see just how badly CHEM Corp. wants to keep me. If you'll excuse me, I'll say good night to Aunt Kate and be on my way." He gently disengaged himself and left the room without a backward glance.

Drew groped blindly for a chair and collapsed onto the cushions. She took several deep breaths to dispel the insistent clamoring of her senses. Casey had taken her close to the edge, but it had never taken much to make either of them desire the other. How many times had she only smiled at him or touched his arm before she'd found herself pinned beneath him in a lover's embrace?

The loud closing of the front door brought her back to the present. Unwilling to see Kate, Drew rose slowly from her chair. She put Shadow back in his cage and made her way wearily up to her bedroom. She wanted only the oblivion of sleep.

Even that wasn't to be. Erotic dreams filtered through her mind, leaving her in a state of anguish by morning.

Just past dawn, while she still lingered in a half sleep, she turned over in bed. One arm was flung out as if looking for something . . . or someone. Then she came fully awake. She realized painfully that she was alone.

Drew didn't see Casey for the balance of the week. Any word from him came by impersonal interoffice memo. She made it a point not to drive by the park in the mornings to watch the joggers—especially one.

Casey picked Shadow up early Saturday morning while Drew was at her exercise class.

She found the two days strangely quiet without the small bird's chattering.

Casey must have been kept informed of Drew's activities, because he returned Shadow Sunday evening, while she was attending a small dinner party.

Monday was as busy as usual.

"Mr. Watson called while you were at lunch," Viv informed Drew at one point. "He asked to be kept in touch about the campaign."

Drew groaned and raked her fingers through her hair. "I keep reminding myself that I got down on my knees begging for this project. I'm really beginning to wonder if I wasn't suffering from temporary insanity at the time."

"You're doing just fine," the older woman reassured her. "You keep saying that deep down he has a soft spot for you."

"Don't ask me how far down that is."

When the telephone rang Viv picked up the receiver. "Ms. Sinclair's office." She listened silently for a moment, then glanced at Drew. "A Mr. Smith is here to see you."

Drew frowned. "What company is he from?"

"He's a messenger and insists that he's to deliver his message personally," the secretary explained.

Drew sighed. Obviously she wasn't going to get any peace this afternoon. If the man turned out to be a vendor he'd be very sorry he'd tried to trick her. "All right, send him in."

Viv left the office for a moment. When she returned she ushered in a dark-haired, good-looking man in his early twenties.

"Drew Sinclair?" His voice was a husky purr meant to send shivers down a woman's spine.

"Yes." She glanced past him toward Viv, but the woman merely shrugged. She didn't understand the visit any more than Drew did.

The man withdrew a small tape recorder, set it on Drew's desk and stepped back a few paces. A rousing tone filled the room. Before Drew's widening eyes, the man began to gyrate to the uninhibited music. Luckily

Viv quickly closed the door, although she remained inside the office to watch the show.

Drew's eyes grew wider as he discarded his navy blazer. The man danced over to her and draped his tie around her neck.

"Wait a minute!" Her protest was halted as his forefinger pressed lightly against her lips.

The shirt was ripped off to reveal a tanned, smooth-muscled chest. The pants soon followed, leaving him clad only in a pair of bright red bikini briefs. Drew couldn't recall where the dancer's shoes and socks had gone to. She could only sit back in her chair in a state of shock.

"No!" She finally managed to gather her wits enough to shriek when it appeared that the minute briefs were going the way of his other articles of clothing. He grinned, but he kept the briefs on. She kept her eyes trained on his handsome face, not daring to look anywhere else.

Not soon enough for Drew's peace of mind, the music stopped. The young man walked gracefully over to a stunned Drew and produced a red rose and a small envelope that rested heavily in her palm.

"Happy birthday, sexy lady," he murmured, placing a warm lingering kiss on her lips. He turned to gather up his clothes, asked an equally speechless Viv where he could dress and walked out of the office.

"He's from Bare Necessities," Viv croaked.

"What?" Drew continued staring at the rose and fingering the round shape of the heavy object in the sealed envelope.

"He gave me his card," the secretary whispered, holding up a cardboard rectangle.

Drew looked up. "If one word about this gets out of this office . . . ." She left the rest of the warning unspoken.

"Are you kidding? No one in their right mind would believe this happened. I'm still not too sure it did, and I watched it. Who sent him?" Viv asked curiously.

Drew shook her head, although a glimmer of suspicion lingered in the back of her mind. "We'll get back to business later," she said crisply.

Viv nodded and walked out of the office, closing the door behind her.

Drew's fingers shook as she ran an apricot-polished fingernail under the envelope flap. The contents fell heavily into her lap . . . a silver dollar. The memory came flooding back in a vivid rush.

Drew and Casey had been living together for almost a year. She had spent all one evening working on a term paper, and Casey had felt a little neglected. He had come up behind her and curved his arms around her breasts.

"Ready for bed?" he murmured, nuzzling her nape.

"Hm? I have to finish this page first," she replied absently, not looking up from her papers.

"Okay, it's your loss," he sighed, straightening up after he dropped a kiss on her temple. "Good night, love."

Drew hadn't made it to bed for over an hour. Thinking Casey was already asleep, she crept through the darkened room and slipped her nightgown on. She had barely cuddled under the covers when a pair of arms pulled her toward a warm body.

"What's this?" Casey muttered, fumbling with the ties to her nightgown. "A chastity belt?"

"Naturally." She giggled at his disgruntled question.

"What does it take—nickels?"

"Nickels!" Drew pretended to be affronted. "Silver dollars only, if you please."

"Silver dollars!" he snorted, moving away. "Well, forget it, then."

Drew had found it hard to keep from laughing. Casey had flopped onto his back, making sure to keep a proper distance from her in the king-sized bed. A moment later he turned onto his side, then onto his stomach. Five minutes later he got up, went into the bathroom for a glass of water and returned to the bedroom. By then Drew had almost exploded with laughter. The loud sighs from Casey's side of the bed were almost her undoing.

"Well," he huffed finally, "how do *you* like rejection for fourteen minutes?"

"Oh, darling!" She hadn't been able to keep back her laughter then. She had slipped off her nightgown and moved into his arms. Any thoughts of rejection were soon forgotten.

On Casey's next birthday one of his presents from Drew had been ten silver dollars, with the injunction to spend them wisely!

A tear appeared in the corner of one of Drew's eyes. She wanted to be furious with Casey for sending her such an unorthodox birthday greeting. She herself had actually forgotten her birthday, what with all that had been going on at work. Casey had even chosen the same music Drew had used when she had delivered his birthday telegram that first time they had met.

The sender had to have been Casey. There was no card, but the silent message was in the silver dollar. Nothing else was needed.

A tiny smile curved her lips. It looked like there just might be a question as to who would be courting whom these next few weeks.

She picked up her phone and dialed a number.

"Mr. McCord's office."

"Hello, Jenny, is he in?"

"Yes, he is." The line clicked, indicating that Drew had been put on hold.

"Hello, Drew." His voice sent shivers down her spine.

"I thought if you didn't have a previous engagement tomorrow, we could have lunch together." Her voice betrayed none of her emotions. "I'd like to start compiling some additional background information on the regional managers I'll be meeting at the conference."

"All right," he replied evenly.

There was silence on both ends. She was waiting for him to mention her unexpected visitor; he was waiting to be blasted for sending the man.

"Will twelve-thirty be all right?" she asked finally.

"Fine."

Drew hung up and jotted a note on her desk calendar, as if she needed a reminder. Then she rang Viv.

"Viv, would you please note that I'll be having lunch with Casey McCord tomorrow?" she instructed.

"Is he the one who sent your—ah—birthday greeting?" the secretary asked.

"I didn't ask."

Drew sat back in her chair and stared with unseeing eyes at the opposite wall.

It was going to take a great deal of self-control for her to finish this project without any damage to her emotions.

That evening Kate fixed one of Drew's favorite dishes for dinner and afterward presented her with a cake and a lacy pastel lilac sweater she had crocheted. There might not have been hordes of people present to help celebrate, or champagne to drink, but Drew didn't care. One of her favorite people *was* there, her stepfather had called to wish her a happy birthday and even Casey, in his own way, had remembered.

The next day Drew arrived at Casey's office promptly at twelve-thirty.

"All the signs of success," he commented sardonically once he was seated in the passenger seat of the Ferrari. "I can't believe this is considered a company car."

"I have a gas credit card and they pay my insurance, which is fine with me." She shifted gears smoothly, not seeing Casey's eyes studying the nylon-covered leg near his own.

"Quite a step up from your little Beetle."

Drew smiled at the memory of her erratic Volkswagen. "My neighbor's son bought it from me about two years ago. He immediately took the engine apart, and how he managed to get all those pieces back where they belonged I'll never know. Now it's painted this horrible shade of orange with black stripes and has a fake tiger's tail hanging on the back."

Casey chuckled at the picture. "It's obviously his first car."

Drew had had Viv make reservations at a nearby restaurant that guaranteed peace and quiet.

Casey raised his eyebrows at the exclusive surroundings. "Amazing how an expense account changes a person's eating habits," he drawled.

Drew flushed. "I'm not showing off," she declared militantly.

He smiled. "I didn't think you were, love. I'm proud of you, Drew. You've worked hard to get where you are, and you deserve the rewards of success."

The headwaiter seated them with a European flourish and a warm smile of appreciation for Drew's golden-blond beauty. Their orders for drinks were taken, and their conversation didn't resume until their drinks were placed before them.

Casey took a sip of his whiskey, set the glass down and studied Drew across the table.

"I trust your birthday gift came suitably wrapped, or should I say unwrapped?" His casual remark caught her attention immediately.

"Oh, it was much more than that." She smiled archly. "He was a great kisser, too."

Casey's eyes darkened with anger. "He kissed you?" he demanded, leaning across the table.

She continued smiling, as if the memory were enough to keep her warm. "He certainly did," she murmured seductively. For once she was rattling Casey's cage!

He scowled as he looked down at his drink. "I told them no kissing," he muttered darkly.

Drew couldn't resist a little prick of the pin. "I'd say that it was entirely his own idea," she replied softly, picking up her wine glass. "And not a bad one, if I say so myself."

For a moment Casey looked as if he wanted to pursue the subject; then he changed his mind. "I understand you were engaged not all that long ago." He was back to taking the offensive in their private battle.

Drew stiffened. "Yes." Why did he have to bring that up? Not to mention, where did he hear it? She wasn't going to give him the satisfaction of asking him to name his source.

"Who broke it off?"

"It was mutual," she clipped, hoping he'd take the hint, although her experience in dealing with Casey told her that he'd drop a subject only when he was ready and not before.

"Then there must not have been that instantaneous attraction that we felt," he murmured. "You have to admit, Drew, that from the beginning we were like a brush fire in the midst of a dry spell. Nothing could have stopped us."

Amber-colored eyes met and clashed with tawny ones. It could have been seconds or hours before the spell was abruptly broken by Drew's harsh words.

"Nothing did stop us, Casey. Nothing but your male ego."

There was a long, tense silence. Casey couldn't present an argument, because he knew Drew spoke the truth; there was no way he could refute it. He sipped his drink as if he had all the time in the world. "Sam Martinson is in charge of our Northeast region," he told her evenly. "He has an excellent record. He's your typical company man and would be at the top of my list of recommendations for promotion."

As far as Drew was concerned, it was all downhill from there.

Chapter Five

*E*arly Friday afternoon Drew threw her small suitcase into the trunk of the Ferrari. She had purposely gone into work very early that morning so that she could leave after lunch with a clear conscience.

"I'll probably be back sometime late Sunday night," she informed Kate.

"I still think you should have called your father first instead of deciding to show up on his doorstep," the older woman commented. "For all you know he may have taken off on a short trip. He travels up to that cabin of his every chance he gets."

Drew shook her head. "Pops is always home unless he's out fishing with his buddies. He won't mind having me on the spur of the moment," she replied confidently.

Kate still looked skeptical of Drew's sudden wish to drive north to visit her stepfather, but she didn't say anything further.

Drew never minded the long drive up the coast to her

hometown of Bakersfield. Her sense of humor tended to surface when the California Highway Patrol officers looked at the sleek black car, then took a second look at the driver, if not a third.

Luckily traffic wasn't too heavy, and by leaving home in the early afternoon she was able to miss the rush hour when she drove through Los Angeles and up over the Grapevine, a steep winding stretch of road leading up into the mountains, then down into the San Joaquin Valley.

After that it wasn't long before Drew turned off the highway. Here the territory was familiar, although there had been many changes since she had left home more than ten years before.

The street she drove down was a far cry from the affluent Spanish-style condominium complex she lived in. Here the homes looked the way they had when they were built in the 1940s and '50s.

The home she had known since childhood was only a few years older than she was. An elderly Ford pickup truck stood in the driveway in front of a detached garage. The hedges were neatly clipped and the lawn recently cut. The stucco house had been repainted white with blue trim a few years ago. Nothing had changed.

Grinning wickedly, Drew roared into the driveway and depressed the horn button. She didn't let up until a tall, angular, silver-haired man ambled out the front door.

"Lordy, woman, it's enough to wake the dead," he grunted, approaching the car. His eyes were wide with surprise at his unexpected visitor. "Don't tell me you were out for a drive and wound up here? Now, cut out that noise! The neighbors around here have enough to prattle about without your foolishness."

"Hm, don't tell me you're having orgies again," she teased, climbing out of the car. She threw her arms around her stepfather and planted a hearty kiss on his cheek. "Pops, you'll never change," she observed fondly, stepping back to study the tall man dressed in his never changing combination of jeans and a plaid flannel work shirt.

"Neither will you." He returned her hug. "I didn't expect you this weekend."

Drew took her suitcase out of the trunk. "What's wrong, are you entertaining a lady friend and hoping to be alone?" she teased, sliding her other arm around his waist and walking with him up to the house.

Marcus Sinclair snorted his reply. "That's the last thing I'd do," he said gruffly, opening the front door and allowing Drew to enter first. "I'll go fix us some coffee."

Drew walked down the hallway to the bedroom she had slept in until she was eighteen. It had gone from dainty peach walls and white ruffles to bright rainbow colors and was now painted a soft pastel blue. She hung her clothes up in the closet, quickly ran a brush through her hair and wandered through the house toward the aromatic scent of freshly perked coffee. Entering the kitchen, she smiled at the sight of a blueberry coffee cake reposing on the table.

"Mrs. Myers still plying you with goodies, is she?" Drew asked slyly, taking a seat at the table. "I'd say she's continuing to work hard to become the next Mrs. Sinclair. You better watch out, Pops. You just might end up to be a newly married man soon!"

Marcus snorted. "That woman has been trying to get her hooks into me for the past fifteen years. If she hasn't succeeded by now, I doubt she ever will. First she claimed you needed a mother's influence; now she says I need someone for my old age! As if I need some sort of keeper!"

Drew smiled fondly at her stepfather. Marcus Sinclair was a man capable of so much love. Her own father had died of pneumonia a few months before her birth. Her mother had met Marcus when Drew was barely a year old, and the warm, gruff-spoken man had captured the widow's heart. Unfortunately, she had died in a car crash a few years later. Marcus had mourned his wife's death deeply, but had had the good sense to realize that Drew needed him more than a woman who could only be a memory.

There had been times when he had made mistakes in raising such an energetic and headstrong girl, but he had always been there when she needed him. No daughter could have had a more loving father.

Marcus's dark gray eyes roamed over Drew's face as he poured two cups of steaming coffee and placed one in front of her.

"You look tired," he said bluntly. "Think this new job might be a bit much for you?"

That rankled. "You sound like some other people I know," she muttered.

"Who am I being lumped with?" He eased himself into the chair across from her.

"Nine-tenths of Fantasy Toys' executives—including Casey McCord," Drew replied grimly, picking up a knife and cutting a slice of coffee cake. She handed the first piece to Marcus and cut a smaller one for herself.

"Casey isn't one to act that way toward you," he argued mildly.

She silently shook her head, wondering why he had said that. Marcus had certainly mentioned Casey quite easily, considering that he hadn't seen him in over five years. The couple had spent two of their vacations in California, and Marcus had flown back to Boston the year Drew graduated. The two men had hit it off immediately; they shared interests in fishing and hunting, sports Drew had no fondness for.

"He's resigning from Fantasy Toys, Pops," she stated quietly, raising her eyes to meet his.

"Did he take another job?" he asked curiously.

Drew shrugged. "Who knows? He's keeping his future plans a deep, dark secret."

"Especially from you," he guessed shrewdly.

She stood up, pushing her chair back loudly. "Casey could have a brilliant career with CHEM Corp.," she declared. "He has more than brains, Pops; he has a driving force that allows him to achieve success no matter what he does. I can't imagine what any company can offer him that we can't!"

"Except your absence?"

Drew's face whitened as the import of his quiet words sank in. She sat back down before her legs collapsed. "No." She shook her head to banish the shocking thought. Another equally painful thought occurred to her. Casey had informed her only that she'd have to court him if she wanted him to remain at Fantasy Toys. He hadn't made any guarantee that he'd actually consider staying. What if he only meant to make a fool out of her? "I'm only going to be there temporarily," she murmured. "Then Marty will be assigning me somewhere else. That's my job. Go in, evaluate the problems, solve them and leave the place in much better shape."

"And this time you plan to leave Casey in charge?" Marcus asked her.

"My boss is in favor of that, yes."

Marcus shook his head as he sipped his coffee. "You're too businesslike these days," he announced. "Damn it girl, you'll end up sharing your bed with a computer!"

"At least there won't be a scramble for the shower in the mornings."

He glowered at her bleak attempt at a joke. He would have continued his lecture if the doorbell hadn't rung.

"Why don't you get that?" Marcus suggested, looking a little uneasy. "If it's that old biddy next door, tell her I'm taking a nap."

"Old faker," she teased lovingly, rising from her chair and heading for the living room. "I bet you didn't take a nap even when you were a baby."

Drew's bright smile froze at the sight of her father's visitor.

"Hello, Drew." Casey looked surprised to see *her* there, also.

"What are you doing here?" she whispered, moving forward to block the entrance.

"Hey, Marcus, call off your watchdog," Casey called out with laughter in his voice, much to Drew's annoyance.

"What is going on here?" she demanded, placing her hands on her hips.

"Casey boy, good to see you!" Marcus greeted the younger man jovially. "I didn't expect you until later in the day."

"Expect?" Drew spun around to face her stepfather.

"Marcus and I have a fishing date tomorrow up in Morro Bay," Casey explained.

Drew turned back to Casey. "How long have you been seeing Pops?" Her eyes narrowed in suspicion.

Laughter assaulted her from both sides. Casey stepped inside and draped an arm around Drew's shoulders; she impatiently jerked away. Marcus groped for a chair while guffawing loudly.

"I think someone disapproves of our friendship, mate." Casey grinned, then turned back to Drew. "He and I don't exactly go out on dates, you know."

She glared fiercely at him.

"You know that the boy and I've always enjoyed a spot of fishin'," Marcus spoke up. "Fred's offered to take us out in his boat tomorrow."

This was clearly something the two men had done before. The strange part was that Marcus hadn't thought to mention Casey's visits before and, ironically, his visits hadn't coincided with hers before. Whose doing was that? She wasn't sure if she cared to find out.

"You never asked me to go fishing with you." God, now she was sounding like a shrewish wife!

"We know better than that, love." Casey chuckled. "You get seasick if you just look at a toy boat floating in the bathtub."

Drew's face reddened. Her tendency toward seasickness was a well-known fact, although Casey had never teased her about it before.

"After my long drive, I hope you have a cold beer for me." Casey turned to Marcus.

"Sure." Marcus rose from his chair and led the way into the kitchen. The men's lighthearted conversation didn't carry into the living room, much to Drew's regret.

"No wonder Pops was so surprised to see me," she grumbled unhappily. "Talk about an unplanned third." She cast a baleful eye in the direction of the kitchen. "I think I'll go to my room now," she called, then sniffed haughtily and left.

Drew unpacked her clothes and hung up the one dress she had brought along. Afterward she pulled off her sea-green sweater and tucked her plaid shirt back into her jeans.

"Very fashionable."

She turned slowly. Casey was leaning indolently against the door jamb, one booted foot crossed over the other. His own jeans were faded, and too snug for Drew's peace of mind as she gazed at the masculine angles of his body, and his rust-colored sweater was one she remembered from long ago. The jungle-cat eyes moved over her slim figure with alarming familiarity.

"Designer jeans from a fancy boutique, designer shirt and sweater, not to mention those fancy boots."

His quiet voice flicked over her nerve endings. "It all goes with the car quite nicely."

"Why didn't Pops ever tell me you came up here to see him?" Drew preferred to ignore his none too subtle sarcasm regarding her choice of clothing.

"You'll have to ask him that."

"Why didn't you mention it to me?" she pressed.

Casey's brief smile didn't offer any enlightenment. "I didn't realize I was supposed to submit a report regarding my private life to you, Ms. Sinclair."

Drew flushed. "We're talking about my father, Casey."

"And my friend," he pointed out, straightening up. "Marcus would like the three of us to go out for dinner." There was a grim sense of waiting in his tense figure. "He won't admit it, but I think he's afraid you'll refuse because of my being here."

Drew's eyes pricked with tears. "Poor Pops," she whispered, reaching out blindly to grip the edge of her dresser. "I wouldn't do that to him. Would you tell him that I'll be ready in about ten minutes?"

Casey nodded and cleared his throat. "Since I usually sleep in here when I visit Marcus, and since I sincerely doubt that you'll invite me into your bed, I'll make up the couch in the living room."

Their eyes met across the width of the room. Drew's breathing deepened, and her body felt lethargic under Casey's intense gaze. It was the same soul-searching stare she had encountered almost ten years ago when she had first seen him.

"The outfit you wore that day left damn little to the imagination," he growled, beginning his mental strip-tease at her toes and moving leisurely upward. "I sat there and prayed you wouldn't dare take off what little you had on, otherwise I would probably have broken some guys' faces."

She smiled, relaxing a little. "Whatever happened to

Gloria?" she asked curiously. Ten years ago she wouldn't have had the nerve to bring up the woman's name.

"Who?" He wasn't feigning a bad memory. He stood there, his thumbs hooked through his belt loops, keeping her attention fully focused on his lean frame.

"Gloria. She was the one who sent you the telegram," Drew reminded him with a teasing smile.

There was no answering smile. "As far as I was concerned, no other woman existed after I first saw you," he said candidly. "I'll let Marcus know you'll be out soon." He moved away, making sure to close the bedroom door after him.

Drew inhaled sharply. That was one reply she hadn't expected to hear. It was going to be a long weekend.

Marcus insisted on treating them to dinner at a nearby Italian restaurant. During the meal Casey treated Drew as the daughter of a good friend, not as the woman who had once shared his life. Marcus watched the couple with shrewd eyes, but gave away none of his thoughts.

When the trio returned to the house Drew retired to her bedroom, leaving the two men in the living room.

"We'll bring home plenty of fish for dinner tomorrow night," Marcus promised.

"Just as long as you're the ones to clean them," Drew informed him, dropping a kiss on his forehead. She ignored Casey's broad grin and subtle hint that he, too, should receive a kiss.

A half hour later, when Drew crawled into bed, she fell asleep feeling strangely comforted by the low rumblings of male voices in the other room.

"Drew."

She had been dreaming again. A dream that had come often over the past five years. She and Casey were back together again. They had spent a warm and loving evening in bed, and afterward she had snuggled up to him, with his arms around her. Now he wanted her to wake up. Oh, the many times they would wake up only to renew the passion that had sent them to sleep hours before.

Drew mumbled sleepily, pushing her head farther under her pillow. "Go 'way."

Warm lips and a silky moustache moved over her bare nape; then a slightly rough tongue traced an erotic pattern on the sensitive skin. "How would you feel about cooking breakfast?" a male voice murmured against her shoulder.

"What time is it?" She rolled onto her back. Her bed was much too warm and comfortable for her to want to leave it.

"A little after four." Casey smiled, looking down at the drowsy features and half-closed amber eyes. He sat on the edge of the bed and braced himself with a hand on each side of her shoulders. One thing in his favor was that she hadn't tried to throw him out of her room yet.

"Too early," Drew muttered, while her brain, still fuzzy with sleep, wondered how Casey had risen without awakening her. With her senses guiding her instead of her logic, she slid her arms around his waist. "I have a better idea," she purred seductively, reaching up to nuzzle her face against his throat. "Instead of my crawling out of this nice warm bed to fix your breakfast, why don't you crawl back in here? I promise you a morning of decadent pleasure."

Casey's expression changed to a confused frown. Something was wrong here. Then it dawned on him. Drew wasn't fully awake yet, and in her somnolent state, the last five years hadn't existed. The feel of her very feminine, half-naked body against him was almost too much to bear. The spicy floral scent of the perfumed body lotion she used mixed with the elusive feminine scent of her skin and drifted upward to his nostrils. He hadn't forgotten the way she fit in his arms, or how soft her skin was under his touch. The tip of her tongue fluttered teasingly against his throat. He swore silently, wishing she would fully awake before this seduction went any further!

"Hell, if you think I'm going to pass this up . . ." Casey muttered fiercely. He lowered his head and took her mouth with a rough urgency. His hands found their way over Drew's bare shoulders and slipped her night-gown straps down to reveal her thrusting breasts. She moaned softly as his questing hands molded the rounded globes to his palms and he rotated the turgid nipples between his thumb and forefinger before drop-ping a moist kiss on each tip.

Drew pulled Casey's shirt loose from his jeans and let her hands skim over his bare back. His weight on her body was warm and welcome. Somehow the bed covers had been pulled away, and the heat of his hands replaced the cool silk of her nightgown against her thighs. She reached for the fastening of his jeans, wanting to feel his bare skin against hers.

"Shake a leg in there!" Marcus's voice intruded with the finesse of a sledgehammer. "Can't you get that girl up, Casey?"

Drew's awakening had been accomplished with a vengeance. She sat up and pushed her hair away from her face with shaky hands. At that moment she wasn't sure if she were more relieved or disappointed that they had been so rudely interrupted.

"Tell Pops I'll be out in a couple of minutes." She spoke quietly, now fully aware of her surroundings. She didn't need to look at Casey's face to know that he, too, was tied up in knots from their preliminary lovemak-ing. After all, he used to tell her that she could arouse him just with her smile, a fact she used to enjoy proving.

He nodded. There was a lot he wanted to say, but he sensed that this wasn't the time to talk. He rose slowly and left the bedroom.

Drew sat quietly, feeling tears fill her eyes. "Damn you, Casey McCord," she whispered fiercely, rubbing her damp eyes with her fingers.

A few minutes later she entered the kitchen, wearing a lilac terry robe. The aroma of freshly made coffee permeated the room.

"I suppose you had a good reason to awaken me at this ungodly hour?" she addressed her stepfather. Now wasn't the time to look at Casey. If she did, she knew that her face would only begin to redden with the memory of what had happened in her bedroom. Not to mention the idea of what else could very easily have happened if Marcus hadn't knocked on her door. At just the thought she could feel a damning flush creep up her neck. "You know how I hate to get up early in the morning if I don't have to."

"Yep, that's why I sent Casey in." Marcus grinned smugly.

Drew made a face, wishing that murder weren't against the law. Why did Marcus have to try his hand at matchmaking? If her mind had been functioning just a little more sanely, she might have decided to give her stepfather a piece of it. As it was, she wasn't sure she had any to spare.

A half hour later the two men had put away four eggs each, a package of breakfast sausage, toast and hash browns. Drew considered herself lucky to swallow a cup of coffee under Casey's intense gaze.

"Thanks, darlin'." Marcus wiped his mouth with his napkin as he rose from his chair. He dropped a kiss on the top of her head and walked out the back door. "We better get rolling," he tossed over his shoulder to Casey.

Casey had also stood up and walked around to stand

behind Drew's chair. She sat stiffly, praying he wouldn't say anything about their kiss. What would she plead? Temporary insanity? Or that her sleep-fuddled mind had forgotten their parting five years before? Neither explanation sounded plausible.

"Think about this, Drew." His low voice drifted downward to her ears. "While I'm out in that boat all day, fishing, drinking beer and trading good-natured insults with your stepfather and his friends, I'm going to be recalling the honeyed taste of your mouth under mine and just how hungry you were for me this morning." With that he was gone.

Drew was very still, listening to the sounds of Marcus's truck as it drove off. For a few moments she was afraid that if she moved she would shatter into tiny fragments. That was something she couldn't allow to happen.

"You're a fool, Drusilla Sinclair!" Kate's voice boomed into Drew's tender ears. The older woman paced the den, all the time muttering under her breath about the insane practices of the young woman she looked upon as one of her own. "You had the perfect chance to sit down with Casey and talk things out, and instead you ran like a frightened little rabbit!"

Drew sat in an easy chair, looking as if she had gone without sleep for days. However much she hated to admit it, Kate was right. She had run. That morning, not long after the men had left the house, she had realized that the worst thing she could do would be to stay around all day allowing her imagination to work overtime. What had happened in her bedroom when Casey came in to wake her up was only a sample of what could happen that night. She was still greatly attracted to Casey, and she knew that that could prove dangerous. Not wanting to find out what would happen that evening, she had quickly penned a note to Marcus, saying that an emergency had called her back to San Diego. She had hurriedly thrown her clothes in her suitcase and taken off without a backward glance. She hadn't left any word for Casey.

Kate was surprised to see Drew home so early and immediately demanded to know the reason for the younger woman's agitated state. Sipping a cup of hot coffee to warm her cold body, Drew recited the events of the weekend in halting sentences, and she didn't leave anything out. Now that Kate knew the whole story, she was berating the younger woman for leaving.

"I want a truthful answer, Drusilla." Drew winced. Why had her mother ever given her such an archaic name? She had always known when she was in some kind of trouble because that was the only time she ever heard the longer version of her name. "Do you still love Casey?"

Drew pushed a stray strand of hair away from her pale face. "It doesn't do any good," she muttered, evading the question.

"Do you?" Kate pressed. She wasn't going to give up until she received a truthful answer.

Drew nodded, looking totally miserable. "That's why I couldn't stay there," she whispered painfully. "I knew that if he came to my room tonight I wouldn't be able to stop him from making love to me. Right now I don't think I could handle that, then watch him walk away from me afterward." She blinked rapidly to hold back the tears filling her eyes.

"Do you honestly think he would do such a thing?" Kate walked over to Drew's chair and sat on the arm. She hugged the younger woman against her, softly urging her to cry and let out all the fears that had been plaguing her during the long drive back to San Diego. "I guess you don't know him as well as I thought you did," she said sadly. "The two of you are still living with your hurts from five years ago, when you should be forgetting them and going on to new and better experiences. I'd like nothing more than to lock the two of you into a small room with nothing more in it than a bed so you could settle your differences," Kate said fiercely.

"Aunt Kate!" Drew looked up, shocked out of her tears by the older woman's unorthodox prescription for clearing the air. She looked up as the strident ringing of the telephone pierced the air. "You better answer it." She instinctively knew who was on the other end.

Kate stood up and walked out of the room. "If you're so sure who it is, you better get it," she advised, a new firmness in her voice. "The two of you aren't going to get anywhere unless you begin doing more than making useless conversation and discussing who gets the bird on weekends."

Five rings. Six. Drew sat in the chair and silently counted them. It had to be Casey, and it was obvious that he wouldn't stop until she picked up the phone. She forced herself out of her chair and walked over to the telephone. Her fingers were shaking when she finally picked up the receiver.

"Hello." Her voice came out in a croaky whisper.

She heard only one soft-spoken word, but it was enough to send shock waves through her body.

"Coward." The click and the ensuing dial tone told her that the connection had been broken.

Chapter Six

The next morning Drew knew that Kate still hadn't forgiven her. The thick silence during breakfast was enough of an indication of the older woman's displeasure. It hadn't helped that Drew had barely gotten any sleep the night before. The husky "coward" rang through her mind again and again as she wandered through the house during the early hours of the morning. Her body ached for the fulfillment only Casey could give her. She had chosen to deny herself what she needed so badly, and she was suffering for it.

"Do you feel all right?" Viv asked with evident concern when she brought a cup of coffee in for Drew on Monday morning.

"I'd feel fine if I could go back home and stay in bed for the rest of the year," she replied, looking over her appointment calendar. "Why does it say here that I have a board meeting in half an hour?"

"Because you do."

Drew wasn't too sure if she would be able to face

Casey so soon. She was going to have to call on every reserve bit of strength she had. "I suppose they'd notice if I weren't there." She sighed wearily.

Surprised by the sound of Drew's tired voice, Viv looked at her boss. "Where's that energetic fireball who came in here two months ago, all prepared to whip us into shape?" she asked, her voice faintly teasing.

"The whip went south for the winter," Drew muttered. It didn't help her frame of mind any when the telephone rang and it turned out to be Marty. "Somebody up there hates me," she groaned, accepting the receiver. "Hello, Marty," Drew said with a false cheerfulness. Her stomach did an Indian war dance as if in anticipation of the conversation ahead.

"Is he staying?" he demanded without any preamble.

"Yes, I'm fine, thank you," she said sweetly. "The weather's just lovely out here. How's Julia?"

Marty sighed audibly. "You know, of course, that no one else can get away with the way you treat me," he informed her darkly.

"That's because they're all afraid of you. You're a male chauvinist of the first water, but you also respect someone who dares to stand up to you." Drew glanced down at her powder-blue silk dress and idly wondered if the neckline might be a trifle too low. How could she have forgotten that she held a board meeting every Monday?

"Just tell me that he's staying and I'll line you up with a sweet little project you'll adore," he wheedled.

"Are you sending me to Paris or London?" Thank goodness talking to Marty could help her get things back in perspective. "You'll have to ship my car over, you know."

"Drew . . ." Marty's low voice held a warning, now. He had already guessed that Drew had no good news for him; otherwise she would have called him immediately.

"Marty, if Casey McCord has already made up his mind to leave Fantasy Toys, you could offer him carte blanche and he'd still do what he wants to do," she replied wearily. "That's the way the man is. There isn't much that can be done to change his mind."

"You can change it."

"I won't be used as a reward for his staying, Marty," Drew stated coldly, sitting up straight in her chair. Her nails drummed on the desk top, revealing her agitation.

"No one knows him better than you, honey," he said quietly, with a silkiness that was deceptive. "He'll listen to you when he might not listen to anyone else."

She stiffened with indignation. "Your insinuation is in the worst possible taste, *Mr.* Watson," she said in a cold voice. "I thought I knew you pretty well, but I can see I was wrong."

"Sweetheart . . ." Why did he always have to use endearments when he wanted something? "So you and McCord lived together while you were in school. No one's going to hold it against you. When I was out there I would have guessed there was either something going on or that something had gone on between you two from the way you acted when I saw you together. I will admit that I'm glad it's a part of your past and not your present. You're much too good a troubleshooter for me to lose you to the marriage market. Men have a funny idea that their wives shouldn't travel."

"You're right, Marty. That's exactly what it was, my past," Drew rapped out, her voice husky with anger. "It certainly has nothing to do with my job now, and it has nothing to do with you as my boss. I resent you checking me out that way, Marty. I resent it like hell!" At that moment she couldn't have cared less if Marty had decided to pull her off the project because she had yelled at him. No, he wouldn't do that, her mind jeered back at her. That would be bad for business. His computerlike mind would tell him that it could prove detrimental to the morale of Fantasy Toys. After all, if he fired her, it would be hard for him to explain that her leaving had nothing to do with the job she had been doing. If Marty had been sitting in the chair across from her, he would have been burned by the flames emitting from her eyes.

"I know that, and I'm damn proud of you for being able to separate the two."

She almost laughed hysterically at his praise. If he only knew how difficult that was to do.

"Then why were you almost ordering me to seduce the man into staying?" she demanded, glancing at the small clock on her desk. She was going to be late to the meeting, but they would wait. This was definitely more important. "Marty, there are times when I don't like you very much, and this is one of those times!"

"Call it a test. I wanted to make sure you still had all your priorities where they belonged. And you do," he concluded smugly. "Also, sweetheart, I don't expect you to like me. Just do the job the way it should be done, and I'll give you that promotion you deserve."

If Marty had been in the room with her Drew would have been sorely tempted to throw something at him.

"We're leaving for Hawaii soon for the sales conference, and I'll be looking over the managers for a replacement," she said crisply. "As you said, I know Casey very well, and he rarely changes his mind after it's been made up."

"This time may be an exception. I saw the way he looked at you during lunch that day," Marty pointed out. "Keep me up to date on your campaign, and don't get sunburned while you're in the islands." With that he rang off.

Drew set the phone down, took a deep breath and gathered up her folders. It wasn't going to be an easy Monday.

The department heads were already in the large conference room when Drew entered. She favored them with a warm smile of greeting and took her seat at the head of the table. Her eyes couldn't help but seek out one person in particular, and she found him a few chairs down the table on her left.

Casey wore a light gray suit with a pale blue shirt and a blue and gray striped tie. Drew bit back a laugh. Even now they tended to wear the same colors without planning to. Casey used to tease her that if they had worn the same size, they would have had a spectacular wardrobe between the two of them. He didn't seem to have suffered any ill effects from her escape on Saturday. Obviously it hadn't bothered him as much as it had her.

Drew sensed a tension in the room, especially between Casey and Raymond Wilson, the production manager. The latter was looking angrily across the table at Casey.

"I've noticed that the production figures are down from last month, Raymond," Drew began conversationally. She might as well get this over with. "I realize that you had some troubleshooters out here from Houston at the time, and something like that can throw a monkey wrench into the works. Or is there a problem I should know about?" She smiled coolly.

"Only one." He glared at Casey.

"Tell her, Wilson," Casey ordered.

"All of a sudden Mr. McCord here thinks he knows the production end," Raymond sneered. "I've been in this business for over thirty years, and he comes from an entirely different field. I'll make allowances for his relative inexperience in toy production, but I think he should not only be told to stay out of something he knows nothing about, but to stick with something he knows best, selling!"

"Selling *this?*" Casey reached under the table, brought out a figure and practically threw it toward Drew.

She stared at the large stuffed animal that slid to a stop directly in front of her. "What exactly is this supposed to be?" She studied the dark brown creature. It had tiny wings sprouting from its sides and a lopsided mouth that looked as if it were giving some sort of horrible laugh. The crossed eyes didn't help its image any more than its ugly color did.

Casey's dark frown invited Raymond to explain. "Delbert Dragon, for ages two and up," he muttered defiantly.

Drew reached out and hesitantly touched the toy. It was soft under her fingertips, the type of cuddly toy a toddler would love—except that its face, not to mention its horrendous color, would be enough to give any child nightmares. Drew remembered being shown all the toys in production when she had first arrived, but somehow this one hadn't been presented at the time. If it had been, she would easily have remembered it and ordered its production halted.

"Who approved the production of this?" she asked quietly.

"Mr. Wakefield." Raymond mentioned the name of the deceased owner.

"And why wasn't I shown . . . ah . . . Delbert when I first arrived here?" Drew knew she was being played for a fool, and she didn't like it. She also knew that she would have to take care of this problem before Marty found out.

"The toy was still in the final stages of design. As I said, Mr. Wakefield had approved him, and we began production a week ago." What he was saying was that there had been no reason to show it to her, since the design had already been approved. While the man had never been openly insolent toward her, he had made it clear that he didn't appreciate taking orders from a woman, and this was just another example of his recalcitrant behavior.

"Raymond, Colin Wakefield is dead, and Fantasy Toys now has a new owner," she began coldly. "As a representative for that owner, I should have been shown this toy before you put it on the production line. As it is, we've wasted a lot of money, because it will have to be pulled. Immediately! In no way does this so-called dragon meet the high standards of Fantasy Toys. If anything, it would do nothing but make us a laughingstock. From what I can gather from Casey's reaction, this was one toy the sales force didn't care to show." She turned to Casey. "Am I correct?"

His lips twisted in a disparaging smile. "Only the staff saw it, and they still haven't stopped laughing. I'm afraid some of their remarks aren't fit for a lady's ears."

Drew sat back in her chair and studied the creature further. "If he weren't such an ugly color, and if his face were softened up a bit, he would be passable," she mused. "The crossed eyes are fine. In fact, they give him a personality. The name wouldn't be so bad, either, if he just had a little more humor in his face. If that were done the retooling would be less expensive, and we could recover a part of the loss we would otherwise sustain."

Incensed at losing the battle, Raymond pushed back his chair and stood up. "I've been with this company from its beginning, and I don't see where a glorified peddler and a dropout from woman's lib can tell me how to do my job! There are many other toy companies out there who would beg for a man with my expertise!" he jeered.

Drew's eyes glowed with the dark lights of an anger that was barely contained. She knew that confrontations were inevitable. She just hadn't figured on the first one being with Raymond. One hand clenched into a tight fist in her lap.

"The last thing I would want to do is keep someone here who is as unhappy as you are, Raymond." Her calm voice belied the storm building up within her. A burning sensation was settling in her stomach and not making matters any easier for her.

The man's mouth dropped open. He hadn't expected her to call his bluff. Now he had to either keep his pride and resign, or forsake it and apologize. He stuck to the former.

"You'll have my resignation on your desk in the morning," he said coldly, then stormed out of the room.

After he left, Drew looked around at the other men, surprised to find several looks of respect and admiration sent her way.

"Raymond has been a thorn in our sides for many years," one man explained, smiling broadly. "It was mighty nice to see him getting some of his own back for once. It may not be very polite to say, but he won't be missed." He glanced at Casey. "His son-in-law was up for your job before you came along, and that didn't improve his so-called good nature any."

After that the meeting proceeded smoothly, although Drew was very aware of Casey watching her with an intense stare. It took all her willpower not to return his intimate gaze.

After the meeting was adjourned the men filed out, but Casey found some excuse to be the last.

"Was there something you wanted to say to me?" Drew asked coolly, standing up and stepping away from her chair. She didn't realize that by moving near one of the windows she allowed the sun to gild her hair and send a warm glow over her face.

"Quite a bit, actually, but I don't think this is the

place to go into it." His words might have sounded careless, but there was no amusement in his eyes. "I do want to thank you for backing me up on that problem with Wilson."

"I didn't back you up," she snapped, ignoring the continuous burning in her stomach. "I did what I thought was best for the company."

"Oh, yes, the company," Casey mused, watching her steadily. "I forgot that your heart belongs to CHEM Corp. now." He stood near the table, legs slightly apart, one hand tucked into his pants pocket, which pulled the jacket away from his hip. He took a step toward her, then paused when he noticed her begin to retreat. "Why did you leave Bakersfield? I hope you realize that you upset Marcus a great deal with your sudden escape."

"I left a note explaining that I was called back," she maintained stubbornly, wishing he would leave so that she could return to her office and swallow a bottle of antacid tablets. "If you have nothing further to say in regard to business, I have an appointment," she lied.

Casey's eyes turned into cold stone chips. "Forgive me, I didn't mean to keep you from anything of importance," he taunted, turning away. "Don't worry, I won't bother you again."

At the point of calling him back Drew moved forward, only to gasp out loud as a knifelike pain shot through her body. She wrapped her arms around her middle, as if to keep the pain from invading her again.

Casey looked back when he heard her cry of pain. Taking stock of the situation, he moved swiftly in Drew's direction to catch her just as she fell into a black void.

When Drew came to she found herself lying on the couch in her office. A pale-faced Casey was leaning over her, and an equally worried Viv stood nearby.

"Wha–what am I doing here?" Drew asked, starting to sit up, but Casey's hands on her shoulders forced her back into a reclining position.

"You fainted," he stated grimly. "Are you on some kind of crazy diet again?" he demanded.

She flushed, remembering the time she had decided she needed to lose ten pounds and had literally starved herself for almost a week until Casey realized what she was doing and harangued her soundly until she began to eat sensibly again. She only wished he hadn't made such a personal remark in front of Viv, in case the secretary figured something out. She shifted her position and winced when a pain, not as sharp as before, sliced through her stomach.

"Maybe it's her appendix," Viv spoke up, noticing Drew's grimace.

Casey shook his head. He knew that Drew had had her appendix out when she was a child, but he kept that piece of information to himself. "The signs are all wrong," he said flatly, his eyes narrowed in concentration. "Although I'd say all the signs are there for the beginning of an ulcer. Especially with that huge bottle of antacid tablets in your desk."

"You had no right to go through my desk," Drew argued.

"For all I knew, you might have been on some special medication." He turned to Viv. "Do you think you can get her in to see a doctor this morning?" He had taken full charge, much to Drew's dismay.

This time Drew did manage to sit up. She looked down in annoyance to find that her shoes were lying on the carpet. At least Casey hadn't tried to loosen her dress. She knew it wasn't because of Viv being present, either. If he had felt that she needed to have her clothing loosened, he would have ripped the dress right off her without regard to propriety!

"I don't need to see a doctor," she stated, noticing

that no one was really listening to her. She leaned over, trying to find her shoes.

"I'm sure I could get her in to see mine," the secretary replied.

"I don't like doctors," Drew announced to no one in particular. Ah, there were her shoes. "All they do is poke and prod and take your temperature. I'm not sick enough to see a doctor," she continued to argue mildly.

"Why don't you call and see if you can get her in and I'll take her over there?" Casey suggested, ignoring Drew altogether.

"I'm the boss here." Drew spoke up belligerently. "And I say I don't need to see a doctor!"

It didn't help to see Casey looking at her with eyes filled with amusement. Drew might have tried to dent his male ego by reminding him who was in charge, but she had forgotten that, when necessary, he always came out on top.

"Shut up," he said affectionately, straightening up. He turned back to Viv. "I'll check in with Jenny, then come back here. I have a pretty strong hunch that she's in the early stages of an ulcer, and her best bet would be to have it treated immediately." He looked down at Drew. "You stay here until I return. The last thing we need is for you to faint again. If you keep it up, the office gossips will have you pregnant!"

"Augh!" Drew moaned, realizing that Casey's teasing remark could be all too true. "Women do faint for reasons other than pregnancy," she gritted. With Casey out of the room, she focused her glare on Viv, who had walked over to her desk and picked up the telephone. "If you make that appointment, you're fired," she threatened.

"That's all right." Viv was unperturbed. "I could use a rest after all the work you give me."

Drew was still muttering her protests when Casey walked back into her office and carefully helped her to her feet. Viv handed him a piece of paper with the doctor's name and address written on it. They had just enough time to make Drew's appointment.

Outside he settled Drew into the comfortable interior of a silver Jaguar.

"And you talk about me coming up in the world," she muttered, looking at the car with undisguised interest. "You haven't done so badly yourself, either."

"Like you, I worked hard to get where I am," he replied, switching on the ignition.

Drew hadn't been joking when she protested about going to see a doctor. Ever since she was small she had disliked the medical profession. Although it wasn't fear, she wasn't fond of the poking and prodding she had to endure during a medical examination.

After she dutifully answered the doctor's questions he gave her the diagnosis Casey had suspected.

"Of course, I should do a few further tests, but I would say you have the makings of a healthy ulcer. And it will only get worse unless you start slowing down at work," he said gruffly. "You're too young and pretty to have that kind of a problem." He proceeded to outline a diet that had all the excitement of toast dipped in milk.

Casey was seated in the waiting room, the object of curious and admiring feminine eyes as he leafed through a magazine. Glad to be free, Drew hurriedly wrote out a check and walked over to him.

"Let's get out of here," she whispered.

He waited until they reached the car before questioning her. "Well? What was the verdict?"

"You should have gone to medical school." Drew searched through her purse for her sunglasses and slipped them on. "What made you think I had an ulcer?" she asked curiously.

He shrugged. "The signs were there." He half turned, one arm placed casually across the back of the seat as he pulled the car out of its parking space. "I remembered the pained look on your face when your boss took us to lunch. The last thing you wanted that day was spicy food. The same thing happened when Marcus took us out to dinner. Italian food is notorious for its spiciness, and you chose the mildest item on the menu. That's rather unusual for someone who was once known for having a cast-iron stomach."

"That was then," she said.

"Did the doctor give you a diet to follow?" Casey skillfully urged the car into the busy street. He seemed to hesitate at the traffic signal, then turned down a street Drew wasn't familiar with.

"After he poked and prodded and took my temperature," Drew grumbled. She turned and looked around at the unfamiliar surroundings. "Are you sure we're going the right way to the office?"

"Sort of." He appeared unconcerned.

"Meaning?" She half turned in the seat to face him. How could she have forgotten how masculine his profile was?

He slanted a sideways glance toward her. "I thought I could tempt you with a nice, bland lunch."

Drew wrinkled her nose. "Sounds boring to me." She smiled impishly. "A pizza sounds great, though."

Casey shook his head. "I wouldn't relish rushing you to the hospital in the middle of the night," he informed her.

"Aunt Kate would be the one to do that," she corrected him.

"I love Aunt Kate dearly, but she's absolutely useless in an emergency. She'd call me." Casey turned into a small parking lot, parked the car and got out to walk around to the other side. He held out a hand for Drew and assisted her out of the car as if she were a prize piece of porcelain. The gesture made her feel very cherished, something she hadn't felt in a long time.

"If they serve health food here, I'm leaving now." She turned to look up at him. "You know very well that I'm your typical junk food fanatic."

"Even going so far as to eat chocolate marshmallow cookies in bed," he said dryly, placing his hand at the back of her waist and guiding her toward the entrance.

"You used to help me eat them," Drew reminded him. For once their differences had been forgotten and they were the friends they had been in the beginning.

The interior of the restaurant was small and homey. Drew ordered a cheese omelet, and Casey ordered a chef's salad.

"Surely you don't have to watch your weight," she commented when she heard his request.

"I still don't like a heavy meal in the middle of the day," he explained. He placed his hands in front of him, the lean fingers laced together. "I've missed you, Drew," he whispered huskily, capturing her eyes with his disarming gaze.

Drew could feel the flush warming her cheeks. She had just opened her mouth to tell him that she felt the same way when another voice wafted over them.

"Casey, *darling!*"

Drew looked up in time to watch a brunette swoop down and plant an all too lingering kiss on Casey's mouth. The warmth she had felt at her own conversation with Casey was now lost. At least he had the grace to look vastly uncomfortable at the dark-haired woman's greeting.

"Hello, Monica," he said politely, once he had gotten his mouth free.

The woman called Monica looked over at Drew, her sharp eyes missing nothing. Drew was positive that the woman realized immediately that her blond hair was natural, that there was a designer name on the label of her dress and that she most certainly wasn't Casey's secretary.

"Business lunch, darling?" Monica purred.

"Monica Jameson, this is Drusilla Sinclair, my boss," Casey said smoothly.

The brunette's expertly arched eyebrows lifted. "So you're one of those professional women I've read about," she drawled. "I'm afraid all that talk of profit and loss statements and annual sales figures is totally beyond me."

"Yes, I'm sure it is." Drew smiled sweetly. She was pleased to note that her thrust had hit home. At least that proved Monica did have a few brains.

Monica's malicious glance could have shot Drew down where she sat. The other woman turned and presented Casey with a smile that was almost cloying. "Don't forget about this weekend," she murmured, ignoring Drew completely. She brushed fingers tipped with bright scarlet polish over his cheek before dropping a kiss on his ear. "See you later, darling." She left in a cloud of French perfume.

Drew wrinkled her nose. She had always hated that scent. Now she knew why.

"An old acquaintance, *darling?*" she drawled with saccharine sweetness.

Casey grinned wickedly. "Careful, I might think you're jealous."

"I don't see what I would have to be jealous of." She smiled thinly. "I think I should tell you that you have lipstick on your mouth."

Unperturbed, he pulled out his handkerchief and wiped the bright red smear from his lips. "I like a pale peach color more," he murmured, gazing at her slightly parted lips. "I wouldn't be tempted to wipe that off."

Drew stared at the entrancing shape of Casey's mouth. She could recall his words about remembering the taste of her kiss. She could also remember the taste of his mouth, and knew she wanted to taste him again. Casey was seducing her just as surely as if they had been alone in a room. Just like that rainy night when he had taken her back to his apartment and made such gentle but possessive love to her. He had seduced her with his husky voice and sexy eyes then, and he could easily do it again now. Drew wanted to cry out in protest, but was silenced by the memory of Monica's mention of seeing Casey this weekend. Somehow she doubted that it would just be for dinner and a movie. She was grateful when the waitress arrived with their meal, although it could have been sawdust for all she cared by then.

"If you don't mind, I'd like to come for Shadow Friday evening after I leave the office." Casey picked up his glass of iced tea and drank deeply. He dug into his salad with obvious enjoyment, but then, he derived pleasure from everything he did.

"I thought you would already have seen how ridiculous this idea of yours is." Drew cut into her fluffy omelet. "If you want a bird so badly, why don't you just buy one?"

"He wouldn't be Shadow, though, would he?"

A tiny smile tugged at the corners of her mouth. "That's true," she admitted softly. "No other bird could be like Shadow."

"You're pretty unique yourself." Casey's hand reached out to cover hers, his fingers laced through her own. At first Drew tried to pull away, but his grip merely tightened. "Don't run away from me, Drew," he pleaded quietly. "Not after all we've been to each other."

"That's all in the past now," she reminded him.

"Moving rapidly into the present," he returned fiercely, his eyes glittering with yellow lights.

"I'm sure Monica will more than adequately compensate for my not returning to the fold, so to speak." Her other hand lay clenched into a tight fist in her lap.

A muscle twitched near the corner of Casey's mouth, a sure sign of tightly controlled anger that was about to explode. "Do you know what happened when Marcus called to tell me you had gotten engaged?" he said thickly. "I went out that night and drank myself into a stupor. I had to numb the pain that was tearing me up inside. Except it didn't work." He swore softly under his breath and dug into his pocket. After throwing some money on the table, he got up and walked around to pull Drew out of her chair. She was too startled to do more than stumble along after him.

"Casey!" She frantically hoped that no one they knew was in the restaurant to see their unusual departure.

He didn't bother to reply as he strode outside, one hand firmly wrapped around her wrist. Instead of walking toward the car he headed for a nearby park. When they reached a group of trees he pushed her against one broad trunk and kept her pinned there with the strength of his body.

"This is what I've always remembered," he growled, looking squarely into her eyes. "My holding you in my arms and your response. Don't deny it, Drew; you remember it just as well as I do. You remember how special we were together."

"No!" she retorted tautly, wishing she could ignore the hard feel of his body against hers. While her mind screamed to reject him, her body instinctively molded itself against him. "That was finished a long time ago."

"I don't think so. We were just in some kind of holding pattern; we were destined to meet again. Destined, Drew, my love." His voice softened. "Don't fight me, Drew," Casey commanded huskily, sensing her indecision.

Drew raised her hands and placed them flat against his chest. "I have to go back to the office." She could feel Casey's body heat through the silky cotton of his shirt. She had a strong urge to unfasten the buttons and spread her hands over his chest.

"We'll be in Hawaii soon, Drew," he reminded her in a raspy voice. "There won't be any office for you to hide in, no board room chair for you to sit in and play the queen. It will just be you and me."

"No!" she denied emphatically, tossing her head from side to side, although she could read the truth of his words in his expressive eyes. "We live different lives now, Casey. We can't go back to the way we were." She gasped as his hands slid down to cradle her buttocks and pull her more firmly against him. His lips feathered moistly along the soft curve of her jaw to her ear. He nipped her earlobe near the tiny gold earring.

"All warm and golden," he whispered, teasing the shell of her ear with the tip of his tongue. He smiled at the shivers that ran through her body and knew he was the cause. "There isn't one cool bone in your body."

For some reason his comment brought Monica to Drew's mind. "Not like some of your other friends," she said bitterly. This time she was able to push him away. "I want to leave now." She forced herself to walk away, and waited quietly at the car until Casey joined her.

The drive back to the office was silent and filled with a thick tension. Drew thanked Casey politely for taking her to the doctor; then she hurried back to her office to escape the knowing look in his eyes. That was the frightening part. Casey knew Drew much better than she knew herself. He held her soul in the palm of his hand, and she sincerely doubted he would ever return it to her.

Chapter Seven

As before, Casey came by to pick Shadow up while Drew was out of the house. They hadn't seen each other in the office for the balance of the week.

Drew and Kate spent most of Saturday shopping for clothes for Drew's trip to Hawaii. First they went to Old Towne to wander through the many shops and gaze in windows that offered anything a person might wish to buy, antiques or clothing or jewelry. It was all there. Drew found a set of old brass candlesticks that she felt would look perfect on the living room mantel. The price tag was a bit higher than she had hoped, but she couldn't resist them, and this was a day to do what she pleased, even if it meant cleaning out her bank account!

The two women lunched at a small restaurant that boasted a patio and umbrella-shaded tables. Under Kate's stern eye Drew chose a crab salad which wouldn't disturb her sensitive stomach. It didn't help to watch the older woman enjoy her taco salad, with its rich and spicy sauce.

"You're sadistic, do you know that?" Drew grumbled, spearing a piece of crab meat with her fork.

"My dear, that's the last word I would use to describe myself." Kate smiled serenely.

After lunch they finished their shopping spree. For reasons known only to Drew, she deliberately chose outfits designed to catch a man's eye. From bikinis to shorts, bathing suits to nightwear, each item was cut to cling lovingly to her body. She also unconsciously searched for something else, a special piece of clothing, but it couldn't be found.

"I wonder if you should be required to carry a permit to wear some of these things," Kate commented when they entered the house later, laden down with packages. "I just hope Casey can handle all the men who are going to be running after you when you show up wearing this stuff."

"Casey has nothing to say about what I wear," Drew said firmly, opening the bags and taking her purchases out, setting some aside to be pressed and immediately hanging others up.

"Don't be too sure that he won't say something when he sees a few of these next to nothing outfits," the older woman said, picking up a few pieces of provocative lingerie and holding them out to Drew.

Drew shot her a dark glare, but Kate was undaunted. As it was, Drew wasn't even sure if Casey was going to the conference alone. Spouses or "friends" were also invited, and for all she knew he might have invited Monica to go along with him. She wasn't about to do any snooping to find out. She might not like what she found.

"What would you say to a movie tonight?" Drew decided she had had enough of listening to the name Casey McCord. "We could go out for dinner first."

"You're much too young and pretty not to want an evening out with a good-looking man," Kate argued.

"I left them in Houston."

The housekeeper merely sniffed with disdain. "Chinese food and that new horror thriller?" She looked at Drew expectantly.

"Ugh!" Drew grimaced. "How can you stand to watch those gory films, especially after eating?"

"I have a strong stomach." Kate smiled serenely, looking very far from the picture of a woman who enjoyed horror movies, the gorier the better.

"How about Chinese food and that new comedy?" Drew coaxed. "We'll even go out for hot fudge sundaes afterward."

"Deal."

After the two women freshened up they left the house for their evening out. Drew hated to admit that there were times when she missed a man's company. After she had been in Houston a little over a year she had met Ron, and she had begun dating him a few months later. After having shared so much with Casey, she hadn't been sure she had anything left to give to a man. Ron had proved her wrong. While he hadn't had Casey's dynamic and forceful personality, he had still made her feel very much a desirable woman. After she broke up with Ron she kept herself too busy to have too much of a social life. It rarely bothered her except on nights like this, when she would think how nice it would be to dress up and go out, with an attentive man at her side.

Would things have been different if she and Casey had talked things out five years ago? That was something that had been haunting her for quite a while. She blamed him for throwing away their relationship, but deep down she knew that she had to share the blame. The sad part was that now it didn't matter, because the past couldn't be recaptured. She would just have to go on from here. Alone.

"Whoever said that movie was funny was talking

through his hat," Kate grumbled when they reentered the house later that night.

"It just goes to show that you can't trust critics." Drew shrugged off her lightweight jacket and hung it in the hall closet.

"It really says something when the highlight of the evening is a hot fudge sundae." She looked up when the telephone rang. "Something tells me that this could be an obscene telephone call to go with the bad movie!"

Drew laughed as she walked over to the phone. "Then I'll take it. Hello?" Her voice was filled with the laughter she had felt. Admittedly the film had been bad, but what had made her evening bearable were Kate's acerbic comments during the movie. It had taken a great deal of willpower for her not to burst out laughing at all the wrong parts.

"Get your butt over here!" The growled command was the last thing she had expected.

Drew looked toward Kate. "You were right, this is an obscene phone call."

"Then hang up!" The older woman hurried over and snatched the receiver out of Drew's hand, then slammed it down. "You shouldn't have to listen to someone speaking filth to you," she scolded.

This time Drew did begin laughing. "Oh, Aunt Kate, you just hung up on your darling nephew!" She gasped for air. She glanced at the phone when it began ringing again. Was it her imagination, or did it have a stronger, angrier ring this time? She picked up the receiver. "Hello, Casey," she said calmly.

"Where the hell have you been?" he demanded, his dark voice slicing through her.

"I had a hot date," she quipped. "We're just getting ready to jump into the Jacuzzi, so if you'll excuse me . . ."

"If you don't want that damn bird fed to the cat next door you'll get over here now," Casey ordered.

Drew's face paled in horror at his threat. "Casey McCord, if you harm one feather on that bird's head, I'll strangle you!" she shouted into the phone.

"I'll see you in ten minutes." The line went dead.

"What is going on?" Kate demanded as she watched Drew run out of the house.

A moment later Drew reappeared in the doorway. "Where does that creep live?" she asked crisply, tossing her keys up and down.

Kate told her, a smile in her eyes.

Drew kept one eye on the rearview mirror as she sped through the deserted streets. The last thing she needed now was a traffic ticket. Thanks to Kate's directions she easily found Casey's small house, built to resemble a French Provincial cottage.

She stopped the car in the driveway and hopped out. She ran up to the front door, which opened before she could hit the doorbell.

"It's about time," Casey growled, gesturing for her to enter.

Drew stepped inside and glanced around, recognizing most of the furniture in the living room.

"What's the emergency?"

"Do you purposely dream up these stunts to drive me out of my mind?" he asked from between clenched teeth.

Drew's head snapped up when she heard a series of high-pitched squawks. She shot Casey a chilling look and headed down the hallway toward the source of the sound.

Shadow stood on top of his cage, his yellow crest standing tall in his obvious agitation, and his beak moving in time to the frightening sounds coming from his throat.

She spun around. "What is going on around here?" She averted her eyes from the slightly wrinkled bed-covers, but something looked very familiar. "The bed!" She sent him an accusing glare. "You told me you sold it!" She gestured toward the king-size ornate brass bed. She had asked Casey if she could have it after she had moved out, but he had calmly informed her that he had sold it. The knowledge that he could so callously have removed an item that had meant so much to them both hurt her a great deal.

"I lied." He shrugged, totally unconcerned by her heated anger. "About that ferocious bird—"

"What?" Drew laughed at his description.

"That damn bird attacked my . . . ah . . . my guest!" Casey exploded, his hands resting on his lean hips.

It was then that Drew noticed that Casey's shirt was partially unbuttoned and hanging outside his slacks. The picture he made wasn't very innocent.

"Perhaps you should explain your problem in further detail," she said icily. She seated herself on the edge of the bed. "Are you trying to tell me that Shadow attacked Monica?"

Casey studied Drew warily. He already knew how dangerous she could be when she seemed to act reason-ably. "What makes you think Monica was here?" he asked all too casually, moving until he stood near the large chest of drawers, out of her line of fire.

Drew's smile reminded him that this was no brainless woman he was speaking to and not to try any tricks. "I didn't realize you had begun wearing perfume," she replied conversationally, although her eyes sent darts through him. She leaned forward, wrapping her hands around one drawn-up knee. "I suggest you look into a better ventilation system if you don't want this place to smell like a bordello every time one of your girlfriends

comes over. So, our big bad bird attacked your girlfriend, did he? I've always thought he fancied himself
an eagle or a hawk. Now I know I'm right. Did she
happen to provoke him in some way?" She felt as if her
smile was plastered on her face and would crack at any
moment. How could he want that she-viper in his bed?
Damn him for this!

Casey began to open his mouth, then shut it up with a
snap. Why should he tell her the truth? She certainly
wouldn't believe it! When he had brought Monica back
for a drink, he hadn't had anything further in mind, but
she certainly had. Monica had maneuvered him into
the bedroom and begun unbuttoning his shirt, all the
while cooing that she knew exactly what he needed.
Fine, so maybe he did need a warm and willing
woman's body, but not hers! Only one woman could
ease the ache he felt. The moment Monica had begun
to pull his shirt out of his slacks, Shadow, who was out
of his cage, had begun shrieking and flown at Monica.
Her usually immaculate hairdo had immediately fallen
victim to the angry cockatiel's beak. Even now he could
hear the woman's screams of outrage. After that it
hadn't taken much to coax her out the door and into the
taxi he had taken the liberty of calling. He sincerely
doubted that he'd hear from Monica again. But why tell
this honey-haired witch that? Why not just brand
himself the Don Juan she probably thought him as?

"I had forgotten he was out of his cage, and
she . . . ah . . . " He frowned, as if needing to choose
his words carefully. "She was taking something off and
he flew at her." He shrugged, all the time watching her
with sharp eyes. The expression on Drew's face wasn't
pleasant, but it told him what he wanted to know. She
cared more than she wanted to!

Drew's insides did a rapid somersault at his implica-
tion. "Perhaps he thought she was trying to attack you

and decided that he should protect you," she joked, although nothing in her manner indicated that she really thought the situation was humorous.

"Damn it, Drew," Casey gritted, moving toward her, his fists clenched at his sides. Why couldn't she just yell at him? Call him names, instead of treating this like some college prank?

"Shadow gets spooked if someone waves things near him. You know that," she explained coldly and concisely. "Next time make sure his cage door is closed, or keep him in another room. After all, there's no reason to give him too much of an education in personal relationships!" she snapped.

By now Casey's face reflected a rage equal to Drew's. He swiftly blocked her attempt to get up from the bed by standing in front of her and leaning over, a hand on either side of her. Her startled eyes focused on the face so close to her own.

"Aren't you afraid your girlfriend will get upset if she finds you in a compromising position?" She couldn't help but breathe in the warm, musky scent of his skin. She could feel a strange tingling sensation along her nerves, and didn't like what it meant.

"I sent her home in a cab." He was busy studying the erratic pulse beating at the base of her throat.

She couldn't keep back her smile. "I bet she was pretty angry at that." The tip of her tongue darted out to wet her lips, an action Casey didn't miss.

Mischievous lights danced in his eyes. "Furious would be more like it." One hand found its way to a jeans-clad thigh. The slow upward stroking motion was deliberate.

Drew's heart hammered so loudly that she feared the world would hear it. "Let me go, Casey," she whispered, wishing it weren't so easy to drown in his eyes. "Don't do this."

"Do what?" He leaned farther forward until she was forced to lie back propped up on her elbows while his muscular thighs trapped her legs between them.

"I won't take Monica's place." Why couldn't she sound more forceful? When had his hand moved up to her midriff? When had her blouse become unbuttoned? When had his hand replaced the lacy covering of her bra?

"I don't remember asking you to replace her." Casey nuzzled the soft curve of her throat. The more he leaned over, the more his body covered hers. A moment later Drew lay back completely, with Casey lying on top of her. "You feel so good to me," he murmured. His hands wandered over her bare breasts, circling the ultra-sensitive nipples, tracing erotic patterns along the undersides and stroking downward to the waistband of her jeans. He pulled the zipper down slowly.

It was beginning to be a repeat of that morning a week ago, except this time Drew was wide awake. She unfastened the rest of his shirt buttons and pushed the fabric away from his shoulders. The crisp dark gold hair she revealed felt familiar under her fingertips; the flexing of his muscles at her exploring touch brought back so many heated memories. She lifted her head and pressed her lips against his damp skin. Her tongue could taste the salty surface.

Casey groaned and gripped her face between his palms. "Open your mouth for me, Drew," he commanded thickly. "Let me taste you."

Their mouths met in a fusion of the senses, their tongues in a heated battle between two people who knew each other's souls intimately. Drew was equally aggressive, her tongue darting into the moist interior of Casey's mouth, pausing only to curl around his tongue and coax it back between her lips. The groans from the depths of his throat were enough to spur her on to further discoveries. Her hands roamed freely over his broad back, feeling the rippling muscles under her fingertips before they slid under the waistband of his slacks to caress his tightly muscled buttocks. She arched up against his potent arousal. She wanted him, all of him, in the most primitive and satisfying way! She wanted that satisfying heat that could drive her to mindless delights.

"I could never forget this, Drew," Casey muttered roughly. "Remember how well we fit together? How well we loved together?" He chuckled huskily. "There used to be a great many days when I'd almost fall asleep at my desk because of the amber-eyed witch who shared my bed each night." He pulled her more fully against his throbbing body. He bent his head and teased her pulsating nipples with his tongue and teeth until she cried out in pleasure filled agony.

"How long has it been since a man made love to you, Drew?" His throaty whisper warmed her swollen breast. "How long has it been since a man had you writhing and purring beneath him?" he pushed relentlessly, hating himself for rubbing salt in his own raw wounds.

"I don't owe you any stories about my past lovers." Drew gasped as Casey's probing fingers sent a searing heat through her body. "Just as I don't ask you about yours."

"You owe me," he told her fiercely, moving his lower torso against hers suggestively. "I was your first lover. I was the man you drove wild when you tried out your powers as the seductress. I was the man who made you a complete woman."

Drew's eyes filled with angry tears. "As far as I can see, all I owe you are my thanks for teaching me so well," she snapped, using all of her strength to push him away. She climbed off the bed and straightened her clothing.

Casey leaned back, making no effort to hide his arousal. "There's no in between with us, Drew. We'll either fight or love with equal intensity. With us, there aren't any halfway measures."

"Then we'd better stick to fighting," she muttered, buttoning her blouse and pushing it back into the waistband of her jeans. If only her body would stop trembling from Casey's caresses. No man could set her body on fire as quickly as he could. Her emotions were begging her to curl right back up on that bed and finish what they had started, but her brain reminded her what a mistake that would be.

"Just how long do you expect us to go on like this?" Casey asked curiously. If he felt any anger at her rejection, he was doing an excellent job of not showing it.

"There is no 'us,' Casey," Drew argued, raking her tousled hair with her fingers and drawing his eyes to the uplifted thrust of her breasts. "Just as there is no 'this.' And don't tell me I'm not making any sense, because I'm perfectly aware that I'm not." She sighed wearily. She turned to the birdcage. "Shadow, when you get home, you'll get an extra-large honey stick for bravery above and beyond the call of duty." She glanced at Casey, feeling more miserable than she had in a long time, but refusing to reveal her true feelings. "I would appreciate never being used as a substitute for another woman again."

He sat up and studied her carefully. "That's where you're wrong. If anything, Monica would have been a substitute for you."

Drew took a deep breath. Without a word she headed blindly for the door. A few moments later Casey could hear the sound of his front door slamming.

"Damn!" He rolled over and drove his fist into the soft mattress.

On Monday morning Casey muttered a greeting to Jenny, his secretary, then went inside his office. The first thing he saw was a large, gaily wrapped package on his desk. Since Jenny hadn't said anything, the gift must have been left there before she came in.

Casey sat down in his chair and picked up the package. There was no card attached. Shrugging, he finally gave in to temptation and undid the wrapping paper. He opened the box and looked inside to find a pile of tissue paper. Under it was a small plastic sign. Taking it out, Casey laughed more heartily than he had in days. He set the small sign on the desk and studied the words.

WARNING: THIS HOUSE IS PROTECTED BY AN ATTACK COCKATIEL

No wonder there hadn't been a note. Only one person could have sent such a crazy gift. Casey loved it—almost as much as he loved her.

Barely a week later Drew sat beside Casey in the jet's first-class section. The rest of their group had already climbed the narrow winding stairway to the lounge for a celebration of their own.

"It sounds as if they're intending to party their way to Hawaii," Drew commented. She turned to lower the porthole shade. She hadn't gotten much sleep the night before, and the last thing she needed was bright sunlight. "At this rate we'll have to pour them off the plane."

"Casey?" A seductive Southern drawl interrupted their conversation.

He turned his head and smiled up at a tall, curvy redhead. "Aren't you joining the party, Chantal?" he asked politely.

"Only if you are," she purred, draping her willowy form over the back of his seat.

Drew hadn't liked the wife of the southeastern regional manager on sight. Chantal Fontaine was the product of an old Southern background combined with modern promiscuity. It had soon become apparent that she intended to make Casey her next victim.

"Maybe later." Casey couldn't seem to keep his eyes from the low-cut neckline of Chantal's black tunic top which left the tops of her breasts in full view. Her white designer jeans looked as if they had been spray-painted onto her voluptuous body.

The stunning woman smiled and tapped a polished fingernail against his nose in a playful gesture. "I'll take that as a promise, ya hear?" The smile she sent Drew was just this side of polite.

"If I hear 'y'all' or 'ya hear' one more time, I'm going to be violently ill," Drew muttered.

"Part of the Southern belle image," Casey replied absently, returning to the business magazine he had been reading.

Drew arched an eyebrow in disbelief. Her own designer jeans might have been snug, but she knew she could sit down comfortably in them, and her leaf-green cotton camp shirt had a modest V neckline. Her wedge-heeled sandals were designed for comfort, while Chantal's spike heels were meant to set off her long, shapely legs.

Casey took two glasses of champagne from the smiling flight attendant and handed one to Drew.

"To warm and sunny days and balmy moonlit nights," he said softly, holding his glass slightly aloft in a toast.

Drew smiled and clinked glasses. "If I remember correctly, you said something very similar almost eight years ago on a flight very much like this." She sipped the bubbly liquid.

"Perhaps there will be other similarities before the trip is over," he murmured suggestively.

Drew's eyes snapped upward. She set her glass on the small tray in front of her seat. "I'm beginning to think you have a one-track mind," she commented tartly, refusing to admit that her thoughts had been running along remarkably similar lines.

Casey's lips curved in a teasing smile. "Usually the tale is about the woman sleeping her way to the top. I always wondered if it would work as well if the situation were reversed."

"Obviously it doesn't, not if the lovely Mrs. Fontaine is the one planning on securing a promotion for her husband in the time-honored fashion," she replied in an acidly sweet tone.

Casey chuckled. "You seem to forget that *I* like to be the one to do the chasing." He finished his champagne and unfolded his length from the seat. Even the first-class seats didn't seem to offer him enough leg room. "I might as well get my socializing out of the way. I do hope you'll be doing some of your own," he said pointedly.

"Don't worry, I'm well aware of my obligations. I'll have an entire week to observe each candidate. Unless, of course, you've decided to stay on?" she asked archly.

He trailed his fingers along her jaw. "Smile pretty and I just might do anything you ask. If you get too bored with your own company, come up and join us."

Drew knew that she'd have little time of her own for the next week, and for the sake of her sanity, that was probably just as well. She already had a strong hunch that it wouldn't take much to have her sharing Casey's bed before the week was out. She smiled, remembering his thank you for the sign. He had told her that he intended to post it on his fence.

She flexed her shoulder muscles and shifted in her seat. The last time she had flown to Hawaii she had been sitting farther back in the jet, but it had been no less exciting. If anything, it had been even more so, with an attentive Casey seated next to her. Her college graduation gift from him had been two weeks in the Hawaiian Islands.

They had swum in the ocean, walked along the beach late at night, visited the tourist attractions, and mainly just enjoyed each other's company. Their lovemaking had been the added spice to their time together. The sigh that left Drew's lips was a wistful one. That was what she had missed the most, Casey's companionship the way it had been five years before.

This wasn't a time to mull over the past. She rose from her seat and headed for the lounge.

Drew was all gracious smiles when she greeted the managers and their wives and girlfriends. She figured that there was some speculation as to why Casey was traveling alone, and herself likewise. Casey had once accused her of worrying too much about what other people thought, and that was just what she was starting to do now. This was not the time to worry about anyone else. She should just settle down and have a good time.

After landing at Honolulu International Airport, they crossed the acres of air terminals to change planes for the last leg of their journey. It was late afternoon when they landed at Lihue Airport on the island of Kauai. A mini shuttle bus transported the group to the well-known beachfront hotel where they would be staying for the next week.

After an announcement that they would meet for cocktails in two hours, they dispersed to their rooms.

Casey glanced at the room key Drew held in her hand and offered to help her with her luggage.

"I didn't come with five suitcases like before," she teased, gesturing to her medium-size case and tote bag.

"No use in your struggling, even with those, since

our rooms are close together." He hoisted the case in one hand and his own bag in the other, leaving Drew to carry her tote bag.

Drew turned out to have a well-appointed one-bedroom suite decorated in cool blues and greens.

"Not at all like the room we had the last time we were here," Casey remarked wryly, carrying Drew's suitcase into the bedroom and setting it on the luggage rack.

She silently agreed with him, although at the time she had cared more about her companion than her surroundings.

"Casey . . ." She walked over to him and placed her hand on his arm. She could feel the muscles tense under her casual touch. "Casey, look at me," she entreated softly.

The jungle cat eyes watched her with an inexplicable sorrow that pierced her heart. "That's the way it's been since you came to Fantasy Toys, Drew." He spoke with a light bitterness. "I can look at you, but I can't touch. All I can do is remember the times when I was allowed to caress you, and so much more. The more I look at it, the more I can see that having you attend this conference was a mistake. You aren't really needed here. If you'd wanted to look over the managers, you could have flown them out to the offices and seen them there just as easily. This was just a crazy plan of mine to get you away from CHEM Corp. and Fantasy Toys. A plan that looks like it's going to fail before it even begins. I should have known better."

Drew wondered if Casey would appreciate knowing that it had been her idea, too. She unconsciously dampened her lips with the tip of her tongue, drawing his sharp eyes to the action.

"Damn it, Drew!" he exploded, jerking away from the hand that was still lying lightly on his arm. "You should know I can't take too much more where you're concerned!"

She stepped back, looking as if she had been slapped. "I'm sorry," she whispered painfully, and turned away from the dark wrath on his face. "I should have realized that you've been experiencing the same hell I've been going through. I can see how thoughtless I've been regarding your feelings. As you said, my coming along was a mistake, but it would look very odd if I left now. I promise to stay out of your way as much as possible this next week."

Casey closed his eyes tightly as if to banish the vulnerable-looking woman before him. Why was it that his schemes wouldn't work out when she was involved? Muttering something unintelligible under his breath, he turned on his heel and walked out, slamming the door behind him.

Drew released the breath she had been holding. She was beginning to wonder who was erecting the barriers now. She might have started their construction when she first came to Fantasy Toys and discovered that Casey was working there, but it looked as if he would complete the job. She couldn't really blame him. Each time he had approached her in an intimate way, she had rejected him. A man could only take so much before doing some rejecting of his own. She remembered him saying that he had hoped things would change between them while they were out here. It looked as if it would have to be all up to her. If so, she had no time to lose. She would start that evening, when the group met for cocktails.

Chapter Eight

$\mathcal{D}$rew chose a black linen halter dress that left her shoulders bare and had a wide ruby-colored snakeskin belt that brought attention to her slender waist. She put her hair in a loose knot on top of her head.

"A-lo-ha!" Sam Martinson greeted her jovially, holding up his Mai Tai.

"I see that you've already gone native," she teased, looking at the gray-haired man's gaily patterned aloha shirt, white slacks and leather sandals.

"He'll probably be weaving baskets and learning the hula by tomorrow," his wife, Polly, piped up. A roly-poly woman in her mid-fifties, she had also opted for the more comfortable style of clothing. In her bright red muumuu she resembled a plump beach ball. Polly's easygoing nature had attracted Drew immediately.

The rest of the group included Charles and Maureen Finch, of the Southeast region, a warm and friendly couple in their forties; Tom and Karla Calvin, from the Midwest, who were down to earth; and Josh and Helen

Randolph of the Northwest region, a couple in their late thirties with a never ending supply of energy. They all had wondered with a growing curiosity if there were an unspoken connection between Fantasy Toys' lovely executive director and its good-looking director of sales.

Casey had changed into jeans and a dark gold cotton knit pullover shirt. He held his usual whiskey and soda as he stood to one side, deep in conversation with Tom Calvin. He gave no indication that he had noticed Drew's entrance, although every nerve in his body was quivering with awareness. He knew immediately that she was behind him and to his right. His senses had always been accurate where Drew was concerned.

Dinner, a vast array of tempting foods, was served buffet style. Three tables, each set for four, had been arranged at one end of the large dining room to be used by the group.

Casey managed to stand in line behind Drew. She took small samples of several salads and headed for a table, with Casey still behind her. Chantal and Paul sat at the same table, due to Chantal's clever maneuvering.

The lovely redhead flirted shamelessly with Casey throughout the meal, leaving Drew to converse with Paul. She hated to admit it, but she felt jealous as she watched Casey smiling and talking easily to Chantal. Drew realized that his smile was not his usual warm, natural one, and that his conversation was stilted, bordering on the formal, but it didn't ease the pain in her heart. Drew found Paul, though he was a quiet man, to be an interesting dinner partner. He was the picture of the Southern Creole gentleman. His dark hair might have been liberally threaded with silver, and the lines in his face showed that he had lived a hard forty-some years, but he was still a handsome man who could attract women's interested glances. It was apparent that Paul wasn't blind to his wife's failings, but if they bothered him, he was able to hide that fact. His rich, melodious voice, with its slow drawl, was a healing balm to Drew's injured ego. Even if Casey were only acting polite, it certainly wouldn't have hurt him to have paid a little attention to her! Instead Drew concentrated on Paul, who had been asking questions about her schooling and what she had done before coming to Fantasy Toys. Seeing his sincere interest, she went on to elaborate about her former projects.

"You're a graduate of Harvard!" Admiration laced the older man's voice. "Your family must be very proud of you. That's a great accomplishment, and I'm not saying that just because you're a woman. I understand it's a difficult school. You not only have to be intelligent but willing to work hard to do well there."

Drew's laughter was low and musical. "I think my stepfather was more relieved than proud when I graduated. It had been a pretty rough four years." Except for the last two, she silently added to herself. "I worked part-time in addition to receiving a scholarship."

"She forgot to mention that she also graduated in the top ten percent of her class." There was a touch of pride in Casey's voice.

Paul smiled slowly. "An interesting piece of information," he remarked with an uplifted brow. What went unspoken was the question of where Casey had heard such trivia about Drew's past accomplishments.

"Marty Watson of CHEM Corp. enjoys lauding Drew's accomplishments to the world," Casey explained smoothly. "Especially when he's speaking to the male half of the population. He thinks it will keep us on our toes."

"If only it were that easy." Drew sighed dramatically. "Thanks to Marty's ground breaking, every time I go in to a new company they expect some dowdy spinster wearing horn-rimmed glasses and sporting a tweed suit."

Chantal sipped her wine, looking a little puzzled by the interchange. "CHEM Corp., that's the new parent company for Fantasy Toys, isn't it? But aren't you Casey's assistant or something like that? You're his secretary, aren't you?" she remarked a trifle maliciously.

"Chantal!" Paul whispered, his dark eyes sending a silent warning in his wife's direction.

At first Drew thought that the other woman was being deliberately rude. Then she remembered that the couple hadn't been present for the initial introductions when the group had met at the airport that morning. She leaned back in her chair, looking totally at ease.

"My official title at Fantasy Toys is executive director, Mrs. Fontaine," she replied matter-of-factly. "Which means that I'm Casey McCord's boss." She met Chantal's gaze head on. "And your husband's boss" was left unspoken, but it was no less understood for all that.

Only the narrowing of the woman's dark green eyes and the tensing of her facial muscles spoke of her agitation. "I see," she said finally. "I must say, you've done quite well for yourself to hold such a high position in what is still virtually a man's world."

Chantal's purring compliment might have sounded sincere to the two men's ears, but Drew read the words the way they were meant to be understood. Chantal couldn't believe that any woman could get ahead in the business world unless she resorted to using her sexual skills.

"Suffice it to say that I have been given *carte blanche* regarding the inner workings of Fantasy Toys." Drew smiled serenely. "In short, my word is law." Her velvety voice carried a steel lining.

The verbal duel was interrupted when two of the other couples paused at their table to suggest that the group go up to the lounge for after-dinner drinks.

Chantal's slightly sullen face brightened when she heard that dancing was also featured there.

"Watch your tongue, Drew," Casey warned in a low voice as they left the restaurant. "I wouldn't care to have to pry Chantal's fingers from your throat after you've pitched her another one of your poisonous darts."

Drew didn't deign to reply. She used a trip to the ladies' room to take her out of his sphere of influence.

Inside the beige and lime powder room, Drew sat on a beige velvet covered stool and stroked on perfume. While she freshened her lip gloss she looked up to see Chantal enter the room.

"You must have enjoyed making me look like a fool," the redhead began without preamble. She dropped into a chair, crossing her long legs at the knee.

Drew turned to face her. "Even nowadays it's common for a woman executive to be mistaken for a secretary. Let's make it clear right from the beginning, Mrs. Fontaine. I would hazard a guess that you participate actively in the furthering of your husband's career. This is one time when your . . . 'assistance' won't work." Drew's eyes glittered with orange-gold lights. She had made her meaning very clear.

Chantal idly studied a fingernail. "Rumor has it that Casey has resigned as director of sales, and that you're here to look over the managers in an attempt to choose his successor." She looked up questioningly. "Paul is an excellent sales manager, the sales reports speak for themselves, but he has no concept whatsoever of how to promote himself. That's where I come in."

Drew's generously shaped mouth narrowed into a thin line. Chantal might think she could explain her actions, but Drew saw them merely as another form of prostitution. Drew pulled the zipper shut on her purse, rose to her feet and headed for the door.

"Then I guess I can just relax and concentrate on

Casey as an extremely attractive man, can't I?'' Chantal's provocative challenge hit Drew right between the shoulder blades.

Drew slowly turned. "I can asily see you as a willful Southern belle during the Civil War," she said quietly. "I just bet you would have been the first girl on your block to invite the Yankees not only into your home, but into your bed. They were the victors, after all." Chantal's gasp of outrage followed Drew out of the room.

The lounge was on the fourth floor, with windows along two sides affording the guests a panoramic view of the beach.

Drew wasn't surprised to find tne seat next to Casey empty or by the fact that the expression in his eyes ordered her to take it. She greeted everyone with a smile and glanced up at the Oriental waitress, who softly asked what she would like to drink.

"I'll have a Tropical Itch," she requested, earning a sharp glance from Casey.

"What on earth is that?" Karla asked curiously.

"Something a little too potent," Casey growled, shifting uneasily in his chair.

"It has bourbon and rum in it, among other things," Drew explained, ignoring his glare. "It's mostly a novelty drink for the tourists. I had it the last time I was in the Islands, and I guess you could say I acquired a taste for it."

The group saw a tall glass arrive, along with a miniature wooden back scratcher to be used as a swizzle stick. Except for Casey, they all decided to try the exotic drink.

The first drink served to relax Drew, but as she began working on her second she could sense conflicting messages being sent to her brain.

"Lady, you're playing with fire," Casey muttered *sotto voce* when she asked for a third. "You're already well on your way to getting tight. You never could hold your alcohol very well."

"Party pooper." She grimaced at his face which appeared just a trifle fuzzy. Her body swayed sinuously in time to the background music. Sensing that someone was standing next to her, she turned her head to find a man of medium height dressed incongruously in a deep burgundy long sleeved shirt, black pants and a fitted vest.

"Would you care to dance?" He smiled brightly, holding out one hand.

"No, thank you," she refused politely.

"Oh, go ahead, sweetheart," Casey urged affably. "I won't mind."

Drew fixed a false smile on her lips. "But I might," she whispered.

"She's just shy," Casey explained in a friendly voice to the other man. He practically pushed an unwilling Drew out of her chair. "Actually, she'd love to dance, wouldn't you, love?" He flashed her a grin.

She shot him a dark glare, then, deciding that a scene wasn't in order, swept out to the dance floor with her colorful partner. As she danced with the energetic man she silently wondered why he wasn't downstairs in the disco instead of up here where the band played more traditional dance music. He was just a bit too flamboyant for her taste. All she could do was force a bright smile onto her face and avoid looking toward Casey. She'd deal with him later. Finally the music stopped. She thanked the man and hurried back to the table before he could suggest another dance.

"I'll get you for this," she threatened under the guise of a warm smile for the benefit of any onlookers.

"Promises, promises."

Drew sipped her drink, then set it down, gazing at it suspiciously. "There isn't any alcohol in this," she announced.

"That's right." Casey's lips twitched with mirth. "And no complaints, okay?"

During the course of the evening Drew danced with each of the men, including Casey. She silently cursed him for choosing a slow melody for their dance, then cursed herself for accepting.

The long flight, coupled with the tension of parrying Chantal's catty remarks during dinner, was telling on Drew's sanity. Using the excuse of weariness, she left the group and headed for her suite. Just as she left the table, she heard Chantal say to Casey, "You're not going to run out so early, too, are you, darling?"

Drew gritted her teeth, made her good nights to the rest of the group and headed for the elevator.

Once in her bed, wearing a peach-colored confection of silk and lace, Drew found that falling asleep wasn't all that easy. There had been no memories to assail her in San Diego. Here on Kauai, in the same hotel they had stayed in eight years ago, it wasn't so easy to ignore him. She could remember how they had gone swimming in the ocean at midnight, then returned to their room to make love until dawn. She was beginning to wonder if it wouldn't be better just to give in to the memories, pick up the phone and call Casey's room. But she shook her head and pounded her pillow into a more pleasing shape. She refused to cede the victory to him.

Since the next morning had been left free for the group, Drew had a light breakfast in her room and decided to spend some of the early morning hours on the beach. She was well aware that the sun was much too strong for the uninitiated during midday. Dressed in her bikini and armed with sunscreen and a book, she went outside.

A number of people were already ensconced on the many chaise longues surrounding the swimming pool or stretched out on cocoa fiber mats on the beach. She adjusted her oversized sunglasses on her nose, commandeered a chaise longue off to one side and smoothed sunscreen on her bare skin. She put her watch to one side so she could keep track of the time. Getting a bad sunburn on her first day wouldn't be her idea of fun.

Later, when Drew met everyone for lunch, her skin glowed the color of rich honey from her short time in the sun. All she needed was a brush of dark mascara and a bright coral lip gloss to brighten the beginnings of her tan.

She had dressed in a turquoise terrycloth tank top and matching shorts with tennis shoes for the boat trip to the Fern Grotto. She had carefully braided her hair down one side of her head so the braid could hang over her shoulder.

"It looks as if you enjoyed some of the sun today," Polly said in greeting. Today the older woman wore a parrot green and yellow muumuu. She had pinned a brightly colored tropical flower in her gray hair.

"Sam might not like you wearing that flower behind your right ear," Drew teased, carefully removing the flower and pinning it behind Polly's left ear.

"Why not?"

"When a woman wears a flower behind her right ear it means she's available. When it's behind her left ear it tells the men she's spoken for." The younger woman's eyes sparkled with mischief. "Of course, you could always wear it on the back of your head."

"And what does that mean?" Polly's eyes twinkled back.

Drew leaned forward and explained in a loud whisper, "That says, 'Come one, come all!' " Polly dissolved in laughter.

"Glad to see you thought to use a sunscreen," Casey murmured, pausing behind Drew's chair.

She looked up and flashed him a smile reminiscent of years ago. He had also dressed casually in khaki cotton shorts and a brightly patterned shirt that would have looked ridiculous on some men, but Casey was able to carry it off admirably. His bare feet were thrust into a pair of disreputable jogging shoes with the laces still untied.

"Aren't you afraid of tripping over your big feet?" Drew glanced down at his shoes.

"I've always been backward when it comes to tying my shoelaces," he admitted with a sheepish grin, then moved on to join Tom and Karla.

"The two of you make a lovely couple," Polly said abruptly.

"Don't tell me you enjoy matchmaking?" Drew accused lightly, wanting to keep things as light as possible.

"Only in beautiful tropical settings," the older woman replied, still smiling.

The minibus took the group to meet the boats that traveled up the Wailua River to the famous Fern Grotto.

"I used to get seasick in the navy. Hope it doesn't happen here," Charles Finch announced when they boarded the long flat bottomed boat with benches running along the sides and in the center.

Casey threw Drew a wicked grin. His thoughts were evident from the mischief dancing in his eyes.

"If you dare say one word . . ." she whispered, leaving the rest of the threat unsaid. At the same time she prayed that nothing would happen. If she got seasick now Casey would never let her live it down!

"You did take your pills before you left the hotel, didn't you?" He was enjoying himself too much to let up on his teasing. "We wouldn't want to put into shore because your stomach decided to do some flip-flops."

Drew sniffed haughtily and moved away, Casey's amused chuckle filling her ears.

The guide kept up a running commentary during the short cruise. When the boat landed upriver at its destination the passengers were instructed to follow a trail through a tangled jungle of ferns and various dark green tropical plants.

"When do the natives surround us, kidnap us and decide to offer you as a sacrifice to the big ape?" Casey asked Drew in a stage whisper. His fingertips traced a light path between her shoulder blades. "Oh, they prefer virgins, don't they? Looks like you're safe, then," he added wickedly.

"Play your cards right and some lovely maiden just might abduct you and carry you off to her hideaway." She wrinkled her nose at him in keeping with the light-hearted mood.

He tweaked the end of her braid and winked at her audaciously before moving on ahead.

Drew noticed Polly's pleased smile and knew that the woman was hoping for a little romance to spice up the week. Her own body and mind were waging a major battle on exactly that subject. To seduce or not to seduce, that was the question.

When the group reached the large cave with its entrance draped with giant, graceful fishtail ferns, a hushed reverence fell over them. No wonder it was such a popular setting for weddings. It seemed more fitting to recite the sacred vows of love here than in a chapel. When the strains of the "Hawaiian Wedding Song" floated over them, everyone felt a special spell.

Drew didn't pull away when Casey's hand captured hers and his thumb traced a circle in the middle of her palm, sending tingles up her arm.

"Casey," she whispered plaintively. Stop. Don't stop. Her mind couldn't decide.

"Ssh, for once just be quiet and enjoy." His murmured words barely reached her ears.

For one wild sweet moment Drew could almost believe that the poignant song was being sung for them alone, just as she had dreamed of eight years ago. It was all too easy to imagine it with Casey's hand warmly encompassing hers, his side brushing against her.

When they returned to the boat Casey refused to release Drew's hand, much to Polly's obvious delight and Chantal's dismay. Drew decided to enjoy his playfulness and Chantal's discomfort to the hilt.

When they returned to the hotel the decision to change into swimsuits and take advantage of the water was unanimous. Drew quickly changed into a honey-gold bikini much the same color as her hair. She wrapped a matching kimono-style robe around herself, and picked up her tote bag that held sunscreen, a mystery book she had been wanting to read for a long time and a towel.

When she reached the swimming pool most of the group was already there, including Chantal, who wore a diminutive emerald-green string bikini. Her sullen features and Paul's angry ones were perfect companions. The couple had clearly had an argument that wouldn't be easily resolved.

Drew walked down the beach a short distance from the others. She spread her towel on the sand and dropped her robe, then ran into the late afternoon surf to enjoy the warm water.

She spent her time bodysurfing, oblivious to the admiring glances sent her way by the men on the beach. She was too concerned with having a good time. Her slim, supple body moved with the water as she swam out time and time again to catch the incoming waves.

"Hey, boss!" She looked up when she heard a man's shout.

Drew waved and struck out for shore. When she

reached shallow water she stood up and waded out.
Casey stood near her towel, his hands braced on his
lean hips. Dressed in navy swim briefs, he embodied all
that was essentially male. His eyes widened as he
watched her approach.

"The water's great," she greeted him cheerfully,
surprised by the tense body and taut jaw. If she didn't
know better, she'd have sworn that he was angry at
her.

"What the hell do you think you're doing, wearing an
outfit like that?" he rumbled, frowning at her.

Drew looked down, expecting to find that part of her
bikini had slipped, revealing more than she cared to.
"What's wrong with it?" she asked, puzzled by this new
turn of events.

"You looked as if you weren't wearing anything
when you came out of the water," he exploded, reaching down for her robe and throwing it over her shoulders. "Look around you! Every man has his tongue
hanging out, hoping some part of your anatomy will do
the same thing!"

Drew flushed at his crude remark, but anger soon
took over. "There are women around here wearing
quite a bit less than I am! Chantal, for one," she
shouted, uncaring who overheard their argument.

Casey looked down at her angry stance. What bothered him the most was the sight of her outthrust
breasts, the nipples boldly outlined by the wet fabric of
her bikini top, and the way the sleek cotton triangle
molded her hips. He smothered a low groan of frustration.

"I wouldn't care if the other women here were stark
naked," he argued, pushing his face closer to hers.
"You're the only one who matters to me."

"I'm not your responsibility anymore, Casey," she
retorted hotly. "Go find someone else to play mother
hen to. I don't need you!" She regretted the callous

words the moment they left her lips, but it was too late to take them back.

Casey's head snapped back as if he had been slapped. "Okay, Drew," he said quietly. "You don't have to hit me over the head. I get the message loud and clear."

"Casey, I'm sorry," Drew apologized, holding out her hand as if to restrain him, but he shrugged and walked off. With sorrowful eyes she watched him head for the water. She hadn't missed his hurt expression. She only wished she hadn't been the one to put it there. "Damn," she muttered, pushing a stray lock of hair away from her face with agitated fingers. "Where's all that fantastic tact I'm supposed to have?"

The beach had lost its charm. She picked up her belongings and returned to her room for a long hot shower.

Drew wasn't surprised that Casey stayed away from her during dinner and the Polynesian show they attended afterward. When he did speak to her, it was in a formal, distant tone that tore at her heart.

"Since the men are taking off for a fishing trip in the morning we'll be left on our own," Polly announced to the other women as they sat in the lounge. "I suggest we do what we know best."

"Spend money?" Drew grinned, noticing how most of the other women's eyes lit up at the idea.

"What better way to salve our abandoned little souls?" Chantal said, entering into the spirit of the game.

"Let's go to the Market Place at the Coconut Plantation. We can be there when the stores open," Drew suggested. "If there's an excellent place to drop a bundle, that's it."

The next morning the women rode the hotel van over to the large shopping plaza, where they wandered through the various shops.

In one boutique a particular item caught Drew's eye. The fabric of the pureau had a swirling pattern of emerald green and gold. It was strapless, and a gold maile leaf clip was its only fastening. The price tag sent a shudder through her body, but the color of the dress had brought back a lot of memories.

"Who knows, maybe it will bring me luck," she muttered to herself, quickly signing the charge receipt before she could change her mind. "A perfect choice for the luau tomorrow night."

During a laugh-filled lunch that consisted of more piña coladas than food, the women began to learn more about each other.

"You really should have gotten that bright blue bikini, Maureen," Drew told the woman in question while she leaned back in her chair and sipped the potent blend of rum, coconut cream and pineapple juice.

"Oh, no, I never wear blue!" Maureen protested.

"Why not? It's a good color for you." Drew was surprised by the other woman's vehemence.

"It's just a crazy superstition of mine," Maureen admitted a little sheepishly. "For a while it seemed that anytime I wore blue, something would go drastically wrong. The last time I wore a blue blouse I had two flat tires in the same day!"

"I only use one particular pen when I write checks, and if I can't find it I go crazy," Karla said.

"I never go out of the house on the fourth of the month," Polly contributed. "Four is an unlucky number for me."

"I only sleep on the left side of the bed," Drew contributed when the others looked at her as if *she* were the crazy one. "I can't get a decent night's sleep otherwise. Honest!" she reiterated, holding up her right hand. She couldn't help but remember Casey's constant teasing about her compulsion for sleeping on the left-hand side of the bed, but she had never given in.

By the time the women returned to the hotel they were feeling no pain. The piña coladas had more than done the trick. They retired to their respective rooms for a well-earned nap before it was time to meet for dinner.

The men returned from their fishing trip late that afternoon, sunburned and slightly the worse for wear after the large quantity of beer they had consumed.

"Just please spare us any stories about the ones that got away," Drew teased the men when they all met for dinner. Her gaze hungrily followed Casey, who was laughing and joking with Polly and Maureen. He took great care to avoid her eyes, much to her sorrow.

Drew returned to her room early that evening. She tried to read her book, but found it couldn't hold her interest. There was only one thing she could do. She picked up the phone and dialed the operator. She only hoped that Casey was in his room.

"Hello?"

"Casey?" Her voice was soft and questioning, as if she were afraid he might hang up when she identified herself.

"Drew?" His voice sharpened with concern. "Is everything all right?"

"No," she murmured truthfully. "I hurt you yesterday, and I didn't mean to. I shouldn't have said what I did, and I'm sorry. If I promise to throw myself into Waimea Canyon, will you find it in your heart to forgive me?"

He chuckled, cradling the receiver against his shoulder as he sat down on the edge of the bed. "I think there's a law against littering."

Drew relaxed at his bantering. He wasn't angry with her anymore. "I wouldn't exactly call myself a piece of crumpled paper," she countered mildly, curling up on the bed, feeling more lighthearted than she had in a long time.

"Are you game for an early breakfast and some windsurfing?" Casey suggested suddenly.

Drew's face lit up. "Name the time," she replied without hesitation.

"Six."

"Ugh," she groaned, falling backward on the bed. "You couldn't make it later in the day, could you?"

"Not when you'd like to believe the day doesn't start until noon," he teased back. "How do you manage to make it to the office?"

"I change the clocks. My mind believes anything it sees," she said lightly. "I've tried to talk Marty into changing the working hours, but he's like you. He believes you're not worth anything if you're not at your desk by seven a.m."

"Think you can manage to be coherent by six?" Casey asked her.

"Sure, I'll live dangerously." She laughed softly.

"Drew . . ." His voice turned into a husky murmur that sent erotic tingles along her spine. "I'm glad you called. You didn't need to apologize. I guess I'm still a little sensitive where you're concerned."

"You know what?" Her tone matched his. "I'm kind of glad you are. . . . Well, if I'm going to be up at such an ungodly hour, I had better get some sleep. Good night, Casey."

"Good night, Drew."

Drew hung up the telephone and continued lying on the bed, smiling to herself.

The next morning Casey was the man Drew had known five years before. He was warmly attentive to her during breakfast and helpful during her abortive attempts at windsurfing. His natural athletic grace gave him an extra edge at the difficult sport, but Drew wasn't as lucky. She finally gave up and sat on the sand, content to watch him fight waves that were intent on washing him off the board.

Drew wasn't afraid that Casey would hurt himself. He had too much common sense to try anything dangerous. Instead she enjoyed watching his lean mus-cled body react as he fought for balance and twisted to catch the wind just the right way. She knew that he still felt a little wary around her, and she could understand why. She was just waiting for the luau that night, when she would spring her new dress on him. If that didn't raise his blood pressure she'd just have to resort to more drastic measures, and in the mood she was in, that wouldn't be too difficult!

Chapter Nine

$\mathcal{D}$rew made sure to take special care with her appearance for the luau that evening.

First on the agenda came a long soak in the tub, with perfumed oil added to the water; then she rubbed an identically scented body lotion into her still damp skin. She washed her hair and blew it dry, then set it on electric rollers. She twisted the resulting curls into a loose, but intricate knot on top of her head. Only a few strategically placed hairpins held it in place. Makeup gave a warm glow to her face. Her only jewelry was a pair of emerald drop earrings.

Once she was properly perfumed and made up, Drew wrapped her dress around her body. The only security was the gold maile-leaf-shaped clip fastened between her breasts. She walked across the room several times, watching the green and gold skirt part to reveal her tanned legs and delicate gold sandals. She glanced at the small travel clock by her bed. Good, by now most of the others would be in the lobby. She hoped that Casey would be one of them.

She injected a new sway into her walk when she entered the lobby. She had timed it just right. She was the last to arrive.

"Sorry I'm late," she called out in a huskier voice than usual.

The expressions on the faces that turned toward her differed. Six men showed frank appreciation for the emerald and gold vision before them. Five women smiled warmly, while one narrowed her eyes with undisguised envy. The one person whose opinion truly mattered to her watched her with a stunned expression that bordered on shock.

"Ah." Casey had to clear his throat before he could speak. "Since we're all here now, I'll tell Maki to bring the van."

"I must congratulate you, Miss Sinclair," Chantal purred, following Drew as they walked out to the van. "You managed to make quite an entrance back there. I can see that I've underestimated you a great deal."

Drew turned, presenting the woman with a feline smile. "Yes, you certainly did, and if I were you, I'd remember that in the future." Then she moved forward and began an animated conversation with Polly, who complimented her warmly on her dress.

"Isn't it amazing how something that just looked like an odd-shaped piece of material can look so lovely on the right person? Of course, my dear, you certainly have the figure to carry something like that off. You don't resemble a potato sack the way I would!" She gave Drew's shoulder a motherly pat as they walked toward the waiting van.

Casey took great care not to sit near Drew for the short drive to the luau. He struck up a conversation with Paul Fontaine, although later he couldn't remember a word he had spoken to the man. Obviously he had given all the right answers, though, since Paul hadn't appeared to notice anything amiss during their talk.

When he had turned around in the lobby to see Drew wearing a dress so similar to the one she had worn eight years ago, he had thought he had been catapulted back in time. Back to the day when they had gone shopping and he had found a dress in emerald and gold that suited Drew's coloring perfectly. A dress that floated about her. She had worn it that evening when they had gone to dinner, and he hadn't been able to keep his eyes off her. In fact, neither could any of the men who had seen her, much to his displeasure. She was *his* woman! He took a deep breath to fill his aching lungs. His body reacted immediately to the sensual picture in his mind. He longed to pick her up and carry her back to his suite. That dress wouldn't stay on a second longer than it would take him to lock the door after them. He'd bet his last dime that she was wearing next to nothing under it. In the closed confines of the van he swore he could smell the spicy floral scent of her perfume, a perfume that hinted of exotic moonlit nights and a soft bed with a golden-haired siren reclining against the sheets. He clenched his hands into fists, cursing the weakness of the male of the species when pitted against a woman secure in her own sensuality. The man would never have a chance.

Drew was busily engaged in her own conversation with Polly, but she could somehow sense that Casey was mentally stripping her. They had always been in tune with each other, and even five years apart hadn't diminished that special mental link between them. From beneath lowered lashes she studied his profile as he turned in his seat to talk to Paul. Casey wore khaki-colored cotton slacks and a white loosely woven shirt that he had left partially unbuttoned in deference to the warm evening air. He could look as devastating in casual dress as he did in a three-piece suit. The deeper tan he had gained over the past few days only served to heighten the potent male sexuality he exuded as naturally as he wore his after-shave. She saw he still wore the narrow gold chain. That chain gave her hope for the success of her plan.

Drew was seated on Casey's right during the luau, but she made sure to treat him the way she would a casual friend. She couldn't tell if he were relieved or disappointed by her attitude.

The pasty concoction called poi was tried by only a brave few, but everybody sampled the various dishes of fish, roast pork, steamed vegetables and fresh fruits. A strong rum punch was also served with the meal.

"After all the food I've eaten this week, I'll probably have to diet for the rest of the year," Polly giggled, her flushed features betraying the amount of punch she had drunk.

By the time the entertainment began after dinner, the conversation had become loud, interspersed with a lot of laughter. Chantal, seated on the other side of Casey, kept him occupied, her low voice bordering on the intimate, much to Drew's disgust.

Three Hawaiian men with guitars serenaded them with Polynesian melodies; they were followed by three women wearing brightly colored pureaus who danced the traditional hula. Afterward they urged three of the men to dance with them. One of the women persuaded Casey to join her in the hip-swaying dance.

Drew couldn't keep her eyes off him as he followed the provocative movements with a natural, lazy grace all his own. The other two men laughed sheepishly and were unable to do much more than wiggle their hips to the music.

"I certainly didn't know my Sam would get up there and do something like that." Polly laughed at the good-natured antics of her husband, who dipped and wiggled with a smiling young Polynesian girl.

"And now it's the ladies' turn," one of the men announced.

Drew and Chantal readily agreed, and even a loudly protesting Polly was convinced to participate.

Drew wasn't surprised to see Chantal throw herself wholeheartedly into dancing with a young man who could barely keep his eyes off her. What bothered Drew was the idea that Casey was watching the redhead with the same absorption. But Drew had a few ideas of her own.

Drew's partner soon learned that she knew what she was doing and after a hurried talk with her, he called some instructions to the band.

In seconds the flowing guitar music was replaced by a hypnotic, and much faster, melody accompanied by the loud beating of drums.

Drew's smile broadened. Almost immediately she was bending her knees and moving her hips in the swift figure eight pattern of the Tahitian hula, a dance that had mesmerized sailors for years. She held her arms out to her partner as if to embrace him. A moment later she turned to the audience, who watched her with fascinated eyes, but there was only one person who interested her.

Casey sat stiffly, his eyes glazed in shock as Drew began to dance in front of him. Her trim hips undulated to the sensual beat as she moved in even closer.

Her skin gleamed gold under the sheen of perspiration from her exertions. Strands of her hair tumbled down, giving her a slightly disheveled but desirable appearance. She was the primitive woman, the sun goddess, calling out to her mate. Drew was dancing just for Casey. She was able to perform this wanton dance because she did it for only one reason—for love. For the love of the one man who could make her whole. That was why she seduced him with the movements of her body and the sensual gleam in her eyes. All because of love.

Casey stared at Drew, swallowing just to make sure his throat muscles still worked. He could feel his chest swelling and cutting off his air. Even if someone had yelled "fire!" he wouldn't have been able to move. He had never forgotten how easily Drew could stir him, the past few weeks had been more than enough proof of that, but those previous times had been nothing more than a kindergarten exercise compared to this! The silk of her dress clung to her breasts, outlining the taut nipples, a reminder of how his touch could send them springing to life. His breathing was constricted, and lights danced before his eyes. He felt as if he were going to pass out right there! And he certainly wouldn't be able to blame it on the rum punch, since he hadn't drunk as much as the others. Damn it, the woman was his boss! How could he feel like that about someone who was his superior? It was easy—because she was also the woman he loved. He was ready to fall into the black abyss of insanity, thanks to her.

Just then the music stopped abruptly. Drew bent down on one knee, her eyes lowered in a submission totally foreign to her personality and the smile on her lips.

The thick silence that surrounded the group was suddenly broken by thunderous applause. Only two people didn't clap: Chantal, who had watched the performance with feminine jealousy, and Casey, who was still in a daze.

"Where did you learn to dance so well?" Polly asked Drew, who dropped into her seat, exhausted.

"I had a college classmate who grew up in Honolulu." Drew reached for her glass of rum punch and drank a little too thirstily. "A lot of our study groups ended up as dancing lessons." Since she had turned to speak to Polly, she didn't see Casey's sharp glance in her direction.

"I'm surprised you did so well in your studies, then," he growled under his breath.

She turned back to flash him a dazzling smile. "Oh, yes, I do a great many things very well," she said throatily.

"I thought it was fascinating that you chose to dance in front of Casey," Polly whispered slyly.

"That's because I didn't think any of the wives here would appreciate it if I danced in front of their husbands," Drew replied serenely. She continued smiling as she accepted compliments from the other members of the party.

Luckily it wouldn't be much longer before they were due to return to the hotel. Again Casey kept well away from Drew in the van. All he wanted was to get to his room and take a long, cold shower!

Just after they returned to the hotel several members of the group proposed a nightcap in the lounge. Drew refused as she watched Casey wish everyone a good night and walk with an unhurried stride toward his suite.

"If I had enough courage I'd just march right up to his room and attack him," she muttered to herself. Not caring to retire to her own rooms just yet, she walked outside toward the small bridge and duck pond. She stood in the middle of the bridge and looked down at the ducks sitting placidly in the water. She had no idea how long she remained there.

"I don't understand it," she complained finally to the ducks, as if they could understand her every word. "I nearly threw my back out doing a dance that raised every man's blood pressure but his. All he could do was sit there like some stone statue!"

"This stone statue was experiencing some pretty stirring sensations."

Drew whirled around at the familiar dry tone. "I thought you had gone to your room." She eyed his wet swim briefs curiously.

Casey shrugged. "I felt like swimming." He stood there drinking in the moonlit figure before him. "That dress reminds me of one you wore about eight years ago."

"I thought the same thing when I first saw it," she said softly, stepping away from the railing and closer to him.

"Until tonight I never thought of foreplay being incorporated in a dance." His harsh voice seemed to be directed more at himself than at her. "You knew exactly what you were doing, didn't you?" He stood barefoot on the grass, the droplets of water on his chest gleaming silver in the moonlight. He had pushed back his wet hair from his forehead with an impatient hand, and his moustache had tiny drops clinging to it. He was all male, primitive and virile, with a masculine sensuality exuding from every pore.

"Yes." Her eyes reflected the same golden glitter dancing in his. There was no point in denying it when he could read her every thought.

Every muscle in Casey's body was tensed with repressed emotion. His hands were clenched at his sides, and he didn't move from his spot, as if he were afraid of entering her sphere of influence and losing his identity. God help him, he wanted her so much!

"Why?" The raspy demand was wrung from his throat.

Drew shrugged, not feeling half as nonchalant as she appeared. "Perhaps I just wanted to go back eight years. We did so much together then, remember? We went sightseeing, we swam and we made love. Well, I went sightseeing this morning, swam this afternoon and now . . ." She met his steady gaze squarely, her meaning very clear.

He expelled a ragged breath. Her words had released him from his self-imposed immobility. His low growl was unintelligible as he closed the narrow space between them.

Casey hauled Drew against his throbbing body as if he never meant to let her go. "You damn little vixen," he muttered thickly, his fingers tunneling up through the sides of her head until the knot loosened and her hair fell down around her bare shoulders. "All I wanted to do these past five years was exorcise you from my mind, but you had to come back, didn't you? You had to return and send me back to hell." His mouth tasted of salt as he devoured her lips with unrestrained hunger.

Drew's tongue darted between his lips to seek out his tongue. She slipped her arms around his still damp waist and pressed herself closer against him. Her hands were splayed out over his back, and she could feel his muscles ripple under her warming caress.

"Oh, Casey," she murmured, mouthing moist kisses along the angular line of his jaw. "You were right. I can't deny what was between us. I don't want to." She gasped when his leg insinuated itself between hers and gently rubbed against her.

"Not here." He breathed deeply to control the raging fire he felt inside. Keeping an arm wrapped tightly around her, he guided her toward the walkway that led to their rooms.

Casey led Drew down the hallway past her door and to his own. He withdrew his room key from a small snapped pocket inside his swim briefs and unlocked the door.

His suite was furnished like hers, but with bright orange, gold and brown in the color scheme.

"How about a brandy?" he asked politely, heading for the bar. Without waiting for a reply he splashed the amber-colored fluid into two glasses and handed one to her.

Drew studied Casey over the rim of her glass as she sipped. She could tell that he was barely in control of himself. It would take very little for her to push him over the edge. She moved toward a chair and sat down, crossing her legs so that the folds of her dress fell away to reveal her legs.

"What are you wearing under that dress?" Casey asked hoarsely, watching her with narrowed eyes as he swallowed the rest of his brandy in one hasty gulp.

She smiled, idly circling the rim of her glass with her fingertips. "That's for me to know," she taunted softly, leaving the rest of the expression unsaid.

The muscles in his throat were working overtime. As if he had finally made up his mind, he set his glass down with a loud clink, strode across the room and pulled her out of her chair.

"Are you saying what I think you are, Drew? That this time you'll allow me to make love to you?" He nuzzled his lips against the sensitive skin just behind her ear. "Because there's no way I'll be able to stop if I begin now."

"Yes," she whispered, tightening her arms around him. "Oh, yes." She buried her face in the crisp curling hair on his chest. She inhaled the musky male scent that mingled with the salty tang from his swim.

Cool fingers grasped her face and tilted it up. His eyes were hot as they swept over her flushed features and parted lips. He lowered his head and dampened her lips with his tongue.

"I like the taste of brandy much more when it's on you," he murmured, then inhaled sharply as his hands wandered from her shoulders to her buttocks. "I was right; you're hardly wearing anything," he accused her. "I like the taste of everything much better when I share it with you."

Drew's eyes twinkled mischievously as she looked up at him. She slid her arms around his neck and massaged the tight cords there. "Once you made a request that we share a meal that way," she teased gently.

Casey grimaced at the memory. "Yes, and it was the longest, most agonizing dinner of my life," he groaned.

She moved against him suggestively. "I never got dessert that night," she murmured, playfully sinking her teeth into his shoulder.

"Sure you did." He grinned wickedly. "It just wasn't one that was listed on the menu, that's all."

Drew delighted in evidence of his arousal. "You're wearing too many clothes," she breathed, sliding her hands under the waistband of his briefs and running them over his skin until the damp material fell to the floor.

"So much for a cold swim," Casey chuckled wryly. He stepped back and gazed down at her dress. With one hand he cupped her breast, rotating his thumb and forefinger around the nipple. "Is there an easy way to unfasten this, or will I have to rip it off?"

"It's very easy." She urged his hands to the gold clip. A moment later a pool of colorful silk dropped to the carpet. She stepped out of her shoes and into his arms.

"Oh, Drew!" Casey rasped, swinging her up into his arms.

"Am I setting up a chain reaction?" she whispered seductively, slithering her tongue down to the hollow of his throat, where his pulse beat erratically.

"Chain reaction?" He laughed hoarsely. He walked into the bedroom, swept back the bedcovers and dumped her onto the bed none too gently. He followed her down swiftly. "Honey, you're setting off a regular series of explosions." His thumbs stroked a soothing pattern along her jawline to her lips. When they parted, he rubbed the smooth surface of her teeth and probed beyond, then covered her mouth with his, his tongue thrusting into the dark recesses.

Drew took open enjoyment in running her hands over Casey's body, reacquainting herself with each line and curve. She relearned the broad shoulders and the chest that tapered to a trim waist and lean hips. She laughed softly and arched against him as one hair-roughened leg slid between her silky thighs.

Casey's head dipped down, and his mouth closed around one swollen breast. "I used to dream of the way your skin smells and tastes," he said huskily, curling his tongue around her nipple. His fingertips feathered over the satiny surface of her abdomen.

"You want me as badly as I want you, don't you?" he murmured, raising his head to look down into her passion-clouded eyes.

"Did I ever have to tell you before?" Drew teased gently, gripping his hips tightly and urging him toward her.

Casey didn't reply. He dropped a light kiss on the tip of each breast, traced the line of each rib with his tongue, dipped into the sensitive center of her navel and farther. Drew cried out when his teeth nipped the tanned skin of her inner thigh. Her fingers raked through his hair. The soft brush of his moustache was an exquisite torture against her ultra-sensitive skin.

"No!" she whimpered, even as her body writhed under his intimate searching. "Casey!" she moaned, tugging at his shoulders. "Oh, please."

"Yes," he breathed, moving up and over her. He entered her with the assurance of a man familiar with the woman who was his other half.

The duel of the senses was only beginning. Drew's body screamed for a quick release. Even as she tried to control the pace, Casey deliberately kept it slow and steady. He laughed low in his throat when she moaned in frustration at his easy rhythm.

"Easy, love," he whispered, framing her face with his hands. "We have all night. I only have so much control where you're concerned. I don't want us to go too fast. We've been apart too long. This has to be very special for us."

She uttered a feminine growl. She sank her teeth into his shoulder, and raked her nails across his back. She recalled every caress that had driven Casey wild. She whispered love words as she touched him and it was more than enough to send Casey over the edge, with Drew tumbling right along with him.

He braced himself on his forearms and looked down at her with bemusement. "It's still there." He brushed his lips across her forehead. It was another few moments before he could catch his breath.

"What's still there?" she asked drowsily.

Casey rolled over onto his back and pulled Drew with him. He shaped her against his side and kept the flat of his hand against her naked hip. "Our magic," he commented matter-of-factly. His other hand brushed damp strands of hair away from her forehead. "That old zip. You always knew how to drive me insane."

"You weren't so bad at driving me crazy yourself."

"Stay with me tonight," he pleaded huskily, tracing the lines of her throat with his tongue. His arms tightened, as if he were afraid that she'd leap out of bed and leave him.

"On one condition," Drew said, nuzzling the hollow of his shoulder.

"What's that?" He tensed, wary of her reply.

"That you," she punctuated each word with a kiss leading up to his mouth, "don't fall asleep until at least dawn. We have a lot of lost time to make up for!"

Casey chuckled and flipped Drew onto her back.

"Insatiable wench." He settled over her like a warm blanket. "That's one promise I think I can keep."

And he did. For hours they lay in each other's arms, murmuring drowsily and making sleepy, satisfying love. Sometimes their loving had an urgent hunger, as if it would be their last time. And each joining turned out to be more satisfying than the one before. It was as if they couldn't get enough of each other.

Casey worshiped Drew's body, encouraged her sensuality and welcomed her participation in their lovemaking. As she eventually fell into a deep sleep she was barely aware of Casey drawing the sheet over them and wrapping his arms tightly around her. It was as if they had never been parted.

Drew woke up mid-morning. It took her a few moments to orient herself. She turned her head and smiled at the still-sleeping Casey. A light kiss on his chin failed to rouse him. He merely shifted his body and mumbled incoherently. She carefully extricated herself from his embrace and slipped out of the bed.

Luckily this was a free day for everyone, so no one would have missed them at breakfast. Her stomach grumbled, a reminder of the late hour and her lack of food. While she wanted nothing more than to wake Casey up in her own special way, she had something else to do.

Drew quietly dressed, dropped a light kiss on his forehead and slipped out of the room. What she had in mind was to take a quick shower and change clothes, then arrange for room service to deliver a romantic breakfast for two to Casey's room. After that, well, anything could happen!

Drew hummed happily to herself as she let herself into her suite. She decided to call room service first, then take her shower. What greeted her when she entered the room was the red light blinking on the telephone, signifying that a message was waiting for her at the switchboard. She picked up the receiver and dialed the message operator.

"This is Drew Sinclair. I believe you have a message for me." Her smile vanished a moment later. "Would you please connect me with the front desk?" She had to force the words past her lips.

An hour later Drew was packed and at the front desk, checking out. Her bags had already been taken to a waiting taxi. She had just started toward the car when a hoarse voice stopped her in her tracks.

"Drew!"

She turned slowly to find a disheveled Casey walking swiftly toward her. He had thrust his unbuttoned shirt into a pair of jeans, and he was barefoot. The fierce expression on his face was enough to scare her.

"What is this?" he demanded in a low voice. "Is this the only way you can handle things? Sneak out of your lover's bed before he wakes up? Can't you take waking up in a man's arms anymore? Or was I just a one-night stand? A roll in the hay for old time's sake?" He bit out each word with dark rage.

Drew's face was paper white under Casey's anger.

Tell him! Tell him! her mind screamed, but her lips refused to form the necessary words. She didn't need his anger right now; she needed his care and concern. Without them, she could only mutter in a toneless voice, "Please tell the others that I was called away on an emergency."

"Sure, just like at Marcus's house." He snorted his disbelief. In his anger he didn't see the pain in her eyes. "I had hoped last night meant as much to you as it did to me. I guess I was wrong."

"It meant a lot!" she retorted in a low voice,

fumbling inside her purse for her sunglasses. "You not only took my body, you took my soul."

"Only in exchange for my own," he returned quietly.

Drew took a deep breath and clenched her trembling hands. "If there are any problems, just call Viv." She blinked rapidly to hold back the tears which threatened to fall. She couldn't think. Her brain refused to function properly. "Good-bye, Casey," she whispered, turning away. The heels of her shoes clicked on the tile floor as she hurried toward the waiting taxi.

Now Casey's face reflected confusion instead of the anger he had exhibited before. When he had first woken up he had thought that Drew was in the bathroom until the silence told him differently. He had then called her room, but had received no answer. When he tried the switchboard he had discovered that she had checked out, a revelation that left him with a raw pain in the pit of his stomach. She was leaving him again! Anger had quickly replaced the hurt. He had hastily pulled on some clothes and made his way to the lobby, hoping to catch her before she left. Then, when he had found her, all he had been able to do was take his temper out on her. Now he remembered the pale features, the unshed tears and trembling chin. Something was very wrong.

"Drew!" he shouted, and began to run after the taxi, but it had already driven off. He turned away and returned to his room, where he stared down at the tumbled bed.

"Damn!" He rammed his fist against the wall. At least the pain would alleviate the numbness he was feeling.

He slumped down on the edge of the bed and buried his head in his hands. The scent of Drew's perfume clung to the sheets and reminded him of their night together. If he closed his eyes he could recall her impassioned cries and the way her body had moved against his. He moaned softly. There was only one way to discover the entire story. He reached for the bedside phone and dialed the operator.

"Operator, I'd like to place a long-distance call."

Chapter Ten

$\mathcal{D}$rew had always suffered from an agonizing fear of hospitals. The small child in her still remembered her mother being taken to one and never returning. And now Marcus lay in intensive care surrounded by machines that looked as if they belonged in a science fiction movie.

It had been a long day. Luck was on her side as she made connections to Los Angeles, then rented a car to drive to Bakersfield. After that, though, it seemed as if the nightmare had only begun. The memory of Casey's angry features still haunted her, but right now Marcus was more important.

"Why didn't he say anything about this to me?" she asked the doctor as he explained that Marcus had suffered a massive stroke. He had also mentioned that her stepfather had been suffering from poor health for the past two years. "He didn't even look sick!"

"It happens that way sometimes," the doctor replied, placing a fatherly arm around her shoulders. "All we can do now is make him as comfortable as possible and pray."

It was night by then. Drew had lost track of how many hours she had spent sitting by Marcus's bedside, silently begging him to wake up. She wanted him to smile at her and let her know that everything would be all right. He looked so pale and so shrunken! He didn't look like the man who had carried her burdens for so many years.

She had just begun to drift off into an exhausted sleep when the monitors began buzzing. In seconds the cubicle was filled with doctors and nurses.

"No, please, let me stay!" Drew pleaded as a nurse gently but firmly ushered her out of the cubicle. "*Please!*" She spun around when a pair of hands settled on her shoulders. "Casey!" she breathed, taking in his taut features with weary eyes.

He instantly took in the situation and steered Drew toward the waiting area.

"I have to stay with him," she protested tearfully, pulling back. "Pops has to know I'm here with him." she insisted.

"He knows you're here, love," Casey said soothingly, sitting on the couch and pulling her down beside him. He cradled her against him and murmured reassuring words in her ear. She buried her face against his shoulder. "Why didn't you tell me?" he asked her softly.

"I was afraid to say it out loud." Her words were muffled against his shirt. "I was afraid that if I told you, it would be true. All the time while I was on the plane and in the car driving up here, I was hoping that it was only a false alarm."

He exhaled deeply. "If only you had told me."

"How did you find out?"

"I called Viv." His breath was warm against her forehead. "I took the first flight I could get to L.A."

Going for too long without sufficient sleep was beginning to tell on Drew. "You didn't need to come," she mumbled, snuggling up against him. "But I'm glad you did."

Casey gripped her tighter while his hand rubbed her nape soothingly.

"Drew?"

She jumped to her feet at the sound of the doctor's quiet voice.

She only had to look at his face to read the answer to her silent question. "No." She shook her head in rapid denial. She backed away. *"No!"* Her voice rose to a scream. *"He can't be!"* The doctor looked as if he were walking through a tunnel toward her. Casey's alarmed voice barely reached her ears before her world went black.

A strong smell assaulted her nostrils, and she tossed her head to evade it.

"Come on, Drew," Casey urged quietly. "Open your eyes."

She obeyed his soft command, but it only served to bring back the pain. Her face contorted in agony.

"I'll take her home," Casey told the doctor.

"I'm going to prescribe a sedative for her," the older man replied. "I think it would be best for her to take one tonight."

Drew was in a state of numbed shock as Casey guided her outside to his rental car.

"I–I have a car here somewhere," she protested in a halting voice, as if it were too hard to think just then.

"I'll call the agency. They can take care of it." He gently pushed her inside the car. "Right now, you're going home to bed."

Casey drove to what had been her father's house and dug into Drew's purse for the key.

"Have you eaten?" She shook her head. "Go change your clothes and I'll see what I can rustle up."

Drew smiled faintly. "My suitcase is still in the car. I don't have any clothes here."

"Not to worry," he said, then snapped his fingers. He disappeared outside and returned with his suitcase. He set it on a chair, opened it and rummaged through the contents. "Not *haute couture,* but they'll serve their purpose." He tossed her a shirt and a robe. "Go take a long hot shower, then come back here. I'll have something ready to eat by then."

She nodded and walked out of the room.

Drew took Casey's advice and stood under the shower until her skin glowed and her fingers began to wrinkle. She gave her hair a thorough brushing and slipped on the pale blue shirt Casey had loaned her, then put on his bronze velour robe over that. Even though the robe probably only reached to mid-thigh on him, on her it stopped just below her knees.

When she returned to the living room Casey had trays set up and plates of chili waiting.

"Hope your stomach can stand the strain," he said apologetically. "The cupboards were pretty bare."

Drew's attention was caught by a photograph on the mantel. She walked over and picked it up, then turned back to Casey. "Did I ever tell you about the time Pops drove my Girl Scout troop to Yosemite?" Her lips curved in a brief smile. "Ten giggling and chattering twelve-year-old girls. We must have driven him crazy, but he volunteered to take us again the next year. He never let me suffer for not having a mother, and he made up for the lack of one as much as he could." Then, under Casey's gentle urging, she sat down and ate a small portion of her dinner.

Afterward he picked up the dishes and took them into the kitchen. When he returned to the living room he found Drew still curled up in her chair, her eyelids drooping with weariness. He picked her up and carried her into her bedroom. He swept back the covers and carefully deposited her on the mattress.

"Go to sleep, love," he murmured, kissing her softly on the lips. "We'll sort everything out in the morning."

Drew's reply was inarticulate as exhaustion overtook her.

Drew was awake. Or was she? It was pitch black, and she was suffocating. There was no air! She couldn't breathe! She gathered all her strength to scream. Someone had to save her!

"Drew! Drew!" She felt as if her body were being shaken to pieces. "It's only a bad dream."

Her eyes snapped open, staring blindly until they focused on Casey's troubled features.

"Oh, Casey," she moaned, throwing her arms around him. "It was awful! I thought I was being buried alive!"

"It's all right now, hon," he crooned, rocking her back and forth in his arms. "It was just a bad dream. Although you did frighten me out of ten years growth when you kept screaming my name. I didn't know what was wrong."

"I called out to you?" She couldn't remember exactly what she had screamed.

"You kept yelling my name over and over again." He used his fingers to wipe her tears away. "Feel better now?"

"Don't leave me," Drew whispered, tightening her arms around his neck.

Casey didn't hesitate. He got up and walked around to the other side of the bed and pulled the covers aside. Once in bed, he pulled Drew against him. She snuggled back in his arms, confident that her nightmare wouldn't return. Casey lay awake for a long time, knowing his nightmare would be of an entirely different nature with a trusting Drew curled up next to him.

When Drew awoke late the following morning she realized that she was alone in bed. She pushed her tangled hair away from her face and slowly turned over on her side. It would be so easy for her to remain huddled under the covers, but her brain kept telling her that she had to get up and make the necessary telephone calls. There were arrangements to be made. She closed her eyes tightly. Where would she start?

"Decided to wake up finally, did you?"

She turned her head at the sound of Casey's gentle, teasing voice. His shirt hung open outside his jeans, and his feet were bare. Casey sat on the edge of the bed and handed her a cup of hot coffee. His matter-of-fact attitude gave no outward indication that they had ever been lovers.

Drew propped herself up on one elbow and accepted the cup for an experimental sip. Just the way she liked it, but then, Casey knew everything about her tastes.

"I hope you don't mind." He spoke hesitantly, as if he weren't sure she would appreciate what he was going to say. "I looked through Marcus's address book and found his minister's telephone number. I called him an hour ago, and I also made arrangements with a mortuary. If it's all right with you, the funeral will be held Monday afternoon at two."

Drew felt some of the heavy burdens being lifted from her shoulders. She reached over and set her coffee cup on the bedside table. Then she sat up and curved her arms around his neck.

"Oh, Casey," she breathed against his throat. "I woke up feeling so scared. I just didn't know what to do."

"Hey, now," he soothed, keeping his arms wrapped

tightly around her. "I'm here, love. You're not alone." He rubbed his chin over the top of her head. "I'll help in any way I can. You know that."

"Then stay with me until everything is taken care of," Drew begged, tipping her head back so she could gaze up at him. "Don't let me go through this alone."

Casey's smile sent a reassuring warmth through her veins. He absently tucked a stray strand of hair behind her ear. "Did you honestly think I'd throw you to the wolves?" he chided gently. "Although I can't imagine why you should have any apprehensions. You forget that I've seen you on the warpath in the boardroom. Honey, there you're a barracuda in a tank full of guppies!"

Drew couldn't help but grin at his bloodthirsty description of her, and Casey was glad to see that he could get a smile from her. She had looked so vulnerable these past hours.

"Barracudas are nasty fish." She wrinkled her nose in distaste. "I guess I should be happy that you didn't compare me to a piranha!"

Casey's smile was that of an indulgent parent, but it didn't quite reach his eyes. He was worried about Drew. Oh, she was smiling and talking in an entirely natural voice, but she was walking an emotional tightrope. Her gestures were rapid and jerky, her eyes a little too bright, and the muscles in her face were taut. The next few days were going to be a strain on her, and he would make sure to be there when she needed him.

When the day of the funeral arrived Drew's emotions were anesthetized. It was Casey who had taken care of all the details. He had met with the minister and with Marcus's attorney, and handled all the funeral arrangements. Casey had also made sure that Drew ate her meals and got her rest. It was he who had called Marty and explained the circumstances. When the older man had pointed out that it would appear very odd to their fellow workers that Casey was up there with Drew, Casey had merely growled that he didn't give a damn what other people thought. He was staying there for Drew's sake, because she had asked him to stay. He had never broken a promise to her yet, and he didn't intend to now.

The funeral was well attended, attesting to Marcus's popularity in the community. Even Mrs. Myers had shown up, a lacy handkerchief pressed to her eyes.

Drew wore a dark gray silk dress and had twisted her hair in a sleek chignon at her nape. With her eyes shadowed from sleepless nights, she looked like someone from another world.

Casey had gone back to sleeping on the couch after that first night. He had only stayed with her to keep away the bad dreams. He had not been asked to share her bed again.

He remained at her side during the funeral and rode with her in the car back to what was now her home. Marcus had left all his worldly belongings to his stepdaughter, Drusilla, except for one item. A cabin he had owned in Arizona was deeded to Carstairs McCord with the hope that he would continue using it with the same joy he had shown during the trips he had taken there with Marcus. Drew felt no jealousy that they had enjoyed each other's company so much; she was glad that the two men she loved so deeply had been such good friends.

"I'm so glad that your young man could be here with you during such a time of sadness." Mrs. Myers laid a comforting hand on Drew's shoulder and cast a sly glance toward Casey, who had been talking with one of Marcus's fishing buddies. "I'm sure he's been a great comfort to you." There was no malice in her voice. "I'll truly miss that man." She dabbed her eyes with her handkerchief and moved off.

It wasn't long before Drew felt as if she would scream if she heard one more condolence. It wasn't that she didn't appreciate all these people who had loved Marcus, it was that the reality of his death was being hammered into her with their each and every word. She drank gallons of coffee, smiled when necessary and spoke only when spoken to. She wasn't able to do any more. Casey looked at her from across the room, saw the desperation in her eyes and quietly but efficiently herded the people out.

Drew sank down onto the couch and pulled off her gray suede pumps. Only then did she realize that her feet hurt.

"Here." Casey sat on the edge of the coffee table and picked up her stockinged feet, placing them in his lap. He expertly massaged her soles and toes, bringing a groan of relief to her lips. She sighed wearily.

"I had forgotten how good you are at that," she murmured, looking at him through half closed eyes. His dark gray suit lent him a new dignity that she couldn't remember ever seeing before. He had shed the suit coat, and the vest hung open. His tie was loosened, along with the collar button on his shirt. For the first time she realized how tired he looked. Poor Casey, he had been thinking so much of her over the past few days that he hadn't been able to give much time to himself. She shouldn't have been so selfish, shouldn't have demanded so much of him.

"Why don't we go out to eat?" he suggested quietly. "You need to get out."

Drew shook her head. "That wouldn't be fair to you. These past few days have been long, especially for you."

Casey smiled gently. "I wouldn't have suggested it if I didn't want to do it, love. Come on, it will do you good to get out."

She looked down at her dress. "I'd like to change

first. And I don't want to go anywhere fancy. Just a hamburger would be fine with me."

"All right." He dropped her feet to the carpet, stood and pulled her up. "You go change, and I'll do the same."

Drew merely picked at her food, unable to eat more than a few bites.

"Try to eat a little more," Casey urged gently.

She took two more bites of her club sandwich and looked up with pleading eyes. "Could we go please?" she whispered.

He nodded and grabbed the check.

A light rain fell over them as they stepped outside. Drew tilted her face back to allow the mist to cover her skin.

"It rained the night you took me to that rock concert, remember?" she mused as he assisted her into the car.

Casey nodded. A moment later he slid behind the steering wheel and switched on the engine.

"My eardrums weren't the same for weeks afterward." His mouth curved in a wry smile.

"I didn't realize until later how much you hated rock music." Drew laid her head back against the head rest.

"I figured there's always a first time."

She turned her head to gaze at his profile which was barely visible in the darkened car. "There were a lot of firsts that night." Her murmured comment easily reached his ears.

A muscle twitched in Casey's cheek, and his hands gripped the steering wheel so tightly that his knuckles were white.

"Casey?"

"Hm?" He didn't appear too pleased with the turn the conversation was taking.

"Did you regret it?" Drew asked in a small voice. She continued watching him as the car stopped in the driveway. "Did you regret making love to me that night?"

Casey reached out to find the door handle, but his hand failed to find its target. "No." His hoarse reply betrayed his emotions. He helped Drew out of the car, but he didn't touch her.

They had left a lamp on in the living room. Drew shrugged off her jacket and dropped it onto a nearby chair. Her numbness was beginning to fade.

Casey pulled off his own jacket and dropped it on top of Drew's. He walked over to her.

"You should go to bed," he advised, brushing his fingertips over the faint violet shadows under her eyes.

"Not alone," she said almost silently.

Casey took a deep breath and closed his eyes tightly. His body was a mass of tension. "Drew, you're over-wrought, and right now you're not sure what you want. This isn't the time," he said slowly, regretfully.

She raised her hand and pressed her palm against the soft wool of his sweater. She could have sworn that she felt the thudding of his heartbeat under her touch.

"I need you, Casey." Her voice trembled. "I need you to show me that I'm still alive." Her arms slid around his waist. She rested her cheek against his chest, inhaling the warm musky scent of his skin.

Casey's arms hung at his side for a few moments, then he slowly lifted them and wrapped them around her. "You have me, Drew, my love," he whispered, placing his cheek against the top of her head. "You have me, body and soul."

They weren't aware of how long they stood there holding on to each other. It was as if the feel of each other's bodies kept them in tune with reality. Casey finally released his hold and stepped back to unfasten Drew's apricot silk blouse and push the edges aside.

"I always liked this color on you," he said, fanning his fingers over the soft lines of her throat. "You used to have a nightgown this shade, and your skin had an added glow when you wore it."

Drew pushed Casey's sweater upward and helped him pull it over his head. Her fingers investigated the dark gold cloud of his hair as he released the catch of her bra and ran his palms over her aching breasts to find the taut nipples. He groaned, bending his head to catch a swollen bud with his teeth. The suckling motion brought a pleasure-filled cry to Drew's lips. Her fingers dug into his hair, and she thrust her breast farther into his hot moist mouth. She threw her head back, her amber eyes closed and her dark lashes feathering over her cheeks. She was the portrait of a woman being truly pleasured.

Casey reached down to unfasten Drew's jeans, then pushed them down to her ankles. They were quickly followed by her lacy beige bikini panties. He trailed warm kisses down her middle, darting his tongue into her navel and scattering love nips along the sensitized skin of her inner thighs.

"Casey!" Drew moaned, digging her fingers into his shoulders.

He quickly shed his jeans and pulled her down to the carpet. She lay sprawled half across him. He framed her face with his hands and brought it slowly toward him.

"Do you want me, Drew?" he whispered in a ragged voice.

"I want you," she replied in a voice that was thick and unsteady. She slowly rubbed her leg against his. The tautening of his muscles told her that he reciprocated those same earth-shattering feelings.

Casey's eyes shone with tawny lights as they roamed over her passion-flushed features. He brought her face down farther until their lips were touching.

"Show me," he invited in a rough whisper.

Drew's tongue snaked out and traced a line around

Casey's lips, then slid between the smooth surface of his teeth. She was the aggressor. She scattered kisses over his face, his shoulders and down to the male nipples that hardened under the rough caress of her tongue.

"Drew!" Casey groaned. He gripped the smooth skin of her buttocks and positioned her over him.

Drew gasped when Casey took control of their loving. With the rhythmic thrusting of his hips and his guiding hands at her waist, he sent her into a world she knew well. She buried her face against the damp skin of his neck, feeling his erratic pulse against her lips. She was unaware of her surroundings; they didn't matter. All that existed for her was the man whose body had overtaken hers. She lifted her head slightly, and their mouths melded. Without him, she was a nonentity. Without her, he was without life.

With Casey's hoarse words of encouragement, Drew fell over the edge. When he was assured that she had reached her goal he fell into that same dark void. She collapsed against him, too sated to move and only vaguely aware of his hands soothing the line of her spine. It was in that position that she fell into a deep sleep.

When Drew next awoke she found herself in bed, with Casey's body curved warmly against her back. Sensing that she was awake, he slowly turned her onto her back.

This time their coming together was leisurely, as if they had all the time in the world. Casey couldn't have been more gentle with Drew if she had been a virgin. Still, the experience was no less shattering to her senses. She clung to him as if he were the only solid object in a sea of sensuality. Every silken thrust of his body, each delicate probe of his tongue and brush of his lips on her satiny skin, was meant to drive her mindless. She cried out for him to end the erotic torture, but he was deaf to her pleas. He continued to drive her further into a pleasure filled agony that only he could free her from. Her fingernails raked along his back and dug into his buttocks, but he was past the point of feeling anything but a special woman's warmth surrounding him. Their cries mingled in the night.

Drew trembled so badly that at first Casey thought she was cold and wrapped his arms around her to keep her close against his damp body.

"Why wasn't it ever like that for us before?" she whispered, smoothing her palm over the flat plane of his stomach.

"Because this wasn't meant to happen until now." He chuckled, capturing her hand. "Sorry, love, if you expect an encore you're going to have to wait. You wore me out!"

Drew's soft laugh mingled with his. Whatever she had been going to say was lost as she drifted into a deep sleep. Casey remained awake for a long time, afraid that sleep would make him relinquish his hold on her.

His time with Fantasy Toys would soon be over. Casey knew that Drew would be upset that he still intended to leave, but how could he explain that he had to go before she destroyed his sanity along with his soul?

It wasn't surprising that Drew slept late the next morning. She slept so deeply that she didn't stir when Casey slipped out of the bed and carefully tucked the covers around her bare shoulders.

When she finally did awake it was with a smile on her lips. She lay still, wondering where Casey was until she heard sounds coming from the kitchen. She stretched her arms over her head and flexed her toes. She couldn't remember ever feeling more relaxed.

She rose from the bed and walked over to the closet

to get her robe. Once it was belted securely around her waist she headed for the bathroom and a hot shower.

Casey lifted his head when he heard the shower running. With a weary sigh he rose from the chair to make a fresh pot of coffee. He had already drunk one pot in the past hour.

"Um, good morning," Drew sang out, dancing into the kitchen and sliding her arms around his waist. Her kiss landed just short of his ear. "Oh, good, breakfast. I'm starved." She laughed throatily, sliding her fingers between the buttons of his shirt to lightly scratch his hair roughened skin.

"Why don't you sit down?" he suggested, mentally withdrawing from her. He hadn't even teased her about suddenly having an appetite for the one meal she usually preferred to miss.

Oblivious to Casey's tension, Drew sat down at the table. She gratefully accepted the steaming cup of coffee he handed her.

"I did some thinking while I was taking my shower," she began, sipping the hot brew.

"Your great ideas always did come while your head was under water," he acknowledged wryly.

"This one is priceless." She looked properly smug.

"I think I'd like some food in my stomach first." Casey placed a plate filled with sausage links and eggs in front of Drew and set his own plate down across from her.

Despite her less than subtle hints, Casey refused to quiz Drew about her new brainstorm.

"I'm so proud of my idea that I feel I deserve a medal." She gave a broad smile as she watched Casey finish his last slice of toast.

"Then tell me about your fantastic idea."

Drew took a deep breath. "I'm going to call Marty and recommend that you be installed immediately as the new Executive Director. Oh, he may want me to stay on another month or two, but I'd make sure that you had all the authority. After all, you certainly know more about the company than I do. Wouldn't that be great?" She waited expectantly for his praise.

Casey stared down at his cup of coffee. "I resigned, remember?" he reminded her quietly.

"Oh, that." She blithely waved his mild protest aside.

"And you?" His reaction wasn't at all what she had expected. "What happens to you, Drew, when all this is accomplished?"

"Me?" She was surprised by his question. "Marty will come up with another project for me. I'll sweet talk him into something in this region." Her smile grew wider, and her eyes sparkled with excitement.

Casey's hands tightened around his coffee cup. "A promotion in return for my sexual favors?" he commented sardonically. "I don't think so, Drew. My resignation still stands. It will be effective next Monday."

Drew couldn't have been more shocked than if he had said, "Last night was fun, honey, but I've got a wife and six kids back home." "But I thought—" she faltered.

"That's the trouble," he cut in forcefully, leaning forward across the table. "You spin all these sugar-coated dreams about my returning to Fantasy Toys without consulting me about my own wishes. You want me to take a position you feel I'm due—"

"Marty feels you're due it," she argued.

"With *your* recommendation," Casey shot back. "Drew, what exactly are you proposing for us? That we have an affair? You'll fly into San Diego when you have some free time, or I'll visit you wherever you may be?" Lines of tension were etched in his face. He shook his head slowly. "That's just not me, love. I called Marty early this morning and suggested Sam Martinson as my replacement. Sam will be given an official offer later today. I also called Aunt Kate. She'll be up late this afternoon to help you settle things here."

Drew could only stare at Casey, unable to believe her ears. "You promised to stay with me," she whispered numbly.

He stood up so suddenly that the chair clattered to the floor. "Then I guess for the first time I'll be breaking a promise to you," he ground out, his hands clenched at his side. "You see, Drew, I had a pretty crazy idea, too. I had hoped that you'd finally come to realize that we had been given a second chance. That we're truly meant to be together. I guess I was wrong. Damn it, Drew, I have my pride! Why can't you understand that? I was brought up to believe that a man takes care of a woman, her material and her emotional needs. Not the other way around. You didn't try to understand that five years ago, and you aren't trying now."

"Meaning that you'd feel much better if I gave up my job. Just the way you implied when I got the transfer five years ago," she said bitterly, as if this were just a continuation of their argument of long ago.

His low laugh was harsh. "You're showing your stubborn streak just as strongly as you did five years ago."

"Stubborn streak! *You're* the one with a bloody stubborn streak a mile wide!" she shrieked at him.

Casey advanced on Drew and bent from the waist until they were at eye level. "You know I don't like you using that word." His low voice was dangerously soft.

She took a deep breath. "Bloody . . . bloody . . . *bloody!*" Her voice rose each time until she all but screamed the word.

Casey's eyes were lit with dark gold lights which Drew militantly returned. Without another word he turned away and stalked out of the kitchen. She could hear the sounds of a suitcase being zipped closed, then the front door slamming. The retreating roar of a car's engine was next.

Drew collapsed back onto the chair.

"Why does it always have to end this way for us?" she whispered miserably, burying her face in her hands.

The only difference was that the last time they had parted, she had been the one to walk out. Now the situation had been bitterly reversed.

Chapter Eleven

$\mathcal{D}$rew was angry. No, she was beyond angry.

From the time Casey had walked out of the house until Kate's arrival, Drew had had plenty of hours to think over Casey's words.

The tears had dried up, the trembling lower lip stiffened, the sniffing silenced and replaced by a stubborn set to her mouth. Carstairs Langdon McCord was in a heap of trouble.

"He really has a lot of nerve!" she gritted, roughly washing the breakfast dishes. It was a miracle that they remained in one piece.

By the time Kate appeared Drew had rained every curse imaginable on Casey's head, including a few never before known to man.

"You're talking from hurt pride, Drusilla," the older woman reprimanded her once the story had been told.

"What makes him think he can calmly walk out of here and out of my life again?" Drew demanded, tears in her eyes. This time they were tears of anger.

"If I recall correctly, *you* were the one who left the last time," Kate said in a quiet voice.

Her blunt statement was enough to puncture Drew's balloon of rage. The younger woman's amber eyes clouded over. She sank down onto the couch, her hands lying limply in her lap.

"I have to stay angry, Aunt Kate," she whispered brokenly. "If I don't, my sanity will go right out the window. I want him to stay, and not just for the company, either."

"Did you tell him that?"

Drew shook her head. "I didn't think he'd believe me."

Kate was amazed at how obtuse her two favorite people were. "Have you ever lied to him?"

"No."

Kate's exclamation was less than polite. "You seem to have been expending your excess energy in maligning my nephew's good character, but now that I'm here I intend to put that vigor to good use. Casey told me that there were some empty boxes in the garage. You begin sorting things out in this room, and we'll go on from there." With that she marched out of the room, leaving an open-mouthed Drew staring after her.

Kate was true to her word. She kept Drew busy every hour of every day. The younger woman collapsed into bed every night with a tired sigh. Drew had no time to think about Casey or how things would be when she returned to San Diego.

Thanks to daily telephone calls to Viv, Drew didn't have too much work to return to. Calls to Marty to keep him up to date on her situation only managed to upset her stomach.

"I'm sure glad to see you back," Viv said when Drew entered the office a week later. "It's been pretty hectic

around here with our new sales director in residence."
She eyed her boss curiously.

Gossip had been running rampant over Casey Mc-
Cord staying with Drew to help her with the arrangements for her stepfather's funeral. Why had he stayed
there, when they had always been at cross purposes in
the office? Was there really something to the rumors
floating around the building? Were they having a hot
and heavy affair? The sight of a dark-visaged Casey
stalking the corridors during the past week hadn't
encouraged anyone to even think about asking him
anything.

"Dare I ask what's on the agenda for today?" Drew
asked, seating herself at her desk.

"Casey McCord's going-away party will be held at
three this afternoon," Viv informed her.

Nothing in Drew's outer demeanor betrayed her
agitation. She had hoped to pretend that it wasn't his
last day. She had told herself that if she pretended hard
enough, perhaps she could make her wish come true.
Not so.

"Would you please see if I can meet with the
department heads sometime today?" she requested in
an even voice, not revealing the churning sensation in
her stomach.

"They'll be in the conference room at eleven." The
secretary flashed a smug smile.

Drew couldn't help but smile in return. "No wonder
you kept telling me you had everything under control,"
she teased, relaxing in her chair. "Talk about the power
behind the throne!"

"I do try." Viv laughed before turning around and
exiting. "It helps keep me out of mischief!"

Drew took a deep breath. She already knew what
was first on the agenda. Marty would be glad to know
that she had come in to work. He had been more than

generous in giving her time off to settle Marcus's affairs, but his goodwill would last only so long before he'd remind her where her responsibilities lay.

"Glad to see you could find time to go into the office." His gruff greeting was just what she needed.

"It's a shame you feel you have to pamper me, Marty," she commented wryly. "I'm a big girl now."

"I don't know why I take this guff from you," he growled. "You're only this brave when we talk on the phone."

Drew smiled. She cradled the receiver between her jaw and shoulder while settling down to hear Marty's famous lecture on how women today didn't have the sensibilities of their foremothers.

"I want you to know that I don't appreciate losing McCord," he grumbled instead. "I also hope you realize that this won't look good on your record."

She absently smoothed the skirt of her pale lilac silk dress. "I guess this means I won't get to go to London or Paris for my next assignment," she said lightly.

"You'll be lucky if you don't get Iceland or the middle of the Amazonian jungle."

Drew wrinkled her nose in distaste. Why didn't his threats bother her? She knew they could easily turn into fact. "I told you before that he's his own man, and he does what he wants to," she reminded him.

"Call me if he happens to change his mind before the end of the day." Without even a good-bye, Marty hung up.

Just before the staff meeting Drew freshened her lipstick and replaced a few hairpins in the sleek coil at her nape.

All the department heads were present when she entered the conference room.

"Glad to have you back." John Landers smiled at her.

"Drew, good to see you again." Sam walked up to her with an outstretched hand and a broad smile on his face.

"Congratulations, Sam." She returned his smile. "How's Polly?"

"Eager to see you again," he replied. "She's been going crazy trying to find a house and get our furniture shipped out here."

The hairs on Drew's nape prickled. Casey was standing behind her. She didn't need the fresh scent of his after-shave to warn her. She spun around.

"Hello, Casey." Her even voice betrayed nothing of her thundering pulse rate.

What she hadn't expected was to see strain on his masculine features and shadows around his tawny eyes.

"Perfect timing, Drew," he murmured for her ears only. "Did you purposely plan your return in time to bid me farewell?"

"I felt it was the least I could do." Her throaty voice danced along his nerve endings.

Casey's eyes narrowed, but any reply he might have made was prevented by the knowledge that they weren't alone.

Drew turned around and graced the men with a dazzling smile. "Gentlemen, since we're all present, shall we begin?"

It wasn't all that easy. Once seated, she found it difficult to keep her eyes from straying in the direction of Casey's seated figure. In turn, his steady stare did strange things to her equilibrium.

Drew's smile wasn't natural, and her husky voice came out a little strained. She spoke somewhat slower than usual, as if it were difficult to find the right words, but she managed to get through the next hour and a half without anyone knowing that her world was falling down around her ears.

When the meeting adjourned she summoned up every ounce of her courage and approached Casey, who was talking to several men.

"Casey?" she began tentatively, waiting for him to turn and acknowledge her presence. "I thought we could have lunch together. You know, sort of . . ." Her words trailed off under his unwavering regard.

"I'm sorry, Drew." It was hard to tell from his expression whether his apology was sincere. "Jenny already asked if she could take her old boss out."

"Oh." Her smile felt stiff. "Of course."

Casey frowned at the bleak expression in Drew's eyes. She had been so cool and self-assured during the meeting that he had figured she didn't give a damn that he was leaving. Could he have been wrong?

Drew was saved when Viv entered the room with a message for her. Murmuring something under her breath, she moved toward her secretary.

She returned to her office, angry at herself for approaching Casey. Why couldn't she just leave well enough alone? After today he would be gone from her life forever.

She wished she knew whether he would be remaining in San Diego. She'd have to find out from Kate. Discreet inquiries to reliable sources hadn't given her any information about Casey's future employment. It was as if he was going to disappear off the face of the earth.

Why couldn't she just remain angry at him? If she did, the hurt would go away. Wouldn't it?

Drew went out for lunch, but only toyed with her salad and returned to her office as soon as she could.

She had barely sat down when Viv entered the office.

"I thought you might be interested in this." The secretary held her hands behind her back as if she were hiding something.

"What?" Drew looked up.

Viv held out a fifteen-inch doll dressed in a ruffled pink gingham dress. Her blond hair, big blue eyes and rosebud mouth made her every little girl's dream.

"Viv, I hate to tell you this, but I gave up dolls when I was twelve," Drew commented in a dry tone.

"I don't think you would have been allowed to keep this one." Viv pulled a tiny ring at the back of the doll's neck.

Drew's eyes widened as the tinny voice used a few choice improper words. "What?" she croaked in shock.

"You really don't want me to pull it again, do you?" The secretary eyed her sardonically.

Drew shook her head. "Dare I hope this is a part of Dunway Toys' new line?" She named Fantasy Toys' chief competitor.

"Her name is Sassy and she's supposed to be part of our Christmas line," Viv explained. "She's supposed to say the usual, 'I love you,' 'Please feed me, Mommy,' etc."

"At least the name is appropriate." An icy smile flitted across Drew's lips. "Whose not so bright idea was the new recording, and have they been handed their final check yet?"

"The recording was the result of a long liquid lunch."

Drew shook her head. What could happen next? "Fine, I want the head of the inspector who passed this doll. I also want the person who made up the recording and anyone else involved. They are to be out of this building before the day is over."

The secretary wasn't surprised by Drew's cold anger. There was no mistaking the glint in her eyes. The people involved would have a hard time finding a job after this mishap.

"You will be attending Casey's farewell party, won't you?" Viv asked, wanting to change the subject.

Drew's hand stilled. "Naturally," she said, although she didn't sound very convincing.

"You don't have to act so excited, Drew." Viv's dry voice was at odds with the sly twinkle in her eye. She had seen the sparks fly between the couple and assumed that there was more there than met the eye.

"Believe me, I'm not," she replied truthfully. "I guess I better dictate that memo while this," she gestured toward the doll, "is fresh in my mind."

The afternoon passed all too quickly for Drew. Before she realized it, the hour was nearing three. Viv had already stuck her head in and announced that she was going downstairs to the cafeteria. "You coming soon?" she had inquired.

Drew had managed a faint smile and a nod. "In a few minutes."

The few minutes stretched to twenty before she finally left her desk to check her hair, freshen her makeup and add a spray of cologne. She studied her reflection in the mirror with a jaundiced eye.

"Bear up, Drusilla," she ordered herself in a stern voice. "Don't let him know how you really feel. Don't worry, you'll survive."

The cafeteria was full when Drew entered the room. She fastened a broad smile on her face and spoke to the various people she passed.

"You'll drink to my well being, won't you, Drew?" Casey pressed a plastic goblet into her hand as he spoke.

She accepted the glass and sipped the champagne slowly. "I see that no expense was spared for your send-off," she murmured, tipping her head back to look up at Casey's face. For a moment her eyes fastened on the blue and pale gray stripes in his tie, idly noting the pale lavender striping along the gray. Even today they were still doing it!

He noticed the direction of her gaze. "We always were a well-coordinated couple. In everything."

Heat stole through Drew's body at the erotic mental

images dancing through her brain. Casey naked, kissing her, caressing her, joining with her. She stifled a sharp gasp at the ache of desire that overwhelmed her.

"When do you begin your new position as . . . ?" Her delicate hesitation was deliberate. "What exactly is your title at your new location?"

Casey knew that innocent smile only too well. "Gentleman of leisure." With that he moved away to speak to someone else.

Drew fumed inwardly. Admittedly, her questioning hadn't been very subtle, and Casey knew her all too well to be taken in by her feigned innocence. Even the office grapevine was falling down on the job. There wasn't one concrete lead as to where Casey was going to be working. Oh, there was a great deal of speculation, but nothing solid. The names of several large toy companies had been bandied about, but it was still only idle gossip. Casey's destination had been kept a closely guarded secret.

Drew circulated, speaking to the many executives, secretaries and various office workers filling the large room. Yet even when she stood at the opposite side of the cafeteria, her senses were aware of Casey's every move.

"Casey!" John Landers shouted above the noise. "We need you on center stage."

Casey walked over to the stocky gray-haired man, who stood holding a large gaily wrapped box in both hands.

"It took a while to find just the right gift for the man who probably has everything." John spoke loudly enough for everyone to hear. "After a great deal of thought, we decided that this was more than appropriate."

Casey's face reddened as he accepted the large box. "I gather it isn't a gold watch," he joked, setting the box on a nearby table, then tearing off the wrapping.

He opened the box and after looking inside began to laugh.

"Appropriate, huh?" He held up a large, bright pink stuffed animal, a feminine version of Delbert Dragon. It had long, thick eyelashes and a bright red puckered mouth. He turned to the new sales director. "Sam, I wish you a lot of luck in convincing the sales force to push this beauty."

"This is one of a kind, Casey," John assured him with a straight face.

"Thank God!" Casey raised his eyes comically, much to everyone's amusement. "Thank you. I'm sure my little friend will be an interesting reminder of my time here." For a moment his eyes met Drew's across the room. The unspoken message was so strong that she stepped back a pace under the force of it. She turned abruptly away to break the spell. She was glad when conversation returned to normal. She'd stay just five more minutes, then make her escape. If she drank any more champagne she'd turn maudlin and normal conversation would be beyond her.

Drew sensed Casey's absence the moment he left the party. With a gracious smile she slowly made her way to the door. She had a strong idea where he might be.

She was right. He had returned to his office and was now filling a large cardboard box with his personal possessions. He had draped his suit jacket over the back of his chair, and loosened the knot in his tie. He looked up at his unexpected visitor, who stood uncertainly in the doorway.

"Just getting the last of my things," he explained in a remote voice, placing a bronze paperweight in the box.

Drew watched Casey with hungry eyes. She didn't know when, or if, she'd see him again, and it hurt so much.

"Watson called me." His lips twisted in a cynical

smile. "If he offered me any more money, I'd own the company."

She finally found her voice. "Would that be so bad? You should be flattered. Marty usually doesn't go to so much trouble for one person."

Casey leaned forward, bracing his hands on the desk top. "Is my staying *that* important to you? Tell me, what did Marty offer you as a reward to keep me here? How far did he tell you to go to accomplish your goal? Funny, Drew, I never thought that you would resort to *tricks* to persuade one poor sales director to stay on the job," he sneered.

She gasped at what he was implying. She had never thought about striking a man before, but Casey was asking for it. It took all her willpower for her to keep her hands at her sides.

"You know I would never do that!" Drew denied in a vehement tone. Her eyes shot fire at him. "All CHEM Corp. gets from me is loyalty. They've done a lot for me. The least I can do is give them my best."

"And they all lived happily ever after," he mocked her harshly, straightening up and walking toward her. "Well, then, my darling, the least I can do is give you my own special good-bye."

"What do you mean?" She eyed him warily as she backed away, only to find herself up against the wall.

Casey's hand shot out and slammed the door shut. His darkened features promised disaster as he bent over Drew, a hand braced on either side of her shoulders.

"I want you to remember this on those long, cold and very lonely winter nights, Drew," he whispered fiercely.

One hand tangled painfully in her chignon as his mouth captured hers. He demanded a surrender she wasn't willing to give. His tongue plundered her mouth, seeking out her tongue and drawing it back into the hot moist regions of his mouth.

Drew moaned, aware of the heat rising in her body. The points of her breasts were pressed against the strength of his chest. As the realization of what she was doing sank in, her body stiffened in shock. Sensing her sudden withdrawal, Casey lifted his head.

"Hate me, Drew," he grated, facing the angry glitter in her eyes. "If it will help to ease the pain any, hate me with all your heart." He pushed himself away, walked back to his desk and picked up the box. Before he opened the door and left the office, he turned to her. "Damn it, Drew, we're only tearing each other apart," he rasped. "I don't know about you, but I can't take the pain anymore." He walked out.

Drew leaned against the wall, not caring that her hair hung in tangled strands to her shoulders and that her lipstick was smeared.

She wanted to hate him. She wanted to despise him with every fiber of her being, but she couldn't. She loved him too much, yet her love couldn't push her into lowering her pride and running after him.

Drew was quieter than usual during the next two weeks. She threw herself into her work with a frenzy that kept her in the office twelve to sixteen hours a day. She grew thinner, and the shadows under her eyes deepened. Even her voice lacked its usual happy sparkle.

Kate tried to talk to her several times about working so hard, but the younger woman only turned away.

"When are you going to snap out of this limbo you're living in?" Kate finally demanded late one evening.

Drew had come home late and refused dinner as she had been doing many evenings, and was now seated cross-legged on the carpet in the den, with papers scattered around her in a half circle.

"I've already apologized for turning down dinner after all the trouble you went to, Aunt Kate," Drew replied in a dull voice, looking up from her work. "I'm just not hungry."

"I can imagine that you weren't hungry for any lunch, either," the older woman huffed, placing her hands on her hips. "Keep losing weight at this rate and you'll have to buy your clothes in the children's section of the store!" Kate scolded, all the while scanning her charge with a worried frown. "It's still Casey, isn't it? And I don't want your stubborn pride answering me this time, either. Tell me the truth."

Drew shrugged. Her voice was a flat monotone when she spoke. "He isn't anywhere, Aunt Kate. His house is closed up, but his furniture is still there, and he isn't working anywhere in the area. No one knows where he is." There was a wistful note in her voice.

Kate stood there, obviously fighting an inner battle.

"Did you think of looking for him outside the state?"

Drew's head snapped up at the quietly spoken question. "Aunt Kate, you know something, don't you? Don't you?" she demanded sharply, drawn out of her lethargy for the first time in weeks.

"And if I do?"

Drew jumped to her feet, ignoring the papers that flew about her. "Where is he?" she pleaded with the older woman. "Please, I need to know."

"Why? So you can hurt him even more than you already have?" The older woman was unmoved by Drew's plea. "You had your chance to iron things out with him more than two months ago. You refused to see it for what it was, and you destroyed it. Why should you be allowed to try now?"

Drew raked her fingers through her hair and shook

her head wearily. "Because I've discovered the hard way that the nights are long and lonely without a special someone to share them with you," she whispered, her words ending with a faint sob.

Kate studied Drew's dejected figure for a long moment. "Casey's in Arizona," she replied finally.

Drew's forehead creased in thought. "Arizona? But there's nothing in . . ." She halted in midsentence. "Pops's cabin!" she breathed in comprehension. "That's where he is, isn't it? You've known where he's been all this time!" she said accusingly when Kate nodded.

"He made me promise not to tell anyone," Kate declared.

The younger woman's shoulders slumped in defeat. "Especially me."

"Yes." There was no reason to lie.

It didn't take Drew long to make her mind up. She headed for the telephone and swiftly dialed.

"Hello, Marty," she replied to the gruff voice on the other end.

"Drew? What the—do you know what time it is?" he growled, all traces of sleep gone from his voice.

"I want to take my vacation time, effective tomorrow," she said crisply without bothering to apologize for calling him so late.

"No way. You have a job to do out there. When you're finished you can take your vacation, but not until then."

"This is an emergency, Marty," Drew argued, desperation in her voice. "Please, I have to go."

"Where? After McCord?" His voice sharpened with interest.

"Yes."

He was silent for a few moments. "I gather this isn't exactly company business," he commented sardonically.

"No." Drew sighed, then decided to push for all she was worth. "Look, Marty, in the past two weeks I've done more than two months worth of work. The dissension within the board dissolved when Raymond Wilson left. There are no major problems to worry about." She waited expectantly.

"By all rights I should keep on saying no, but I have an idea you'd go anyway," Marty grumbled. "One week, no more, and it will begin next Monday, not tomorrow."

Drew exhaled the breath she had been holding while waiting for his decision. "You won't regret it, Marty," she vowed.

"Damn right I won't!" he rumbled. "While you're at it, you can persuade that young fool to call me and we'll discuss something I have in mind for him."

"And if I can't persuade him?" she dared to inquire.

"Pick up suitable clothing for Iceland, because that will be the site of your next assignment. And next time, don't call me in the middle of the night!" He slammed the receiver down, the loud sound echoing in her ear.

Drew set her phone down. With that out of the way she only had one more obstacle to overcome, and that would be the hardest.

She and Casey were very much alike, and when their iron wills clashed it was a battle in which no one could guess the outcome. She turned to Kate, who had stood nearby, listening unashamedly to the telephone conversation.

"Casey once told me that all we were doing was tearing each other apart," Drew said quietly. "The time has come to heal the wounds."

Chapter Twelve

The Ferrari sped along the remote desert highway, its driver's hair a golden banner in the wind.

Drew preferred an open car to air conditioning, even when it was as hot as it was today. Despite the wind her powder blue cotton tank top was sticking moistly to her skin, and her white jeans were colored a pale beige from a fine layer of dust.

She had worked doubly hard the latter part of the previous week. Everyone had been surprised to hear that she was taking a few days off. Everyone but Viv, that was. But if the secretary had an idea where her boss was going to, or to whom, she kept it to herself.

Drew slept very little the Friday night before she left. She got up at dawn, finished her packing and ate a breakfast that Kate insisted she consume.

She drove steadily, not stopping until just before she reached the California–Arizona border. Then she had dinner and found a motel room for the night.

She spent the evening watching an old movie on

television and studying an Arizona road map. She had had to go through some of Marcus's papers to find directions to the cabin. She hadn't been there since her early teens, and she didn't want to trust her memory and end up lost.

Later the next morning Drew pushed her sunglasses back up on her nose and used a tissue to blot her perspiration streaked forehead and cheeks. Traffic was sparse that day, and she was glad that she'd had the car thoroughly checked out before she left. This wasn't the place to have a breakdown. She glanced at the gas gauge and knew she would have to stop at the next service station. The last sign she had seen had read thirty miles, which meant she had about another fifteen to go. She pressed the accelerator just a little harder. Humming a popular country-and-western tune under her breath, she concentrated on reaching what should be her last stop before arriving at Casey's cabin. It was time to begin thinking about what she would say to him before he decided to throw her out. She sincerely doubted that her surprise visit would merit the red carpet treatment.

"Speed limit around here is five-five," a disembodied voice called from above. "You've been doing six-five for the last ten miles. Want to drop back and try the speed limit for a while?"

"Oh, no!" Drew moaned, staring into her rearview mirror, then turning her head carefully to scan the deserted road around her. Where had that voice come from? The only thing that saved her sanity was the familiar whirring sound overhead. She glanced up to see a highway patrol helicopter flying to her right. That explained the disembodied voice. From then on she was careful to keep an eye on the speedometer.

The gas station was in a small desert town, the rest of which consisted of a small general store and a restaurant, with a sprinkling of houses off in the distance.

The man in charge of the gas pumps was of indeterminate age, with a beard, and a wad of chewing tobacco puffing out a corner of his mouth. He walked out of the garage, his grease-covered fingers scratching his overall-covered chest.

"Fill 'er up?" He eyed the sleek car curiously.

"Yes, please." Drew looked around. "Is there a restroom around here?"

"Around the back."

A splash of cool water on her heated face and a cold can of soda from a dilapidated, dust-covered machine helped boost her tired spirits.

The man had just finished cleaning the dust-covered windshield when she returned to the car.

"What kinda car is this?" he drawled, accepting the money Drew handed him.

"A Ferrari," she replied absently. Right now all she cared about was arriving at her destination before she melted in this heat!

"Ferrari, huh?" He scratched the top of his grizzled head. "That's what that Hawaiian detective fella on TV drives, ain't it? 'Cept his is red."

"That's right." She waited impatiently for her change. "No offense, but I'm in kind of a hurry," she prompted.

"I've seen that show a coupla times," the old man informed her, taking his time in handing her several grubby bills. "Trouble is, we don't always get good reception out here. We either get a fuzzy picture or no sound. Sure do enjoy that fella, though." He chortled, then warned her with a friendly wag of the finger, "You be careful out there on the road, Miss. There's some crazy people in this world, and you're too purty to have something happen to you."

"Thanks." Drew smiled, stuffing her change in her wallet. "I'll be cautious." A moment later the powerful engine roared to life and she pulled out onto the highway.

In a couple of hours she slowed down as she drove through the town of Sedona, heading for Oak Creek Canyon, where Casey's cabin was located.

Marcus had gone there at least twice a year for trout fishing. It wasn't until after his death that Drew had discovered that Casey had accompanied the older man on those trips for the past few years.

Drew stopped at a small coffee shop, deciding that she needed something solid in her stomach before facing Casey. She preferred to ignore the fact that she was only putting off the inevitable. She didn't want to think that he just might refuse to see her. Worse yet, what if Kate was wrong and Casey wasn't there, or he had already left for home? She would have made the trip for nothing.

She sat at the small round table, idly fingering one of her french fries. The cheeseburger she had ordered was large and juicy, more than she was used to eating these days, but she couldn't seem to work up an appetite for it, though she ate it anyway. She took her time drinking her iced tea and finishing her lunch. All too soon her plate was empty, and there was no reason to wait around any longer.

Drew took some extra time to brush her hair into a loose knot on top of her head and apply a fresh coat of tinted lip gloss. Her clothes still stuck to her damp skin, but there wasn't anything she could do about that. She replaced the top on the car. She didn't want to arrive looking too windblown.

After studying the directions one last time, she steered the car onto the main street and headed for the canyon area. With luck she'd arrive at the cabin within the next forty-five minutes.

"Hi, Casey," she muttered to herself. "I just happened to be in the neighborhood and thought I'd stop by. How's it going? Nope, that will never do." She grimaced. Flippancy was something he didn't appreciate, but she wasn't sure if he would want to hear the truth, either.

Drew had forgotten how beautiful this area was with its trees and fast running streams filled with trout for the avid fishermen. She drove slowly, enjoying the scenery and putting off the moment of reckoning.

She soon turned off the main road onto what seemed more like a dirt path. She winced as the powerful car jerked and bumped its way along the rocky track. There wasn't any way she could call this a road! Dust rose in her wake as she made her way slowly up the steep incline.

Drew wasn't prepared when the car bucked and the wheel jerked out of her hands. She hastily downshifted and pressed the brake, praying she would be able to keep the car on the road. The ditch on either side could easily tear the bottom out of the low slung vehicle. When she came to a full stop she found her hands shaking in reaction.

She got out of the car and walked around to assess the damage. The flat tire told her the whole story.

Drew wiped her arm across her forehead and looked at the steep hill. It was going to be a long walk. It would be an even longer one if Casey weren't there and she had to hike down to the main road to find someone to help her.

She rolled up the windows and locked the doors as a precautionary measure before striking out. She hadn't gone very far before her leg muscles began protesting.

"I paid out all that money for those classes and I can't even walk up one stupid little hill," she panted, concentrating on putting one foot in front of the other.

It seemed like hours before the road finally leveled off. Just ahead, in the middle of a clump of trees, stood a small wood frame building with a covered porch in front. Drew looked around to see if she could find any signs of life, but all was quiet. An unfamiliar tan and white dust-covered Bronco sat in front of the cabin.

"Terrific," Drew groaned, slowly approaching the building. "I came all this way and he isn't even here."

"It depends on who you're looking for." She spun around at the sound of the husky male voice.

Her eyes widened at the sight before her. The man standing before her was Casey, yet he wasn't. This man wore a pair of heavy jeans that had seen better days, hiking boots and a well worn plaid cotton shirt, partially unbuttoned to reveal his sweat-streaked chest. His face was shadowed by the beginnings of a beard. As was true of so many blond-haired men, Casey's beard had a reddish hue to it.

She found it hard to breathe as she faced the man she had driven hundreds of miles to find. Where was the pat little speech she had rehearsed so carefully during her trip? Gone, with the rest of her sanity.

Drew continued studying Casey. It wasn't just the rough clothing and beard that made him different. There was more, much more. The wary stance, the cat's eyes watching her with caution in their tawny depths, the lack of expression on his face. He *wasn't* surprised to see her!

"Did Aunt Kate tell you I was coming?" she blurted out suspiciously.

The smile on his face wasn't welcoming. "Since this place isn't modern enough to have a phone, she would have had to go to a great deal of trouble to get in touch with me." He didn't move from his wide-legged stance, his arms crossed in front of his chest.

"It's—it's just that you don't seem surprised to see me." Drew felt on the defensive because of Casey's impervious manner.

"Where's your car? Surely you didn't hitchhike out

here from San Diego," he said politely, ignoring her comment.

She wanted to scream at him for always being in control of any situation. She was hot and tired, her feet hurt, and her new Italian sandals would never be the same.

"I had a flat tire down the road, if you can call that pile of rocks a road," she announced flatly.

Without a word Casey swung around and walked away.

"Where are you going?" Drew called after his retreating figure.

"To take a look at your car," he shot back.

Drew tried to hurry after Casey, but had to stop to pull a pebble from her sandal. The words she muttered under her breath were indicative of her temper.

It didn't take as long to walk down the hill as it had to trudge up it.

"Flat tire, all right," Casey muttered after examining the car.

"No kidding!" Drew took a deep breath. "Did you think I couldn't tell?"

He shot her a level look that instantly silenced her. He held out a hand, palm upward. "Keys."

She pulled them out of her pocket and tossed them to him.

"How you got those things in that pocket I'll never know," he muttered. "You probably had to use a shoe horn to get them on." He opened the trunk and looked inside, muttered a curse and then turned toward Drew. For a moment he was torn between yelling at her for taking a chance on this road in a car without four-wheel drive and walking over to her, throwing her down to the ground and making violent love to her. Even in dust-covered clothing, her face shiny with perspiration and her hair limp with heat, she was the most beautiful woman he had ever seen. His jeans suddenly felt tighter under the strain. "Why the hell are you carrying around a flat spare tire?" he rapped out, bracing an arm against the upflung trunk lid.

"What?" Drew's dismay was evident on her face. She ran forward and looked inside the trunk. "But I had everything checked out before I left!"

"Under the hood, perhaps." Casey shook his head in disgust. "How many times have I told you always to check things out yourself? You can't leave it up to the garage. What if you had been out on the highway, miles from anywhere?"

"It didn't look flat when I left!" she argued, waving her arms in frustration.

"The windmill act isn't going to work," he grunted. He continued shaking his head as he pulled Drew's suitcase and tote bag out of the car. "Here." He handed her the tote bag. "I'll have to take your spare into town and have it fixed before we can do anything." He picked up the suitcase and walked up the hill without bothering to see if Drew was following him.

Not anxious to stay there alone, she hurried after him. Her mind raced with questions. Who was this new Casey McCord? Where was the gentleness she had always associated with him? He might not have been surprised to see her, but he wasn't exactly welcoming her, either.

When Drew reached the cabin the front door stood open and there was no Casey to be seen. She entered and dropped the tote bag on the smooth wood floor.

Nothing had changed. The old-fashioned braided scatter rugs were still on the floor, and there was the stone fireplace, blackened by the many fires that had burned in its interior. She knew there were two bedrooms and a bathroom down a narrow hallway to her left. A tiny kitchen was situated off to her right. There was an old temperamental gas stove, and electricity was courtesy of a generator out back.

Casey appeared in the kitchen doorway. "You'll probably want to wash up."

Drew didn't need his suggestion to remind her of how grubby she must look.

"I'm going to take your spare tire into town now and have it taken care of for you," he informed her as he walked toward the front door. He would have continued past her if she hadn't impulsively put out her hand to detain him.

"Casey . . ." She spoke softly, while her eyes pleaded silently with him to answer her. "How did you know I would come?"

His own eyes were dark golden pools as he gazed down at her. "Souls don't use the ordinary forms of communication, Drew," he replied quietly, then swiftly walked out the door. A few minutes later the Bronco's engine roared to life, and then the sound receded as he traveled down the hill.

Drew went into the kitchen and poured herself a tall glass of cold water. Drinking deeply, she wandered down the hall and found her suitcase in the first bedroom. Casey must be occupying the larger bedroom in the rear.

A terrifying thought occurred to her. What if he wasn't alone? For a moment she was tempted to peek in the rear bedroom to see if there was any evidence of a woman's presence, but she swiftly banished the thought. If he were there with someone else, he would have told her right away and probably bundled her off as fast as possible.

Drew sat on the edge of the single bed. It wasn't until then that she realized how tired she was. She wanted nothing more than to sink back down and sleep her tensions away, but she knew that she needed a shower first. She wearily rose to her feet and shed her clothing.

The water was lukewarm and erratic, but to Drew it was sheer heaven. She stepped out of the shower stall and reached for a white towel hanging on a nearby rack.

Back in her bedroom, she put on a cotton robe, flopped down onto the bedspread and burrowed her face into the pillow. Despite Casey's less than enthusiastic welcome she felt more relaxed than she had in a long time. Her eyelids slowly drooped, then remained closed.

It was a couple of hours before Casey returned. The silence in the cabin bothered him. Drew wouldn't have wandered off on her own, would she?

"Drew?" he called out, glancing in the kitchen but finding it empty. "Drew?" He raised his voice as he hurried toward the back of the cabin.

The open doorway to the first bedroom beckoned to him. He stood there drinking in the sight before him.

Drew lay curled up on the bed, her robe bunched up, leaving her slender legs bare to the thigh. The neckline gaped open to reveal one rounded breast to his hungry gaze. The small room was already filled with the sensual floral scent of her perfume.

How many nights since the last time he had made love to her had he dreamed of seeing her this way? How many nights had he tortured himself with memories that only sent him reeling into a black pit of despair? This was no dream, but the reality could be just as frightening.

"Drew," Casey whispered with an ache in his throat. Even in the sleep of innocence, she personified desire and a deep sensuality. No woman could arouse an aching fire in his loins as swiftly as she could.

He crossed the room and sat carefully on the edge of the bed. One hand wrapped itself around the side of her throat.

"Drew, love," Casey murmured, bending his head to caress her temple with his lips.

"Um." She stirred sleepily under the warm brush of his beard against her skin.

"Naptime is over." He lay down beside her and tickled the tip of her ear with his tongue while he slid one hand under the cotton robe to rediscover the enticing contours of her body.

Her body acknowledged his more than effective way of waking her up much faster than her sleep-filled brain did. It didn't take long for her arms to circle his neck and pull his face down to hers.

"It's just beginning," she breathed against his lips, while she wiggled closer against his body. His shirt buttons were easily unfastened, while he pulled her robe from her naked body.

Nothing mattered but the present. Drew's tongue teased Casey's lips open and delved into the warm interior. He stiffened under the sensuous onslaught of her hands as they deftly unbuckled his belt and slid the zipper to his jeans downward. She feathered her fingertips over the flat surface of his stomach, then they darted lower in ever widening circles.

"Oh, Casey," she murmured throatily, glancing up from under coyly lowered eyelashes. "You never could hide anything from me."

"Drew, you're making this very hard," he warned in a raspy voice.

"Uh-hmm." She got up on her knees and proceeded to push his jeans and jockey briefs down to his ankles. "Kick them off, darling," she instructed matter-of-factly, as if undressing him were an everyday occurrence. Of course, it *had* been one of her chief pleasures five years before. "Now, sit up so I can take off your shirt."

Casey's mouth was suddenly very dry. "Drew." He had to concentrate in order to force her name out. "I don't think this is a very good idea."

She grinned impishly and leaned forward to drop a moist kiss on his nose. "I do."

From past experience Casey knew that Drew could be totally unpredictable at times, and this was one of those times. When he had first seen her on the road looking tired, dusty and cranky, he had figured to have a fight on his hands. That was why he had escaped into town so quickly. It appeared that she had used that time to shower and get some rest. How could he have forgotten the womanly scent of her skin?

Now as naked as she was, he lay half over her body, crushing her full breasts against his chest, the taut nipples pressing into his skin.

"Something tells me that you're one very frustrated lady," he remarked, placing a warm hand over one silken thigh and moving it upward.

"You're so right," she purred, mimicking his action with a caress of her own. His velvety skin throbbed to life under her touch. "I've missed you, Casey."

He smiled with a warmth she hadn't seen in a long time.

"What took you so long?" he chided, probing farther and eliciting a sharp gasp from Drew's lips. His mouth left a searing brand on her breast as he traced the sensitive skin with his tongue.

She blinked, finding it difficult to think coherently while Casey was finding all sorts of new erotic spots on her skin. "I-ah-I have a stubborn nature."

"No kidding!" he teased. His tongue had now discovered the inner shell of her ear.

"Also, you-ah-you weren't the easiest person to find." His leg was lying nestled between her smooth ones and proving to be very distracting. She focused on his chest, hoping to remain coherent for a few more moments. Without warning she laughed and reached toward the matted hair. "Look, I found a gray hair!"

"Hey!" Casey yelped and pulled back, scowling at this swift turn of events. "I hate to tell you this, but I was attached to that," he informed her.

"Not anymore!" she sang out.

Casey growled, reached for Drew's wrists and pinned them over her head. "Now that you've got me all hot and bothered, you're going to have to finish the job." He captured her mouth in a kiss designed to destroy her sanity.

Drew's tongue slid back into the darkened regions of Casey's mouth to tease and parry. She was quickly remembering how much they had both enjoyed it when she played the aggressor. The groan that came from the depths of his throat told her of his arousal. The tip of her tongue darted into his mouth only so far, then withdrew. Casey could take only so much before he took over.

He taunted her with the virile strength of his body, the arousing caresses of his hands and the moist heat of his tongue.

"How did you manage to get away from your office?" he asked hoarsely, thrusting gently at her arching hips.

Drew laughed softly. "I guess Marty thought I would be able to persuade you to come back." Her hands roamed over Casey's muscular back and down to his tightly muscled buttocks.

His body tensed, but not from desire. "Watson sent you?"

She was too lost in a haze of sensuality to notice the abrupt change in his demeanor. "Hm, I think I like you with a beard," she murmured. "It makes you look very sexy!"

"Watson," Casey prompted tersely.

Drew reached up and linked her arms around his neck. "Perhaps he would let me write this off as a business trip," she joked.

But Casey didn't see any humor in her statement. He levered his body away from her and sat up.

"Casey?" Drew was puzzled by his withdrawal.

"I guess I was wrong after all," he said in a low voice as he got off the bed and picked his clothing up from the floor.

"What do you mean?" She propped herself up on one elbow. "What are you talking about?"

Casey pulled on his briefs and turned around to face her. "You didn't come here on your own, did you?"

"Of course I did." She still couldn't understand what he was trying to say. "What are you getting at?"

There was a hurt expression in Casey's eyes that bothered Drew. Why this sudden change? A moment ago this passionate man had been ready to make love to her. Now he only looked sad. He looked as if he had just lost his last friend, a fact she mentioned aloud.

Casey smiled bleakly. "Yes, I guess I did," he mused. "I lost her five years ago, but then I thought I had found her again. Now I know differently." He shook his head in sorrow. "I thought you had come here because you wanted to, because you wanted me, not because your boss sent you." He took several deep breaths. "Your tire's been fixed and put back on your car. When you get into a larger town, I suggest you see about replacing the other one."

Drew felt chilled to the bone. "Casey, I can handle your anger, but not this-this . . ." She was at a loss for words. "Talk to me, Casey. What have I done?" Her expressive face reflected her bewilderment. "Why are you doing this to us?"

His harsh laugh cut her to the bone, as did his words. "Tell Watson I can't be bought at any price. I never realized you'd go so far as to prostitute yourself for CHEM Corp.," he said sadly. He turned away and headed for the doorway.

"What?" Drew sat upright, shocked by his condemnation. She dragged her robe over her bare shoulders as if she were suddenly ashamed of her nudity.

"I'm sure you can find a motel room in town for tonight. You'll probably want to get an early start back to San Diego. Tell Aunt Kate I'll be in touch, and tell Watson you didn't fail. I just intend to stay here for reasons of my own." Casey didn't even turn to face her as he spoke.

Drew stared at the bronzed skin of Casey's back, dark against the stark white of his underwear.

"You can't want me to leave!" she protested. "Not after—we almost—"

"That's exactly why I think you should leave now," he cut in sharply. "Good-bye, Drew." He walked out of the room.

She sat very still, unable to believe her ears. Funny, she hadn't stopped to think rationally once Casey had begun making love to her. All that had mattered was his love, his warmth, his tenderness. She had come to see him for one very selfish reason: because she still loved him and wanted to be with him. For the first time in five years she had put CHEM Corp. second in her life.

The trouble was, she knew that no matter what she said, Casey wouldn't believe her.

Injecting some iron into her spine, Drew scrambled off the bed and opened her suitcase to find fresh clothing. As she dressed her brain was in full gear. If Casey thought she was going to meekly walk out of his life, he had another think coming!

Casey went into his room and dressed rapidly. He had come to the cabin because there were no memories of Drew here. Now there wasn't one place on earth where he could be free. The woman who owned his soul still hadn't learned to share her life, and probably never would. He stiffened when he heard the sound of the front door closing; the click of the jamb seemed so final.

"Damn her!" he groaned, closing his eyes tightly.

For one brief moment Casey had dared to hope. To hope that Drew had come here on her own, not because Watson had ordered her to, but because she loved him. Casey knew Drew loved him! So why couldn't that stubborn little witch tell him so without making all this trouble between them? Apparently fate was working against them. Drew was meant to go her way, and he was meant to go his. Each alone.

Chapter Thirteen

"Some help you turned out to be. Now the car won't work at all!" A belligerent Drew faced a stunned Casey. Without waiting for a reply she swept past him into the cabin. "I certainly wasn't going to drag that heavy suitcase back up here, so I left it in the car until morning. Unless these woods have elves, I doubt that anyone will find it."

"I'll drive you into town," he offered instantly, a hint of desperation in his voice. He just couldn't let her spend the night! Not if he wanted to retain his sanity.

"No way!" She flounced over to the couch, prepared for the argument she knew she was going to get. "I was up at five this morning in order to get an early start and escape some of the midday heat. I'm tired, my feet hurt from all the rocks I've climbed over, and I'm hungry. I want some food, another hot shower and some sleep," she announced imperiously. Luckily he hadn't seen the wary look in her eyes. She'd had no idea what kind of reception she'd receive this time. She did know that he wouldn't be above bundling her into his Bronco and driving her into town if he didn't want her there. They said the best defense was a good offense. Well, she was more than ready to prove that point.

Casey studied Drew's set features. Her speech was just a shade too pat. She seemed to have forgotten that he knew every trick in the book when it came to dealing with her.

He walked over to the couch and leaned over, placing one hand on either side of her shoulders.

"What did you do to the car, Drew?" he asked in a rough velvet voice, making sure she looked him squarely in the eye.

"Nothing." Her reply was too swift to be true. "I don't know anything about cars. You're more than aware of that."

Casey's uplifted eyebrow and the skepticism on his face told her that he didn't believe her gaze of wide eyed innocence.

"It looks like you're stuck with me, like it or not," Drew announced, flopping back on the couch. "What's for dinner? I'm starved!"

He grumbled something under his breath and stalked off toward the kitchen. His reply was the metallic rattle of pots and pans. He clearly wasn't pleased by Drew's reappearance or her smooth explanation.

She reached down and kicked her tennis shoes off, then stood up and walked barefoot into the kitchen.

"Can I help with anything?" she asked brightly, standing in the doorway.

"No, thanks," Casey growled, pouring barbecue sauce over two thick steaks.

"If you like, I could make the salad," she offered, managing to keep her voice pleasant despite his surly manner.

He set the basting brush down and turned to her.

"Why don't you go take that shower you wanted so badly?" he asked tautly.

"Good idea." Drew's face lit up as if that hadn't ever occurred to her.

"It's going to be a long night," Casey muttered between clenched teeth as Drew headed off.

Dinner was silent save for "pass the salt, please," and "may I have the butter?" Drew glanced at Casey's stony features and knew that this wasn't the time to push her advantage.

When her offer to wash the dishes was coolly rebuffed, Drew retired to the living room and curled up on the couch with a paperback book she had found under the coffee table. Casey must have read it and tossed it there when he had finished. If the lurid cover was anything to go by, she'd be disgusted by page two. Drew tucked her bare feet under her and began reading. In no time she was engrossed in the adventure story.

"What are you doing?" The book was rudely torn out of her hands.

Drew looked up, surprised by the dark anger in Casey's eyes.

"I'm reading," she replied, determined to be as reasonable as possible.

"This is *trash!*" He glowered at her, furious with her for no apparent reason.

"Actually," she tipped her head to one side in thought, "it was very informative. Is it really possible to make love in that position?" she asked curiously.

"Drew!" Casey roared in shock. "This isn't the kind of book you should be reading." He threw it across the room.

"Oh? I didn't realize I was only supposed to read certain novels," she drawled. "You act as if I don't know the first thing about the birds and the bees. Well, buster, I want you to know that I do know that babies don't come by way of the stork!"

Casey ground his teeth in exasperation. It didn't help to see that Drew wasn't wearing a bra under her cream colored T-shirt. The thrusting outline of her coral nipples had been only too apparent during dinner. And her jeans were so tight that they looked as if they had been painted on her. On top of that, did she have to wear the same damn perfume that had been haunting him all these years?

"This is nothing more than pornography," he pointed out, glaring darkly at her. "It's filth, trash; it's—"

"It looked as if you had been reading it." Drew's smile was just this side of angelic. Inside, she was laughing herself silly. Casey was so upset over *nothing!* Admittedly, the book in question was written in the worst possible style, and the plot, or lack thereof, focused mainly on the main character's sex habits. She found it more amusing than disgusting, all the while wondering where these people came up with enough energy to hop in and out of so many beds when they couldn't seem to engage in one meaningful conversation!

"That's different," he snapped back, still standing over her looking very much like an aggrieved parent who had found his child reading adult magazines. "Those are men's books. We're expected to read them." Somehow that explanation didn't sound very plausible even to his own ears, and the expression on her face told him that she didn't see it that way, either.

"And I'm expected to read all those sweet women's magazines, and books dealing with skin care and diets, not to mention twenty thousand ways to fix hamburger." It was a major miracle that she was managing to keep her temper. "Actually, that book was proving to be highly educational." She leaned back, stretching her arms over her head, fully aware that the action only caused her breasts to thrust out more. Strangely, the idea of flaunting her body before him was enough to stimulate her nipples into pouting buds that pushed against the soft cotton of her shirt, something else that Casey couldn't help but notice.

A muscle twitched at the corner of his mouth, indicating that his temper was becoming greatly strained. Cursing fluently under his breath, he twisted away and stalked down the hallway. A few minutes later Drew could hear the sound of running water. She'd bet everything she owned that Casey's shower was a very cold one. While he cooled his temper in the shower she escaped to her bedroom and carefully shut the door. She was smart enough to know when to quit pushing.

Drew was awakened the next morning by the aroma of bacon frying. She got out of bed and pulled on a pair of navy cotton walking shorts and a white and yellow striped pullover. She was surprised to find her suitcase standing outside the bedroom door. Obviously Casey hadn't trusted himself enough to even bring it inside her room.

"Do you have to cook food so early in the morning?" Drew demanded, walking into the kitchen.

Casey barely glanced at her from his position at the stove. "Since it's past ten, I'd say it's hardly early." He gestured to the coffeepot. "Want some?"

Drew raked her fingers through her still tousled hair. "I didn't realize it was so late," she murmured, pouring herself a cup of coffee.

"I can only guess that you still don't believe in eating breakfast," Casey said politely. He looked altogether too sexy in tight jeans, no shirt and bare feet. His hair gleamed from a recent shower.

"You gather correctly." She sat at the small table,

watching him place three eggs and four slices of bacon on a plate, along with several slices of toast. She could remember watching him eat a large breakfast like that every morning.

"Drew, my love, what did you do with the distributor cap?" His casual question was meant to catch her off guard.

Drew looked up with a deceptively innocent expression. "What's a distributor cap?"

"A part that's pretty important if you want your car to run." His eyes met hers across the table. "I had to make arrangements to have your car towed into town, since that was the only way I could get it off the road."

"What!" She slammed her cup down on the table top. "Casey, you can't just hook a Ferrari up to a tow truck like some beat-up old jalopy!"

His lips tightened at her lack of trust in his common sense. "I'm aware of that." He spoke with a cold, concise snap to his words. "I supervised the loading of your car myself. Of course, if I had known that you didn't trust me to do the right thing, I would have woken you up. Since you had insisted you were so tired last night, I thought a few extra hours of sleep would be beneficial to your well being." Not to mention your temper, his manner implied.

"No, you're right," she replied swiftly, ashamed of her rude outburst. She reached across the table for his hand and laced her fingers through his. "I'm sorry, Casey; of course you would know exactly what to do."

"Naturally."

The arrogance in that one word was too much for Drew. Her eyes narrowed to golden slits. "Isn't it rather boring to be right all the time?" she asked with saccharine sweetness. She propped her chin on one palm, looking at him with wide eyes. Only the dancing glitter he saw there was evidence of the sarcasm she had left unspoken.

Damn, why did she have to be the woman to drive him past the limits of rational thinking? Casey demanded of himself, gazing down into her delicate face. The face of an angel, the temperament of a virago and the body of a sorceress all rolled up into one neat package.

Drew couldn't help but recognize the desolation in Casey's eyes. "We're tearing each other apart again, aren't we?" She sighed and pulled her hand away from his. She covered her face with her hands. "Casey, I'm sorry; I don't even understand myself anymore."

Hearing the pain in her voice, he stood up and walked around to her chair, then squatted down next to her.

"Drew," he murmured, gently taking her fingers, then tightening his hold when she tried to pull away. "Just answer one question for me. Did Watson send you here? Was he the only reason you came?" He silently pleaded with her for the truth.

She looked up and studied his face. There was no harsh anger in his eyes, and she knew that he would listen to her this time. "I called Marty and told him I was taking my vacation time now. It didn't take him long to figure out that I was coming to see you. He did suggest that I try to persuade you to come back to Fantasy Toys, but I told him that I wouldn't come here for that reason. I'm not here as a representative for Fantasy Toys or CHEM Corp.," she said honestly. "I'm here because I—" She almost told him the real reason, that she still loved him, but this didn't seem like the time to divulge that piece of information. "I missed you," she said, settling for a half truth.

Casey bent his head and nuzzled Drew's palms with his lips and tongue. His beard tickled the sensitive skin. He didn't doubt the truth of her words. He only knew that she hadn't told him everything.

"After I finish my breakfast, how about a walk?" he suggested softly.

She caught her lower lip between her teeth. "On one condition." She drew each word out slowly.

Casey was instantly wary. "What?"

"That I won't have to walk either up or down that damn hill!"

Casey's laughter was rich and full. "Deal," he agreed, leaning forward and dropping a light kiss on her lips to seal their bargain. He pulled back before the kiss could deepen.

Her lips tingled from the brief touch. Perhaps it would help both of them to get out of the confines of the small cabin.

Their sexual attraction was as strong as ever, but there was too much between them that had to be resolved before they could think of returning to their former relationship.

"I think I'd better get something to eat." Casey's hoarse voice sounded as if it had been forced from his throat.

Drew's eyes followed the line of Casey's throat down to the dark gold whorls of hair on his chest. How she used to enjoy combing her fingers through those crisp hairs, burying her face in them and inhaling the musky scent that was uniquely his. How soft those hairs were where they arrowed down to his stomach, how—She jerked away from her erotic thoughts. She pushed herself out of the chair with a muttered excuse about refilling her coffee cup, although it was nowhere near empty.

Casey watched Drew's uncertain movements but said nothing. He still had his own devils to deal with. He wanted to believe her when she said that Marty hadn't sent her. What he wanted to hear from her was that she had come here because she loved him. Why was it so

hard for her to say the words? Damn her! When wo[...]
she free him from the hell she kept him in? No wom[...]
would drive that many miles to see a man just becau[...]
she "missed" him. There was more to it than that, a[...]
he wanted her to admit it. He wanted her to be me[...]
honest with him, as well as with herself. He only hop[...]
they could settle this soon, before the damage v[...]
beyond repair.

"You better put on jeans and boots if you've [...]
them," he advised brusquely, tackling his now c[...]
eggs. He didn't look up, but he could sense the look [...]
puzzled hurt she flashed him. Right now, he wasn't s[...]
if he cared. Let her get back some of the pain he h[...]
suffered thanks to her. "The woods aren't very kind[...]
bare legs, no matter how good they look."

After Drew finished her coffee she rinsed her cup [...]
and placed it on the drainboard. "Since I didn't di[...]
any of the breakfast dishes, I guess I don't have to wa[...]
them," she announced cheerfully, hoping to break [...]
silence that had fallen between them. When he did[...]
answer she headed for her room.

Ten minutes later she reappeared wearing jeans[...]
pullover sweater and a pair of tennis shoes, and w[...]
her hair tied back in a casual ponytail.

Casey had pulled on a tawny lightweight sweater t[...]
matched his eyes, and wore a pair of sturdy hik[...]
boots. He carried a small knapsack that fitted ea[...]
over his broad shoulders. Again Drew saw him a[...]
man of nature. Why hadn't she noticed that about h[...]
before? After all, he had grown up on a ranch. T[...]
type of life couldn't be all that strange to him, ev[...]
though the house he had lived in in Montana wa[...]
great deal larger than this cabin.

Walking outside, Drew breathed deeply of the fre[...]
woodsy air.

"No smog or pollution here," Casey told her, wat[...]
ing her enjoy the warm sunshine.

"That's why Pops enjoyed coming here so much." There was no sorrow in her memories, only the remembrance of the good times. The smile on her lips was natural, her movements unrestrained. "I'm glad you were able to share it with him," she said sincerely.

For a few moments Casey saw the energetic college student he had met ten years before. The faint lines of strain were gone from her face, and her eyes were clear and sparkling. She had never looked more beautiful.

"Come on, Drusilla Louise." He held out his hand, palm up. "We've got some exploring to do."

Drew wrinkled her nose at his use of her full name. "Anything you say, *Carstairs Langdon,*" she couldn't resist jibing back.

"God save us from family names," Casey groaned.

"Anything has to be preferable to Drusilla." She took his hand and walked by his side, secretly pleased to note that he had shortened his normally long strides for her. "It always makes me think of a wicked witch from a fairy tale."

"Oh, you're a witch, all right." He looked down at the top of her head, a strange glint in his eyes. "But not a wicked one," he finished in that sexy, husky voice that always sent shivers along her spine.

Drew studied Casey out of the corner of her eye. What kind of person was he going to be today? When she had showed up last night he had looked as if she were the last person he wanted to see. This morning he had been just a step short of rude. Now he sounded like the friend and lover she remembered from so long ago. She only wished that the spell would last.

Judging from Casey's confidence as they trudged through the woods, he had learned the surrounding land well. After about an hour of steady walking Drew discovered leg muscles she hadn't known existed.

"Can we stop?" she pleaded, already beginning to slow down.

"Soon."

"Now?" Drew pressed again.

"Not yet." Casey continued walking forward.

"Ca-sey!" she shouted in protest five minutes later. "My legs are ready to fall off!"

"I thought those exercise classes you take were supposed to build up your stamina." He halted long enough for her to catch up with him.

"That doesn't mean I'm in training for the Olympics," she puffed.

"It's just a little farther," Casey coaxed. "Don't worry, Drew, it's worth it," he promised with a dazzling smile.

"It had better be," she muttered, following him through a dense section of trees.

When they stopped at the edge of what looked like a miniature meadow she knew he had been right. This had been worth the long walk.

"How did you find this place?" Drew breathed, walking out into the grassy area and spinning around with her arms lifted as if to embrace the sun.

"Just happened on it during my wanderings." Casey slipped off the knapsack and dropped it to the ground. Kneeling down, he pulled out a blanket and spread it out over the grass. "I thought you were tired," he teased, watching her playful antics.

"Um, this is better than a shot of adrenaline." She dropped down beside him.

"There's more." He grinned, reaching back into the knapsack. *"Voila!"* He held up a bottle of wine and a corkscrew. "Don't worry, I also brought some solid food. I don't want to carry a drunken woman all that way back to the cabin."

Drew checked the contents of the knapsack and found thick roast beef sandwiches and potato chips. "You forgot glasses," she pointed out.

Casey shook his head. "When you're in primitive

surroundings you have to give up a few luxuries." He deftly pulled the cork and lifted the bottle to his lips.

Drew gazed at the way Casey's throat muscles worked as he swallowed the wine. It took a moment for her to realize that he was holding the bottle out to her.

"Sorry I wasn't a gentleman and didn't offer it to you first." He grinned unrepentantly at his lack of manners.

Drew accepted the bottle and sipped cautiously. White wine might not go with roast beef, but the dry, tangy alcohol hit the spot. For a moment she imagined that she could taste Casey's mouth with the wine. She thought of the warm, masculine taste she knew so well. As she tipped her head forward again she found Casey's eyes, full of agony, riveted on her mouth.

"Why are you back in my life again, Drew?" he rasped, leaning forward and placing a hand on her leg, his thumb rubbing seductively along her thigh. "Why did you get rid of the distributor cap and insist on staying here last night?"

She shifted uneasily under his erotic caress. "I've been wrong about you in so many ways," she told him in a low voice. "I kept thinking I could mold you into something you weren't. You had your reasons for resigning, and I had no right to give you a hard time about them. As for Marty throwing in his own two cents' worth, well, he's very much like you." She smiled at his grunt of disgust. "Oh, yes, he is, Casey. The two of you always think you're right whether you are or not, and the both of you will always hold out to the very end."

Casey's hand slowly inched up her thigh. "And you?" His warm, wine-scented breath teased her face. "Do you hold out?"

"Not with you," Drew whispered, unaware that her arms were circling his neck, her fingers tangling in his hair. "Never with you." The words were swallowed by the hungry force of Casey's kiss.

Her lips parted, asking for the kiss to deepen, but he ignored her unspoken plea. Casey preferred to cover every angle of Drew's face with light kisses while his hands freed her hair. His fingers dug gently into her scalp, not to inflict pain, but to knead and massage her tension away.

He carefully eased Drew onto her back, then followed her down. "So sweet," he muttered thickly.

"Casey," she murmured as she lifted her face to his.

He nuzzled the soft lines of her throat. "You're not wearing a bra," he groaned, molding a soft breast against his palm.

"No, I'm not. Does that mean I'm seducing you?" She couldn't resist teasing him.

"In the best way possible." He lowered his head so that his lips could capture the cotton covered nipple. The gentle tugging of his mouth brought a moan of longing to her lips. "You've always been a narcotic in my blood, Drew. One habit I've never been able to break." With that his mouth moved over hers with an urgency meant to send her whirling into a world of lights and colors.

"You're the true essence of femininity, Drew," Casey rasped, sliding his hand under the heavy denim of her jeans and the soft lace of her bikini panties. His probing fingers sent new shock waves through Drew's body.

"Am I?" she breathed, gasping under the sensual nip of his teeth as his mouth traveled along the soft skin of her throat.

"Um, you're warm, pliable." Each word was punctuated with a love nip as his mouth trailed down to a passion-swollen breast. "So very receptive," he murmured, finding the sensitive tip.

Drew could feel herself melting under Casey's verbal and physical seduction. Her fingers dug into the muscled hardness of his back as he lay fully over her, his masculine heat scorching her with its special brand.

"Possessive as hell, too." He chuckled throatily, noting her passion-glazed amber eyes with male satisfaction. "There's only one problem."

"What?" She found it hard to form the one word.

His tongue traced a lazy circle around the pulsing hollow of her throat. She couldn't stop her shiver of anticipation and undulated seductively under him.

"As much as I'd enjoy making love to you in this meadow, the clouds overhead tell me there's a storm on the way. And not even for you would I care to have my bare backside caught by a stray bolt of lightning." Casey grinned wickedly. He moved off her and repacked the empty wine bottle in the knapsack. He gazed up at the storm clouds hovering nearby. "We'd better get back to the cabin in a hurry."

Drew breathed deeply to dissipate the cataclysm her body was experiencing. She had been so lost under Casey's spell that they could have been caught in the middle of a blizzard and she wouldn't have noticed! It took her a little longer to gather her wits together as she sat up and pushed an unruly strand of hair away from her face. She moved off the blanket and picked it up, giving it a good shaking before folding it and handing it to Casey.

When they reached the cabin Drew fixed a hot lunch of cream of mushroom soup and grilled cheese sandwiches. After their meal Casey built a fire to ward off the sudden chill in the air. He had already exchanged his lightweight sweater for a bulky knit pullover.

"This is all very relaxing," Drew declared, curling up on the couch after she had finished washing and drying the lunch dishes. Casey had declined her suggestion that he help her by using the excuse that he had done the breakfast dishes without assistance. She held a mug of steaming coffee, allowing the heated ceramic to warm her hands. From beneath her lowered lashes she watched Casey stretch out on the rug before the fire. Despite what had been on his mind not all that long ago, he now acted as if a nap were more important than making love to her. She noticed how the orange and red flames played over his face as if paying homage to a golden god. At that moment he looked very virile and dangerous.

"That's why I came here," he mumbled in reply. His eyes were closed, his hands lying loosely on his chest. He looked extremely comfortable. "I needed to re-charge my batteries, and this was the best place to do it. I've discovered that I'm not as young as I used to be."

Drew allowed a small smile to curve her lips. "You're not ready for a wheelchair yet, love," she promised.

His answer was a soft, but very identifiable snore. Casey was sound asleep! Drew settled back on the couch and watched him with loving eyes. She was beginning to wonder if fate had stepped in to give them another chance. Was it fate that had decreed that she would travel out here to the middle of nowhere to confront Casey again? Was it fate that had decided it was time these two headstrong individuals should get together, because no one else would be able to put up with them? She only wished she knew. She also wondered what Casey would think of her thoughts at that moment. She had a lot of questions to ask him, but they could wait. She had plenty of time.

Chapter Fourteen

For the next hour Drew continued to watch the soundly sleeping Casey. The shadows outside deepened, and the chill in the air increased, but that didn't matter.

She pulled a blue and green afghan around her shoulders and tucked the ends over her bare feet. It wasn't long before her own eyelids closed.

Dreams were nice. They involved the hard warmth of a man's arms cradling her. Something soft and furry brushed over her face in a gentle caress. She murmured and snuggled even closer against her dream. Then there was a floating sensation and she was lowered onto something soft.

Her jeans were unsnapped, unzipped and pulled off without her even stirring. Her shirt was similarly dispensed with. She was barely aware of the quilt that was draped over her half-naked body and the pair of lips that feathered over hers. She succumbed to full slumber before she could question her dream's actions.

When she awoke the next morning she could hear the incessant drumming of rain on the roof. She lay huddled under the quilt, listening to the melodic sounds.

How had she gotten to bed? The last thing she remembered was lying on the couch and draping the afghan over herself.

No, Drew hastily corrected herself. That wasn't the last thing. It appeared that her dream had been real after all.

She assumed that Casey must have awakened and found her asleep. He had carried her into the bedroom, undressed her and covered her up against the cool night air.

She stretched her body under the warm covers.

"I could go for this total relaxation," Drew murmured to herself.

After checking her watch and seeing that it was just past eight, she got out of bed and dressed in jeans and a lime green velour top. She pulled on heavy socks to keep her feet warm.

"Good morning," Casey greeted Drew when she entered the kitchen. "There's coffee on the stove." He too was in jeans and a flannel shirt, with only socks on his feet.

She glanced out the small square window, but all she saw were silver sheets of rain and a heavy mist hiding the nearby trees. "It's really coming down hard, isn't it?" she commented while retrieving a coffee mug from the cabinet.

"The road is more mud than dirt," he replied, seating himself at the table.

Drew spun around. "You mean we're stuck up here?"

Casey grimaced. "It's nice to know my company will be appreciated," he intoned dryly.

"You know what I mean," Drew stammered, taking the chair across from him.

"It's a good thing I had your car towed into town." He spread orange marmalade over his buttered toast. "With all this mud, it probably would have slid down into the ditch."

She nodded. "How long do you think this rain will last?"

Casey shrugged. "Hard to say. I have a multiband radio, and I've been using it to check on the weather conditions. You might as well know that we could be stuck here for several days."

Drew took an experimental sip of her coffee. "Then I hope you won't mind if I continue reading that *fascinating* book I began earlier." Her eyes danced with laughter. "I never read about a human pretzel before."

"Why read about something you could try out for yourself?" Casey murmured, glancing up. "There were quite a few snowbound weekends when we used to enjoy our"—hesitation—"privacy. Those were good times, Drew."

"It probably wasn't a habit you gave up, either."

He set his coffee cup down and leaned forward in his chair. The intense expression on his face was frightening. "What do you want me to tell you, Drew?" he gritted. "That I've been celibate these past five years? For God's sake, woman, I never thought I'd see you again! I had to make some sort of life for myself. You can't tell me that my past sex life bothers you that much?"

Drew's emotions had been on such a see-saw that Casey's caustic words were just too much for her to handle. She averted her face to hide the tears that were beginning to form in her eyes.

"What would you know?" she whispered brokenly, jumping to her feet. Ignoring his command to stay, she retreated to her bedroom. With the door closed, she was able to allow her tears to fall. She lay face down on the bed, crying into her pillow.

"Drew . . ." Gentle hands wrapped themselves around her shoulders and carefully turned her over. She was pulled onto Casey's lap and cradled against his chest. "Don't cry, sweetheart," he crooned in her ear as he rocked her in his arms.

"Damn you!" she sobbed. "What comes next? A listing of all the women you've made love to in the past five years? That could take days!"

Casey was stunned by Drew's vehemence. "If I didn't know better, I'd think you were jealous," he accused.

She sat up, glaring at him. "Then you're right, because I am jealous. I'm jealous of all those women who have shared your bed!" she cried out. "I'm jealous of them sharing you! Of knowing you the same way I used to know you!" She beat at his chest with her fists, all the time crying angry tears. Casey made no movement to stop her; instead he waited until Drew collapsed against his chest, gasping for the air her crying had restricted. "It hurts so much," she sobbed, curling her arms around his neck.

"It can work both ways, Drew," Casey interjected quietly. "After all, you were engaged for a while. You can't tell me that you didn't find out how he was in bed."

That one statement effectively dried Drew's tears. As always, Casey's logic held a spark of truth that couldn't be denied.

"I had to know," she mumbled against his chest.

Casey stiffened. He already knew that he wasn't going to like what he was about to hear, but his masochistic side insisted that he find out.

"Know what?" It took a great deal of effort for him to force the question past his lips.

"Ron is a very nice man, has a good job and would make a wonderful husband, but I couldn't be the wife he wanted," Drew breathed. "He made me feel warm and desirable, but he couldn't make me forget myself the way you could. He knew right away that I was going to give him back his ring."

Casey couldn't remember ever feeling such a strong urge to kill a man. How dare another man touch his woman!

"It-ah-it looks as if we're even then, doesn't it?" He cleared his throat, knowing full well that he was lying through his teeth. The old double standard still hadn't died within him.

"At least we were engaged to be married," she maintained stubbornly, tipping her head back to look at him.

"And how did your ex-fiancé make love?" Casey grated, the primitive half of his personality surfacing again.

Drew looked away, unable to answer his question. Not so gentle fingers gripped her chin and turned her face back to his.

"Tell me, Drew," Casey ordered, punishing himself as well as her.

When she answered him, her voice was so low that he had to lean forward to hear her words. "After– afterward, I–I became violently ill." Her thick lashes lowered to hide the bleak expression in her eyes.

Whatever Casey had been expecting to hear, that wasn't it. "Oh, Drew." His voice broke. He folded her in his arms and pressed her tightly against him. "How did he take it?"

"How do you think? Oh, he was very nice and understanding." Her voice quavered. "He also suggested that we have a long discussion on where our relationship was going. I told him we didn't need to talk. I gave him back his ring; he dressed and left. I didn't see him again after that."

Casey rubbed his chin over the top of Drew's head. "For six months after we parted I found it impossible to make love to a woman," he reflected. "I'd always see your face superimposed on someone whose name I couldn't even remember five minutes later."

His harsh confession sent her arms slipping around his waist.

"We're hating each other for doing something that was natural," Drew murmured, burying her face against the hollow between his neck and shoulder. "We never thought we'd see each other again and, as you said, we knew we'd have to make new lives for ourselves without each other."

Casey gripped her shoulders and pulled her upright. "If you hadn't gone to bed with him, would you have gone through with the marriage?" He had to know.

"I don't know." She shook her head slowly, looking utterly miserable at the memories he had stirred up. "I just don't know."

"I do." His quiet voice held no sign of his usual arrogance. "You would have called the engagement off sooner or later."

Drew's laugh turned into a strangled sob. "Your self-confidence is overwhelming."

"It has nothing to do with self-confidence, Drew," he continued quietly. "You forget that I know you very well. I admit I don't like the idea that you allowed another man to make love to you, but I can understand your reason for doing so." He grimaced. He sincerely doubted that she'd believe him when he didn't believe himself. "If he had been all that you wanted in a husband, and you had loved him a great deal, then you would have had the shortest engagement in history." For all his calm exterior the telltale muscle beside his mouth twisted in agitation. "But he wasn't what you needed."

"When will it end, Casey?" Drew sighed against the warm skin of his throat, inhaling the clean scent of soap and masculinity. "When will we go back to being friends? You've always been my best friend, did you know that? No one ever mattered to me as much as you, except for Pops." She could feel him nodding.

"You've been the same to me," he admitted softly.

"Remember all those nights we stayed up late talking?" she recollected, closing her eyes to visualize the sweet memories of the past. "You'd explain your new designs to me, and I'd tell you how one of my instructors had driven the class crazy with some insane assignment that had to be done in record time. Or how unsure I was of my job in the beginning, and you'd reassure me and tell me I'd do just fine if I'd relax more and not worry so much about everyone else."

Casey grinned. "What about that time you were so offended when someone asked you to fix coffee because they thought you were one of the secretaries? You came home hopping mad that night."

She laughed softly. In a short time they had reverted back to the close relationship they had shared so long ago. They had shared laughter, jokes, tears and pain during their years together. Now they were sharing special memories.

"I can still remember that night you went out with some of the engineers from your department for a bachelor party and came home so drunk you tried to get into the wrong apartment." Drew was warming to the subject. "Miss Bird had been shocked enough to have an unmarried couple as next-door neighbors, but the sight of you trying to get into her apartment . . . !"

Casey's hand moved over her back. "I felt pretty low the day Brenton Engineering laid me off," he began, speaking of the subject they had been carefully avoiding for so long. "And it didn't get any better when I realized that the engineering field was tight and jobs were at a premium. Getting that sales rep's job at Sundance was only a matter of being in the right place at the right time."

"But it upset you because you had to take such a drastic cut in pay, didn't it?" Drew asked.

He twisted a lock of her hair between two fingers, savoring the silky texture against his skin. "I enjoyed taking care of you, Drew," he said softly. "Basically I'm a pretty selfish man. I never really cared about a woman before you. I always felt that you were a part of me. And when you left I felt as if that part of me had been torn from my body without the benefit of anesthesia."

"I didn't dare pass up that transfer to Houston," she explained. "I was just starting out in their training program. All I heard was how much promise I had, and how in five to ten years I'd be sitting in a choice position." What she didn't tell him was that during that rough period in their lives she had fervently hoped that Casey would ask her to marry him. She had pretended that she was more than happy with their relationship, but deep down she had to admit that she had been ready to settle down. Perhaps she had pretended too well.

"It looks as if you reached your goal."

Drew shook her head, not wanting him to interrupt. "I also knew you weren't happy at Sundance, and that engineer's positions were rare in Boston then. I saw Houston as a new chance for both of us." Her fingers idly smoothed the soft flannel of his sleeve.

"With you running all over the country ten months out of the year?" Casey asked icily. "At least when you were in statistics you stayed in one office most of the time."

"Casey, I didn't become involved in the new projects department until six months after I transferred to Houston," she explained.

"Another promotion?"

"A request."

Casey frowned at her reply. "Why? You seemed happy enough in statistics."

Drew nuzzled her cheek against his shirt front. "I had too much free time," she whispered. "Too much free time to think."

"About us?" His arms tightened into a vise.

"Yes." That one word said it all.

They were unaware of time passing. All that mattered was that their arms were wrapped around each other and their shared body warmth comforted them. The hours ticked by, but they didn't notice. They needed only the emotional sustenance they got from each other.

The rhythmic pounding of the rain was soothing. Drew and Casey didn't want to speak for fear of breaking the spell that surrounded them.

"I really hate to say this"—Casey's low voice held a thread of amusement—"but my right arm has gone to sleep and feels about ready to fall off."

"Oh, I'm sorry!" Drew immediately shifted her position on his lap. She looked up and uttered a soft laugh of embarrassment. "I guess I'm too heavy for you."

"Oh, you may have put on a few extra pounds in the past five years." He cast an assessing eye over her slim figure. "But I'd say they've been distributed in all the right places." One hand moved up from her waist to the underside of her breast.

Casey was right. Drew's once angular girl's figure had matured over the years. Her pert breasts were still firm, but they had become fuller, and her hips were now a bit more rounded. Her figure was still slender, but now it was softer, with the bloom of maturity on her clear skin.

"They'd be in all the wrong places if I didn't keep up with my exercise classes," she rejoined dryly, moving off his lap to sit cross-legged on the bed. "I don't have to run all over a college campus now, or even from office to office, as I did when I worked in Boston."

Casey merely grinned. "How about a game of cards?" Being so close to her on the bed was beginning to take its toll on his nervous system.

"Gin?"

"You always cheat at gin."

"I do not!" Drew denied, fixing him with a glare. "You always accused me of cheating, but you could never prove it."

"I could, I just didn't bother to," he returned equably. "It was always more enjoyable to watch you twitch your luscious little body to get my mind off what you were really doing."

Drew picked up the pillow behind her and began hitting Casey over the head with it. "As if you never cheated!" she screeched. "What about all those times we played strip poker?"

"Hey!" he laughed, trying to dodge the soft missile. "Be careful with that thing!"

Drew wasn't sure just when the playful game changed into something else. Casey playfully lunged for her and pinned her against the quilt.

All of a sudden their laughter stilled. Their eyes met and held in unspoken communication. The tension in Casey's body communicated itself to her.

"It always comes back to one thing with us, Drew," he told her in a hoarse voice. His hands pressed lightly against her hips to bring them more fully against his. "We can't deny this."

"Do we want to?" She reached up and smoothed a stray lock of hair away from his forehead, then slid her fingers around to the skin of his nape. The tiny hairs teased her fingertips. "I want you, Casey." Her eyes didn't waver from his steady gaze.

His slow smile did strange things to her equilibrium.

"Casey!" Drew's protest when he moved away from her was halted by his fingertips brushing against her lips.

He picked her up, not at all deterred by the few extra pounds he had accused her of gaining.

"Why contort ourselves in a single bed when there's a perfectly good-sized double one down the hall?" he pointed out, carrying her out of the bedroom. "We might as well be comfortable."

"Um," she agreed all too readily, nipping his earlobe in punishment for allowing her to think he had even contemplated leaving her.

"After all, you are past the big three-oh," Casey teased as he dropped Drew onto the middle of the large bed in the rear bedroom.

"Meaning that I'm in my prime," she reminded him in a haughty manner. "Whereas you've been past yours for a good twelve years or so."

"Oh, yeah?" he growled, dropping onto the bed beside her. "We'll see about that!"

Drew's shirt and jeans were pulled from her body without ceremony. There was no force involved. Not when she was just as eagerly stripping Casey's clothes from him.

"Now we can get down to some serious kissing," Casey murmured once there wasn't one item of clothing between them. He lay half over Drew and framed her face with his hands. His thumbs brushed provocatively over her lips and pulled down gently at the corners. "One very delectable mouth." His tongue imitated the soft motions of his thumbs.

Drew was amazed at the restraint Casey exerted over himself. His kisses started as a gentle, exploratory skimming of his mouth over hers. Very gradually his tongue slid over her lips to the smooth surface of her teeth. When they parted to allow him entrance into the darkened cavern he drew back, not wanting to deepen the caress just yet. There was no teasing in his actions. He merely intended this to last as long as humanly possible.

Casey leisurely delved into the outer regions of Drew's mouth, then moved on to the delicate lines of her jaw and up to her ear. Each crevice was examined by both his fingertips and the tip of his tongue. Drew shivered at each caress. Casey ignored her murmured pleas for him to touch her swollen breasts. When his hands finally moved to cup the ultra-sensitive skin she cried out with relief even as his tongue laved a white hot path to the turgid nipple. The suckling motion of his lips brought a new sensation to the center of her being. His fingers reached up to tunnel through her hair in an attempt to keep her head still, while one leg hooked over her two restless ones.

"There's plenty of time, my darling," he said, calming her with the soothing motions of his hands.

"No," she protested weakly. She needed him now! Her body spoke more eloquently than any words could. She arched against him and moved her hands down his sides to his hips.

Casey chuckled and easily captured her seductive hands, then pinned them up over her head. "Little witch," he rasped.

This time there was no soft seduction in his kiss. His mouth opened over hers and his plundering tongue urged her lips to part. His free hand roamed over her body, tracing and probing each responsive spot.

Drew's own ardor was rising to meet Casey's. Her hands explored his lean muscled frame. Her tongue darted into his mouth, marking his teeth and beyond.

"Oh, Drew," Casey groaned, pulling away for a moment and feeling the molten invitation in her trembling limbs. "I can't wait any longer."

"I don't want you to." Her hands circled his neck and

brought his head back down for the kiss that would initiate the vibrant lovemaking to follow.

Casey lay between Drew's thighs and entered her with the fluidity of a lover familiar with his mate. Familiar, yet experiencing their love anew.

This time their lovemaking was heightened by their new awareness of each other. Each thrust and stroke was choreographed to carry Drew to a new level of sensuality.

Drew was clay to be molded to Casey's specifications. She held on to him with her arms and body, afraid that somehow she might lose him as he took her into a glittering new world.

At that moment Drew experienced more than the ultimate step. She experienced ecstasy in its purest form. With her own cries of joy came Casey's groans of fulfillment.

He shifted his weight, balancing himself on his elbows. He looked down at Drew's face, shimmering with the same perspiration that covered his own body. Her eyes were liquid with her joy.

"Tears?" he asked, catching a salty drop with his tongue.

Drew shook her head, unable to speak just yet. "I never—" Her voice broke with this new emotion.

"Me, neither," Casey agreed, rolling over onto his side and pulling her with him. He arranged the tumbled quilt over them so that the cool air wouldn't chill their damp bodies. "I think we broke the record."

"For what?" It was too difficult to raise her head when she could just as easily burrow into the hollow of his shoulder.

"Give me time, I'll think of something." He chuckled softly.

"Um, I love your Western accent. It sounds so sexy." She gave a feminine growl of appreciation.

"What accent?" He pretended to be puzzled. *"You're* the one with an accent."

"In Montana I would have an accent. Here, you do," she corrected.

"Argumentative wench." Casey yawned. He couldn't remember ever feeling so at peace with himself.

"Casey?" Drew turned so that she lay half over him, her crossed arms resting on his bare chest. "Why didn't you want me to read that book? I want the truth now!"

He grimaced at her sudden switch in topics. "It's not a book for ladies," he mumbled, refusing to look at her. "There's too much graphic violence."

"Violence!" she hooted. "The first three chapters dealt with Kordell's sexual habits! The man spent more time in bed than he did chasing criminals!"

"How far did you get?" Casey eyed her suspiciously.

"Until just after he meets the Countess."

"How far after?"

"Far enough," she sang out, dropping a kiss on his nose and laughing.

"I knew you were trouble from the first moment you showed up here," he groaned.

Her laughter died abruptly. "Are you really sorry I came?" Drew whispered sadly.

Casey recognized the hurt in her voice and wished it hadn't been his thoughtless remark that had put it there. "No, baby." He hugged her tightly. "I admit I was leery in the beginning, but now I feel very flattered that you came all this way to see me. By the way, how *did* you manage to get here without getting lost? You never were any good at reading a road map."

"It wasn't easy," she admitted ruefully. "I did get lost once, but luckily I only went a hundred miles out of my way."

Casey roared with laughter at that. "When did you

find out you were wrong? When you ended up in Florida?"

She aimed a playful fist at his jaw. "When a very nice man at a gas station asked me where I was going and said I was going too far south. He got me headed in the right direction."

"Thank goodness for nice men in gas stations." He shifted her more comfortably against him. In no time they were sleeping deeply.

"I can't believe that Jack and Irene got a divorce! They were always so happy together." It was a few hours later, and they had fixed a quick lunch of waffles and sausages. "What happened between them?" She sat in the kitchen, wearing the shirt Casey had worn earlier.

"His assistant." He raised his eyebrows comically. "You know, the one with the big—"

"The bow-legged one?" she hastily interrupted his more explicit description. "She also had a horrible overbite!"

Casey's grin was lecherous. "Yeah, but she also had a great pair of—"

"*Carstairs Langdon!*" She fixed him with a warning glare.

"You can't fight Mother Nature, love." He was unrepentant of his wicked thoughts.

Drew speared a piece of sausage with her fork and lifted it to her lips. They had been catching up on their activities for the past five years, with Casey updating her about some of their friends.

Casey leaned forward to pick up the coffeepot and refill his cup. He was finding it difficult to concentrate on his meal when he could see Drew sitting across from him wearing only his shirt and a pair of lacy bikini panties. Right now he wanted nothing more than to run out in the rain and shout, "Hey, world, this woman's all mine!"

"I've got this brilliant idea," he said in that familiar husky tone.

"Oh?" She propped her chin on her fist. "And what could that be?" The seductive purr in her voice and the dangerous sparkle in her eyes told him that she'd agree to whatever his suggestion might be.

"Being as it's a rainy day and we don't have a television or too much in the way of modern entertainment, I thought we could take an old-fashioned nap."

Drew's smile was as wide as Casey's. "Before or after?"

"After."

"On one condition."

He groaned audibly. "What is it this time?"

"That during our nap you make sure I get the left side of the bed," she informed him in her efficient businesswoman's voice.

"Does this agreement need to be in writing?" Casey asked.

"Mm." Drew considered him through half-closed eyes. "I think I can take your word for it."

"Fine, if I let you sleep at all, you can certainly doze on the left side of the bed." Casey stood up and leaned over to pull her out of the chair.

"The dishes!" she protested when he swung her up into his arms and carried her out of the kitchen.

"Don't turn practical on me now or I may forget my good intentions," he warned her with a growl.

"Oh, well, if there are good intentions involved, forget it." Drew giggled, nipping his earlobe. "I prefer a man whose intentions are far from honorable."

Casey planted a swift kiss on her lips. "Then, my lady, you have the right man."

Chapter Fifteen

The rain had stopped by the next morning, leaving a sea of mud instead of a road to the main road.

"I'll need to go into town for supplies if we expect to keep on eating. And with all our activities lately, we're going to need to keep up our strength." He grinned wickedly, enjoying Drew's blush.

"But you said that it's all mud out there." She carefully sipped the hot coffee she had just poured.

"That's why I bought a four-wheel drive vehicle," he explained, accepting the coffee cup she had handed him.

"I'll need to check on my car."

Casey nodded, keeping his face averted. In the space of twenty-four hours he had come to expect that Drew would stay with him as long as possible. He had forgotten that she had another role in life. He had no wish to come between Drew and whatever goal she was seeking. He couldn't force her to make a choice

241

between himself and her career. Casey wanted Drew to come to him of her own free will.

An hour later the now silent couple rode in the Bronco down the muddy road. The rain had been a hard one, judging from the terrible road conditions.

"Uh-oh," Casey muttered when they reached the outskirts of town.

"What's wrong?" Drew asked, turning to him.

"It looks like some flash flooding went on." He gestured toward several partially collapsed buildings. "We better head for the garage first."

Drew looked around at the mud-filled streets and buildings. When Casey muttered an explicit curse under his breath, she glanced in the same direction he was looking.

"Oh no-o-o," she moaned, reaching for the door handle and scrambling out of the truck. She ran through the mud toward the broken-down building where a car's black hood peeked out from under a pile of mud and loose boards.

Drew stood in front of what had once been a garage, but now was only a pile of rubble. Her arms hung loosely at her sides, and the expression on her face could only be described as stunned.

"It can't be," she whispered. She spun around to face Casey, who had walked up behind her. "That's not my car in there, is it, Casey?" she appealed to him.

"There ya are, Mr. McCord." A short stocky man in mud-splattered jeans and boots approached them. "Sure sorry about your car. That flood hit us before we knew what was happening. I'm afraid the car's a total loss."

"But you're insured," Drew spoke up hopefully.

"That's the problem, little lady." He scratched the top of his head. "There's never been any reason for us to have flood insurance out here. At least, not until now."

"I don't feel very well," she moaned, turning back to gaze at the broken down building.

"Course I will check with the insurance company to see what they can do," the man hastily assured her.

"Drew, I'm sorry." Casey put his arm around her slumped shoulders. "I never thought this would happen."

"I saved up my bonuses from four projects to make the down payment on that car," she said woodenly. "They wouldn't take my Volkswagen as a trade-in. I even gave up membership in my health club so I could afford the payments." She turned to gaze up at him with blank eyes. "That was my first new car."

"I know, babe," he soothed, cupping his hand around her nape and drawing her face against his shoulder.

"I washed and hand-polished it every weekend," she babbled into the soft fabric of his jacket, still unable to believe the scene before her.

"Let's go get some coffee," he urged gently, steering her back toward the Bronco.

"My mechanic is going to be so mad," Drew mumbled in a numb monotone. "He treated it as if it were his own."

"He'll get over it." Casey got behind the wheel and switched on the engine.

"My car payment is due next week," she continued in that same flat voice.

"Don't worry, honey; I'll take care of everything." He leaned over and patted her knee. She was really worrying him. If only she'd scream or rant and rave! That kind of scene he could handle.

Drew sat stiffly in the truck, staring straight ahead. She didn't stir until a solicitous Casey appeared at the passenger door and assisted her out. He ushered her into the coffee shop and steered her toward a nearby booth. He requested two coffees and danishes from the waitress who hovered nearby.

"Drink this," he ordered gently when the coffee arrived.

Drew obeyed, then put her cup aside. She looked around her.

"What's wrong?" Casey asked.

"I didn't bring my purse." She frowned in annoyance. "Could I borrow a dime, please?"

Casey obliged by handing a coin to her. Drew slid out of the booth and headed for the back of the coffee shop.

Casey spread butter on his warm danish and bit into it. As the minutes ticked by he resisted the urge to turn around and discover where Drew had gone to. When she finally did return the dazed expression in her eyes was gone and a smile was on her lips.

"That's a quick switch," Casey commented, gesturing for the waitress to refill their cups. "What brought about the happy face?"

"I called Marty." She bit hungrily into her danish. "Um, this is good!"

Casey tensed. "I didn't realize a dime could cover a twenty-minute phone call to Houston," he said quietly, with a trace of sarcasm in his voice.

"I called collect. Oh, here's your dime." She handed him the coin back. "Thank you."

"Why did you call Marty?" he asked casually.

Drew looked surprised by the question. "To have him take care of the car, of course."

The muscle next to Casey's mouth twitched. "Didn't you think that I could take care of it?"

"I'm sure you could, but Marty knows who to contact," she explained logically.

It bothered Casey more than he cared to admit. Oh, sure, Marty Watson was hardly the kind of man to appeal to a woman like Drew, but Casey could still remember a time when she used to automatically turn to him when she had a problem. For a while it had seemed as if they had returned to their former relationship. It didn't seem so now.

"If you've finished, we'll get going," he said abruptly, pushing his coffee cup to one side.

Drew was mystified by Casey's swift change in moods, but she didn't question him. She took the last bite of her danish and stood up.

Casey was silent during the drive back to the cabin. He might not actually have exceeded the speed limit, but the expression on his face said that mentally he was going over a hundred miles an hour. The cold front was still in effect when they entered the cabin.

"Casey, what's wrong?" Drew watched him agitatedly pacing the floor.

"You still haven't broken free from CHEM Corp., have you?" He stopped his pacing and looked at her as he spoke.

"Broken free? I took my vacation time; I didn't resign from my job," she replied. "I don't know what you're trying to get at. Would you mind clarifying this a little more?"

"You—me—Watson—CHEM Corp.—everything!" Casey roared.

"Casey, you're shouting." Drew spoke in a quietly reasonable tone.

"I have a damn good reason for shouting," he gritted, walking over to her.

"Fine, I'd like to hear it." She faced him, her arms crossed in front of her.

"I told you that I'd take care of your car, but you felt you had to go running to Watson instead of letting me help," he replied sulkily.

Comprehension dawned quickly. "You're jealous of Marty!" she accused.

"Jealous, no. Envious, yes." He quieted down.

"There was a time when you'd automatically turn to me when you had a problem. Now you run to him as if he were your husband or something."

"I had to learn to do things on my own, Casey," Drew told him. "In many ways it was good for me to have these five years, because they gave me the opportunity to do that. Pops was there for me from the beginning, then I had you. Oh, you urged me to think for myself and follow my own initiative, which really helped, but you were still there if I hit a snag. Now I make my own mistakes and I learn to rectify them without any help. Contrary to anyone's opinion, Marty does not help people get out of the messes they get into. You're on your own as far as he's concerned. I called him because the company takes care of my car insurance. His secretary will handle it from there."

That piece of information should have made him feel better, but it didn't.

"I think I should tell you the real reason why I came out here, and why no one knew where I was going to work next." His voice was so low that she could barely hear him. "Actually, I'm not going to work for another toy company, or any company, in my former capacity."

"I'm afraid you've lost me."

Casey turned to her. "Six months ago a friend of mine from my college days came to me with a proposition. He was starting up a consulting firm and wanted me to come work for him. He needed someone with a strong sales background. It pretty well entails doing what you do: going into a company, analyzing its problems and showing the executives how to correct them. The idea appealed to me, and I told him that when the time came to put the company together to give me a call and I'd let him know my answer. That time has come."

"It's a risky venture," she commented softly.

Casey nodded. "That's why I wanted to think it over before I made a decision."

"And now you've made it." It was a statement, not a question. He nodded again. "You're going to do it, aren't you?"

"Yes." He turned away. "It's a big step, and it scares me, but I need to find out if I can make a go of it."

"You will," Drew said, confident of any decision Casey might make. "You've always done well in anything you've attempted. Why should this be any different?"

He shook his head, laughing bitterly. "Because I also had this crazy idea of telling you how much I love you and asking you to marry me. Now I don't know if I can ask you to share my life if I may not have a job by the end of the year."

Drew wet her lips. "Did you ever think of asking me for my opinion? After all, this would involve my life, too. What makes you think I wouldn't be in favor of you branching out?"

"This company could fail, for all I know. I can't take that chance," he said vehemently.

"You still could have asked me!" she argued.

"I'd be traveling, and you seem to have to do your own share of that. What kind of marriage could we have when we'd be miles apart?" He turned away.

"Damn you!" Drew shouted, her temper flaring. "There you go, making decisions for me again. Well, fine, I'll make it real easy for you." She spun around and stalked off toward the back of the cabin. Five minutes later she came back carrying her suitcase and tote bag.

"What do you think you're doing?" Casey demanded.

"I'm going home to people who allow me to make up my own mind," she snapped.

"You're not going anywhere." He glared at her.

Drew faced him with a cool smile. "Want to bet?" She opened the door and carried her bags outside. A moment later Casey heard the Bronco's door slam. Drew reappeared in the doorway. "I'm going to the bus station. Are you going to take me, or do I have to hitchhike?"

"Neither." He looked to be at his most stubborn.

"Fine." She hastily opened a drawer in the nearby table and extracted the extra set of keys that she knew was there. Casey lunged toward her, but she evaded him and ran back outside.

"Come back here!" Casey yelled.

Drew made sure to lock the door. She unrolled the window a bit and looked out. "Why don't you go back to Montana? I'm sure they appreciate the big he-man attitude there!" she shouted over the engine. After a loud grinding of gears the Bronco lumbered down the road, leaving an angry Casey behind. "You'll find your truck at the bus station if you want it badly enough," she called back to him.

Four days later Casey parked the Bronco in the driveway to his home. He sat there for a while and stared out the windshield. It was so quiet! He groaned and laid his head on his crossed arms which rested on the steering wheel. Perhaps it wasn't macho for men to cry, but that didn't stop the dampness around his eyes.

It had taken him most of a day to get his Bronco back. As Drew had promised, it had been left in the parking lot next to the bus station.

The days had never seemed so lonely. Casey thought over what Drew had said and silently admitted that she had been right. He had been in the habit of doing her thinking for her. Oh, sure, it might have looked like she had all the independence a woman could want, but when it came down to a crucial decision, he had always made it for her. Drew wasn't that young unsure woman any longer, and Casey was going to have to realize that. If only their tempers hadn't erupted that day. Maybe they could have worked out a compromise. Now he doubted that she'd be willing to see him, judging from her anger the day she had left. Oh, well, he could always check with Aunt Kate. If nothing else, he wanted to tell Drew that she was right. He should have talked his plans over with her sooner. It had sounded as if she would have been more than willing to take a chance with him in this new venture. He should have given her the choice, just as she had offered him a similar choice five years earlier, when his stubborn pride had gotten in the way. He had lost her then, and due to that same pride, he had lost her again now. And this time he might not be given another chance. He couldn't blame fate if that happened. He could only blame himself.

Casey's movements were slow as he climbed out of the vehicle. There was no need to hurry. Only an empty house waited for him.

He unlocked the front door and entered the dark house. He switched on the lights in the living room and looked around with a puzzled frown.

Funny, he'd swear he could smell Drew's perfume. Maybe she was right about needing a better ventilation system. No, it had to be his imagination.

He sighed wearily and headed for his bedroom. Maybe, just maybe, he'd be able to sleep tonight.

It wasn't until he entered the room that he noticed a light burning in the bathroom.

"What the . . . ?"

"It's about time you got home!"

Casey swung around. There was Drew, dressed—or more accurately undressed—in a flame-red silk and lace teddy, with her hair tumbling down around her shoulders, a picture of vibrant feminine sensuality kneeling in the middle of the bed.

"What? How?" He shook his head, as if he were unable to believe his eyes.

"We need to have a discussion about this bed," Drew began crisply, sitting back and drawing up one leg in a provocative pose.

"The bed?" Now he knew he was dreaming!

"It's only fair that if you get Shadow every other weekend, I have visitation rights to the bed," she went on blandly, clasping her fingers around her drawn-up knee.

Hope filled Casey's body. "Every other weekend?" A smile teased his lips.

Drew chewed her lower lip reflectively. "Not exactly." She cocked her head to one side. "I thought about visitation rights *every* weekend, and week nights, too." She smiled warmly. "Also . . ."

"There's more?"

She nodded. "It's a good thing you keep such good records. I found the name of your consultant friend and gave him a call. He was very interested in acquiring someone with an administrative background. Of course, I'll have to fulfill my contract with Fantasy Toys, but that should be tied up within six months. I don't have to tell you that Marty was thoroughly displeased with my letter of resignation. He called me every kind of fool he could think of, but he knew he couldn't change my mind. His last remark was that I'm too stubborn for my own good, and you more than deserve me," Drew said smugly.

"Why?" Casey's eyes narrowed. "Why did you call Jeff?"

"I told him that you would take the job, but that we came as a package deal," Drew said. "He was all for it. With luck, when I begin working there, we might get some assignments together. He explained to me that he'll be concentrating basically on Southern California, so we wouldn't have any transportation problems. Aunt Kate can keep house for us, since you aren't exactly the picture of neatness, and she can look after Shadow when we're out of town." She smiled, obviously proud of herself.

"You're making my decisions for me, Drew," Casey growled.

She shook her head. "All I did was give him the acceptance you had planned to give him all along. So, is it a deal, Mr. McCord?"

Casey laughed, walking over to the bathroom and turning off the light. His next stop was the bed. He took Drew's hand and pulled her up into his arms. "Deal, Ms. Sinclair. Now help me get out of these damn clothes!"

Drew's answering laugh was smothered by Casey's hungry mouth. She wound her arms around his neck and pressed her silk-clad body even closer to him. "If necessary I'll just rip them off," she murmured against his lips. "It will certainly save a lot of time."

When Casey was finally naked and lying next to Drew their love showed in their worship of each other's body. Every curve and angle was stroked and caressed with loving hands. They murmured praise into each other's ears and moaned softly when one of them found a particularly sensitive spot on the other.

When they joined together Drew felt more loved than she had all the other times Casey had made love to her. This time was special. This was a time that had never been equaled. He led her farther and farther into a world of pure sensation, and she didn't want to come back. Not as long as he was there with her. When the time came for them to float back to earth they were more fulfilled than they had ever been before.

"You know, of course, that this time I'll expect you

to marry me," Casey said quietly. "I can't go through the hell I've been going through for the past four days."

Drew breathed sharply. She had been afraid that he wasn't going to repeat his proposal. "On one condition."

Now he was wary. "What?"

"That I always get the left side of the bed!"

Silhouette Special Edition. Romances for the woman who expects a little more out of love.

If you enjoyed this book, and you're ready for more great romance

…get 4 romance novels FREE when you become a Silhouette Special Edition home subscriber.

Act now and we'll send you four exciting Silhouette Special Edition romance novels. They're our gift to introduce you to our convenient home subscription service. Every month, we'll send you six new passion-filled Special Edition books. Look them over for 15 days. If you keep them, pay just $11.70 for all six. Or return them at no charge.

We'll mail your books to you two full months *before they are available anywhere else.* Plus, with every shipment, you'll receive the Silhouette Books Newsletter absolutely free. *And with Silhouette Special Edition there are never any shipping or handling charges.*

Mail the coupon today to get your four free books—and more romance than you ever bargained for.

Silhouette Special Edition is a service mark and a registered trademark of Simon & Schuster, Inc.

Silhouette Special Edition

$2.25 each

111 ☐ Thorne	133 ☐ Douglass	155 ☐ Lacey	177 ☐ Howard
112 ☐ Belmont	134 ☐ Ripy	156 ☐ Hastings	178 ☐ Bishop
113 ☐ Camp	135 ☐ Seger	157 ☐ Taylor	179 ☐ Meriwether
114 ☐ Ripy	136 ☐ Scott	158 ☐ Charles	180 ☐ Jackson
115 ☐ Halston	137 ☐ Parker	159 ☐ Camp	181 ☐ Browning
116 ☐ Roberts	138 ☐ Thornton	160 ☐ Wisdom	182 ☐ Thornton
117 ☐ Converse	139 ☐ Halston	161 ☐ Stanford	183 ☐ Sinclair
118 ☐ Jackson	140 ☐ Sinclair	162 ☐ Roberts	184 ☐ Daniels
119 ☐ Langan	141 ☐ Saxon	163 ☐ Halston	185 ☐ Gordon
120 ☐ Dixon	142 ☐ Bergen	164 ☐ Ripy	186 ☐ Scott
121 ☐ Shaw	143 ☐ Bright	165 ☐ Lee	187 ☐ Stanford
122 ☐ Walker	144 ☐ Meriwether	166 ☐ John	188 ☐ Lacey
123 ☐ Douglass	145 ☐ Wallace	167 ☐ Hurley	189 ☐ Ripy
124 ☐ Mikels	146 ☐ Thornton	168 ☐ Thornton	190 ☐ Wisdom
125 ☐ Cates	147 ☐ Dalton	169 ☐ Beckman	191 ☐ Hardy
126 ☐ Wildman	148 ☐ Gordon	170 ☐ Paige	192 ☐ Taylor
127 ☐ Taylor	149 ☐ Claire	171 ☐ Gray	
128 ☐ Macomber	150 ☐ Dailey	172 ☐ Hamilton	
129 ☐ Rowe	151 ☐ Shaw	173 ☐ Belmont	
130 ☐ Carr	152 ☐ Adams	174 ☐ Dixon	
131 ☐ Lee	153 ☐ Sinclair	175 ☐ Roberts	
132 ☐ Dailey	154 ☐ Malek	176 ☐ Walker	

SILHOUETTE SPECIAL EDITION, Department SE/2
1230 Avenue of the Americas
New York, NY 10020

Please send me the books I have checked above. I am enclosing $_____
(please add 75¢ to cover postage and handling. NYS and NYC residents please
add appropriate sales tax). Send check or money order—no cash or C.O.D.'s
please. Allow six weeks for delivery.

NAME _____

ADDRESS _____

CITY _____ STATE/ZIP _____